THE BEST FOOT FORWARD:
The James T. Medak Anthology

NOTE: Under no circumstances should you read this book unless you yourself are barefoot.

TABLE OF CONTENTS

INTRODUCTION

It really is a strange thing, to be writing this.

You see, after years and years of working on higher-minded, academic writing, it is amazing how quickly I adapted to writing what is essentially really hot foot fetish porn. In the early days, there was a good deal of tickling as well, but over time, it's become very foot-oriented, which I quite frankly don't mind given the way that fetishes evolve and change over time.

However, to have this, to have an honest-to-goodness anthology is something altogether different. In truth, this was a choice I made because after my third book came out, I had a lot of foot fans ask me on my blog "Hey, I see you're an author -- which one should I pick up first?" Although I am always a fan of *Getting Off on the Wrong Foot* if not just 'cos it was the first one to get published on my own imprint, they all indicate where I was at the time sexually, and each have their own charm (although to be fair, I do feel like the writing on *GOOTWF* was the best overall).

As much as I'd like to think that there are people who go out and grab every single thing I write, people just don't have the time or money to buy an author's entire bibliography, so I created this anthology more out of convenience than anything else. Here is the best of the best: my absolute favorite stories as voted on by me and me alone. Now don't get me wrong: I do love all of them in their own way (and, simply 'cos I just finished working on it shortly before writing this, my full-length novel *How To Be a Footpig* is one I am absolutely beaming with pride about), but I really wanted to go for a real diversity of stories, featuring tickle ones and foot worship ones and edging-oriented ones and just about every other variant there is imaginable. If I went a bit overboard, fuck it: it's my own goddamn imprint, so I'll publish what I want. I'll even put some emoticons right here 'cos I can ;-) :-P

In all seriousness though, one of the most amazing things to come out of writing these books is just hearing from guys with foot fetishes the world over, all of them telling me how being as public as I am with my foot fetish has given them strength or encouragement or just made them not feel as alone as they are with their strange attraction to male feet. It's a hard thing to quantify for sure, and to be honest, when I was in high school, I fought the living fuck out of it, refusing to accept it and hating myself for seeing feet in the sexual way that I did. However, that moment when I stopped fighting it and crossed over to the other side, out-and-out embracing it in all its weirdness and wonderfulness -- man, it felt like a weight was lifted off of me. I love the fact that I *love* male feet as much as I do. I make sure that the fetish doesn't define me (again, who wants to be known around the office as "the foot guy"?), but that I have a healthy relationship with it. You aren't weird. You aren't a freak. You're a guy that's got a foot fetish -- so what?

I don't look back all that favorably on *How to Be a Tickle Slave* as, well, that was my first effort ever. I though the publisher would do more to correct my numerous typos but they didn't, so that's very much on me. There's a bit of an amateurish quality to it but the enthusiasm, as well as that initial attention to story, characters, and detail was there. *My What Ticklish Feet You Have* was very much a continuation of that but I made sure to have both "tickle" and "feet" in the title as the way my fetishes were evolve absolutely required me to make sure I was giving equal treatment to each. Thus, *Getting Off on the Wrong Foot* has long been my favorite, as the stories and characters felt more mature, more lived-in, and while the giddy enthusiasm of my first two books was replaced with more nuanced growth in the third, I'm still happy with all of them, and most especially happy with the fact that I made damn sure to never repeat the same story twice. I suppose it's an easy thing to do (and lord knows I've seen tons of other fetish authors do so), but to constantly push and challenge myself, both with narrative structures and unique scenarios, was part of what I felt made me different from other writers, even as I still took notes and lessons from all of them, because good lord there are more than enough out there that are way better at this than I am.

Still, it is a pleasure and a joy to write about a fetish that I hold so very near and dear to me. At the time of my writing this introduction, I can't tell you what will happen after this or what forms my work will take, but the one thing to know is that I am grateful for every fan that ever bothered to reach out to me, to every person that ever bought a physical version of my books with their own money in actual bookstores, and those people who are reading my stories without ever posting as much as a single internet comment about their fetish but savor the the tales regardless. Trust me: if my books have impacted you in any positive way at all I would love to hear from you, but no matter what, know that you are not alone in your love for all things podiacal. There are literally thousands upon thousands of people who share the same feelings with you, and as my inbox has shown me throughout the years, that number is only growing from there.

None of this would be possible without the numerous incredible authors that came before me, and know that I'm not joshing you when I let you know they are all better than me at this. Truly, seek out the works of Wayne Courtois, Keith Steeclif, Christopher Trevor, and any of the Jack's Male Tickling Rack-era stories from an author simply known as Eddie. Truly, dig into these classics all, as these authors paved the way in so many ways for others like lil' ol' me.

With that said, please dig in to what lays before you: a detailed catalog of stories that stretch over five years celebrating tickling, edging, sex, and -- most of all -- male bare feet in all their glory. As you drift off to sleep finishing one of these stories late in the night, all I have to say in response is simply ... "Feet dreams ..."

--James T. Medak (July 2014)

This book is dedicated to Michael K.: friend, confidant, and one of the kindest fetish friends I have ever had the pleasure to meet. You've gone above and beyond on every project we've ever done, and it would be remiss of me if I didn't thank you for it. This is for you.

FOOT CLUB

(originally appeared in *How to Be a Tickle Slave*)

+ + +

Oh, the very first effort. The story of its creation itself has somewhat become legend in and of itself, but that's only 'cos it's absolutely true: I was housesitting and was bored, so, being the responsible lad I am, decided to smoke some weed. Eventually high and horny, I had access to a computer but definitely didn't want to leave a trail of porn on their comp. So I just decided to try my first ever stab at writing fiction, thinking nothing about my raging hardon as I did so. Thus, "Foot Club", although a bit obvious in its intent, was still a significant step to take. When I woke up the next day, I liked what I did but had to go over a lot of the mistakes someone would make while writing stoned: names being mixed up, some mis-typed words, running sentences, etc. The end result was the first thing I ever posted on a forum that was of actual substance, and the reaction was significant enough that it gave me the confidence to actually do more. Thus, everything starts right here. It is ground zero and it is horny as all get out ...

And Todd was found out, his greatest weakness suddenly exposed at the moment he least expected it, realizing now that he would be a perpetual footslave to the person who he thought would least control him ... and there was nothing he could do about it.

+ + +

1. "What the fuck is 'Foot Club'?"

"Dude, just drop it, OK!" sneered Zach, the skater punk that sat in front of Todd every day during his Philosophy of Art class. Todd looked pleading with his blazed blue eyes and collegiate-handsome good looks, but Zach wasn't going to budge. When Zach left to use the restroom in a class two days prior, Todd managed to sneak a peak into Zach's planner during a planned writing exercise. It said that next Tuesday would be a meeting of 'Foot Club'. Todd was a bit intrigued to say the least, and the very fact that Todd even mentioned it to Zach was obviously breaking some taboo -- yet that only intrigued Todd more.

Admittedly, Todd didn't care much about forming a friendship with Zach -- after all, the dude wore skater shoes -- but Todd couldn't help but be a bit fascinated by what was transpiring. When Todd was a teenager, he began developing his strong, powerful male foot fetish, which started during a Scout camping trip in which he lost a bet, was hog-tied in his tent, and forced to smell and worship the feet of the senior Scouts (aka the ones nearing Eagle). It was a one-time, isolated event designed to humiliate the newest members of the Troop, but its effect still had a powerful effect on the young Todd. He started out seeking revenge -- wanting to do the same thing to his captors that they did to him -- but soon his desire to get back at the senior Scouts turned into an all-out obsession with men's feet.

It was kind of weird for Todd, as he still liked girls and wound up (surprisingly) being quite the ladies man during his senior year of high school, but when you came right down to it, Todd got turned on the most by guys feet and the very thought of worshiping, tickling, and massaging them. Guys in flip-flops were his favorite, and even though he had a few discreet, intoxicated experiences with some "foot guinea pigs" during his freshmen year in college, the idea of sex with a guy just didn't do anything for Todd. He just wanted feet, plain and simple. It became somewhat of an insular sexual conquest for him, and one that he wasn't able to satisfy for months on end. He had an "understanding" with one of the gay guys on campus, who kindly let Todd worship his feet for hours on end, but as soon as actual emotions were beginning to emerge between them, Todd cut it off -- he just wanted foot action with no strings attached (which, incidentally, proved to be a very, very hard thing to get). It was a weird, complicated experience that wound up polarizing his friends around him, but Todd knew he couldn't change who he was: it was better to accept who he was than to fight what he was always secretly thinking about.

Even now, watching as Zach glanced over his shoulder at him every few minutes just to scold him, Todd began wondering what this "foot club" experience was. Oh yeah, he got the reference: *Fight Club* and all that. Hell, he didn't even think it was that tacky of a name. He just wondered what if there were guys around here that shared his fetish? He had a crush on every perpetually sandal-clad frat boy that walked by him, unsure of whether he wanted to dominate them or be dominated by them. Every once in awhile some guy would catch him staring at their bared feet, but Todd was never sure if the glance he got in return was a look of disgust or a wink of acknowledgment. Either way, Todd's feet -- in flip-flops and blue jeans for every day the temperature was over 50 -- were exactly the kind to get those kinds of glances: size 12 monsters with absolutely perfectly rounded toes. He just got a profile on a fetish-based social networking site the other week, and already he had made some 30-odd friends, including eight right here in this very state! As turned on as he got by others podiacal treasures, it was kind of surprising how turned on Todd was getting by exhibiting his own soles for unknown horny masses ...

The sharp buzz of the between-classes bell snapped Todd back into reality, and he seemed dazed, just having woken up after dreaming of feet. The small hard-on in his pants simply disappeared the second that Todd saw what was scrawled on the blackboard: "THREE PAGE ESSAY DUE TOMORROW!" That was the most terrifying thing of all, as Todd had *no* idea what the prof was referring to.

As he wandered across the spring-licked campus, nodding at friends and classmates, Todd gradually came to a decision: tomorrow night, he would follow Zach to "Foot Club."

+ + +

2. By the time that Tuesday had rolled around, Todd had gotten nervous. He was thinking of nothing but possible worship opportunities, often fantasizing about being tied up on the floor of a fraternity basement, sandaled and barefooted fratboys tickling, poking, prodding, and teasing him, all filming it and putting it up on YouTube in an act of great humiliation. In truth, Todd didn't know why being subjugated to such degradation was appealing to him, but for the time being, that fantasy was all he could think about.

Todd was still reading an incredible new TKLFrat story at 2AM, losing track of time while trapped in a horny state of mind, jacking himself off in nothing but his computer screen glow ... at least until his roommate burst in. "Still up?" said the bearded, handsome Doug, as Todd quickly Alt-Tabbed his screen and covered up his massive hardon as non-chalantly as possible. "Oh yeah ... you know how Googling yourself can lead you to weird places on the internet." "Ha ha, yeah," sighed Doug in agreement.

Todd hated Doug: not because of who he was (he actually was a well-tempered guy who never got agitated by any of Todd's habits regarding hanging clothes up), but because of what he wore. That's right, Doug wore Chuck Taylors every day. Ever. In his life. He was somewhat of an overachiever and a drama nerd to boot, so between the early classes and late rehearsals, Todd was usually in bed during anytime that his buddy would be unshod. The few glimpses of Doug's foot flesh that he saw were too much for him -- he had an unbelievable crush on Doug's feet (and to a lesser extent, Doug), so seeing them as infrequently as he did just drove him up the wall. He & Doug chatted for awhile, but before long they both had turned the lights off and went to bed. Todd, awash with fetish fantasias, wouldn't fall asleep for another three hours.

When he woke up the next day, it was 1PM. He didn't know how he did it, but here was, awake and having just missed three of his classes. Well, fuck. Tonight was Foot Club -- he could give himself the day off. After grabbing some cereal, he waded around in his dorm room trying to kill time, popping in some *Doctor Who* but then regretting it 'cos he forgot the Season Three opener had David Tennant barefoot for half the episode, further propelling his fantasies. He tried to do some Spanish homework, but still couldn't get his mind off the topic at hand. Time inched by, but by 5PM, he was saddling up to do some Zach stalking. As he was putting on his hoodie (yes, even with jeans and flip-flops still), Doug walked in.

"Hey man ... where you off to?"

Todd remained coy: "I don't know, I just need to go out. Some nights you just need an adventure, you know?" Doug laughed, "Yeah, I know that feeling. Well best of luck." Doug went to his computer and was reaching for a beer in his under-the-counter fridge right as Todd was closing the door.

This was going to be interesting no matter what happened, Todd thought. After getting out of the cafeteria before 6PM (aka before "the rush"), Todd wound up walking near some of the dorm apartments before he found Zach kicking around in the parking lot of the science building. He was with some skater buds, and Todd sat next to a tree in a distance, just waiting for the guys to finish up. Yet they kept skating and skating, and Todd went from sitting to slumping, from slumping to sleeping. When he woke up, he had no sight of Zach nearby. He glanced at his cell -- it was 9:43PM. Shit. He then heard what he thought was Zach's voice echoing between the apartments down the road. He clenched his toes together around sandal's toeholds and began running as fast as he could in Zach's direction.

When he finally got Zach in sight, he was down to only one other friend who Todd couldn't recognize -- all he could tell was that Zach's friend was in flip-flops, and that's all Todd needed. He began walking slowly and less conspicuously behind them, the now-present moonlight helping on the visibility front. After a minute's walking, Zach was soon entering through the ground-level door of a frat house. Todd looked around -- no one was watching. After about 30 seconds, he entered the same door, unsure of exactly what building he was entering (Todd never went to many frat parties) or what was to be expected inside. Either way, his heart was beating a lot faster than it normally did.

He heard some noise coming from the basement, and began heading down the creaky frat-house stairs. He was walking one flight down ... and there was a second? Man, this was a deep basement. Yet there was a room down there of what looked like ... hard concrete ... but covered by sand? In this room, there were wooden support pillars scattered around, and in the middle of the sand-accented floor, there was a bunch of barechested guys, forming a circle around a single swinging lightbulb. Todd looked right next to the base of the stairs: a series of discarded A&F t-shirts, hoodies, jackets, and shoes. Yet his inquisitive eye jumped right for the signs, and there were no sandals to be found. None of the guys in the circle had noticed him, so Todd quietly removed his hoodie and undershirt, and walked calmly in his leather sandals towards where the guys were gathered. Much to his surprise ...

... they were just talking. Looking at the abs of his fellow peers, he found more six-packs than the Stop-N-Go convenience mart. All these guys ... looked good! And were barefoot! There were still quite a few guys in flip-flops, so Todd just assumed that as long as your feet were exposed, you were OK. Todd caught bits of conversations about classes, girls, the kegger this Friday, etc. He was mainly just intrigued by the number of guys around him, all drawn by some strange homoerotic impulse. Oddly, Todd felt safe around here, but he wasn't sure why.

"LISTEN UP!!"

The voice came from Gregg, the tall, dark-haired kid who always wore a suit to his classes. Now, he was down to nothing but his jet-black dress pants, but never had he looked more commanding. The conversations quickly died like ambers in a fire -- all eyes were fixed on the half-nude Gregg. "OK, ladies. Good turn out tonight, I must say. But I'm somewhat disappointed, as this means a lot of your are violating the first two rules of Foot Club." That last sentence came out sternly, and the gravity of it had an obvious impact on all. "So let's review," started Gregg. "The first rule of Foot Club is ... you do not talk about Foot Club." Just like the movie, Todd thought. "The second rule of Foot Club is ... *you do NOT talk about Foot Club* -- unless you *want* to get punished. The third rule of Foot Club is that if someone is begging for mercy, you stop. The fourth rule: only two guys to a match. The fifth rule: one match at a time. The sixth rule of Foot Club is ... no shirts, and no shoes." The guys let out a holler to this one.

"The seventh rule," Gregg continued, "is that a match must go on as long as it needs to.

And the eight rule is ... if this is your first night at Foot Club ... you *have* to take part in a match. With that said ... who here is at their first Foot Club?" Todd was tempted to raise his hand, but was too timid. He was standing behind a row of guys, so perhaps he could just quietly slip out and get back to --

"I KNOW SOMEONE!"

Todd perked up -- it was Zach's voice. "Todd is here!" All the guys turned in the direction of Zach's finger, pointing directly at the flip-flopped Todd, his toes clenching at the sudden attention. "All right!" shouted Gregg. "Zach, since you pointed out the newbie, you gotta match him. Todd! Get over here!"

Todd was frozen. He couldn't move. He couldn't bring himself to do anything, but the group of guys parted like the Red Sea to let him into the center of their sweat-drenched circle. Zach had entered the center, and he never looked more fetching, donning nothing but jet-blue basketball shorts. "C'mon!" he cried, and soon Todd began dragging himself to the center, almost as if by an unconscious force. Next thing he new, he was there, facing Zach, with a sea of hungry, lusting eyes looking at every inch of his boyflesh. He slowly slipped out of his flips -- it just seemed like the natural thing to do -- and suddenly he saw himself at the first match. Gregg was getting ready to shout "Go!" when Todd stopped him. "Hold on, hold on, hold on!" Todd screamed. "Guys, I don't know what's going on ... I ... I just got here. I ... I found Zach's thing about Foot Club and got intrigued and ... I'm sorry, I don't know what I'm doing or even what's happening right now."

There was a pause. Gregg just smirked at him. "Well, you're about to find out what's happening. GO!"

+ + +

3. Zach began running at Todd and instantly tackled him to the ground. Todd, totally unaware of what was happening, soon sound himself horizontal in sand and panting for breath.

In the struggle, Zach was soon sitting on top of Todd's lap, using his beautiful blond boyfeet to hold Todd's arms to the ground. Todd's legs could flail but that's about all that they could do. With his free hands, Zach suddenly dug right into Todd's exposed ribs. "*Oh my god*!" screamed Todd, the last word breaking like a laughed syllable. He had never been tickled in his life. Oh sure, Todd loved dishing it at times, he loved watching others get tickled, but he had never experienced this sensation. It's like electricity was being whipped inside his body, and it was nice ... and terrible! Todd began laughing, but he couldn't stop! His emotions ... they were being turned on him. He tried to move, but Zach's strong, powerful feet were driving his wrists into the ground. Todd couldn't believe it. He couldn't move. He tried bucking his hips but Zach's weight was too much for him. The fingers began crawling along his ribs and up to his armpits, and Todd began spasming hard. He was laughing and laughing and *holy hell he couldn't stop laughing*! He wanted to say something, provide a coherent argument as to why he didn't deserve this, but the tickles were short-circuiting his brain, destroying any chance to develop a thought or say a word.

He heard the faint sounds of the guys hooting and hollering around him, but Zach's perfectly stiff fingernails were turning Todd into a vessel for tickle ghosts to emerge. He couldn't believe it. He was helpless and laughing and getting more exhausted with each passing second. He wanted it to stop so badly but his massive, raging hardon was saying otherwise. No doubt Zach could feel it underneath him as he tortured the helpless Todd, but there seemed to be other things on his mind: turning Todd into a helpless Tickle Toy.

Time blurred, his senses got fucked up, and he couldn't tell how much time was actually passing during his tickle episode. He wanted to scream and pass out, but it was impossible. He then had a small burst of energy and mustered up a shout: "GOD, I GIVE UP!!" "You have to do better than that!" sneered Zach. "Whahahahat do you want me to haha say, Zach?!" "That you are my footslave!!" Without even thinking Todd screamed at the top of his lungs "*I am your footslave Zach*!!"

...

It stopped.

It actually stopped. Todd couldn't believe it. Zach stood up and left Todd's weak body laying there in the middle of this circle of horny guys. His lungs were taking in bucket breaths, and then he turned onto his side, curled up in exhaustion. He had never been hornier in his life. As his head laid down on the sandy floor, he saw a virtual plethora of frat-toes gradually encroaching on him, and with weak breath just muttered a "feet ..." before he passed out. He wasn't in shock, he just needed to sleep.

+ + +

4. Todd woke with toes in his mouth.

They weren't too far deep, but there was a salty taste right at the front of his lips. He tried to move. He couldn't. His hands were tied behind his back with zip-ties, and his ankles were bound together with the same. He moved a bit, and after a few seconds, realized he was completely naked. The toes drew out from his mouth and his blurry vision gradually came into something clear: Zach's sole was hovering above him. Zach was in a chair, and Todd was on the floor of some room of the fraternity, a cheap rug keeping his naked body from the glossy hardwood. He moved his head around -- there was music in the background, guys were drinking, but their attire hadn't changed. They were all proudly barechested and barefooted, and even though he was embarrassed to be nude, Todd felt his cock twitch just a bit.

"Hey everyone!" shouted Gregg, "Zach's Tickle Toy just woke up!"

The guys standing around soon sat down, and Zach could see clearly now: he was in a small room, where two couches were facing each other against the near walls, and in-between the couches (on either side) were chairs, one which housed Zach and one which housed Gregg. Todd, horrifically, was at the center of all this, about a dozen pairs of bared and sandaled feet on each side of him, only a foot away. Todd's cock twitched again. Todd tried moving one more time, but he was toast: there was nothing he could do.

"What's going on?" asked the weak, still-recovering Todd.

Zach just laughed. "You're in hell now, my friend."

"What happened?"

"I dunno," started Zach. "Hey Bill -- mind playing back that footage?" Out of the corner of his eye, Todd could tell that some guy was at a computer in the corner of the room, and Todd thought he could see the YouTube logo on one of the pages there. Some buttons were pressed, and then out of the tinny computer speakers, he could hear his own voice scream out "*I am your footslave!*" Then it all came back to him. Oh shit.

"Yeah," started Zach, "up for one hour and already gained 200 hits. You're a cel-web-rity, footslave!" Todd just groaned, half-out of worry, half-out of exhaustion. "So," Zach continued "we broke out the beers and got some time here. I wanted to ask you a few questions, footslave. Why'd you come here tonight?"

The embarrassment was seeping in. "I'd rather not say ..." started Todd.

"C'mon!" started the guys on the couches. Their toes began prodding Todd, who was writhing around on the floor, helplessly bound. Some guys just wanted to poke Todd's helpless ribs. Some were wiggling their toes into his flesh, making him laugh, while a few just wanted to fondle their new erotic plaything. It was like an army of sweaty college feet had been unleashed on the poor boy all at once, hounds from hell traced on to his nervous sweat. The twitch was even bigger this time 'round.

"Not a good answer, Todd ..." sneered Gregg. "Now tell us ... why did you come here tonight?"

Todd blurted out "I have a foot fetish! I'm sorry, I just ... god, I just ... I have a major foot fetish, guys. There. I said it."

"Really?" stated one of the anonymous guys on the couch. "Zach, make him prove it."

"With pleasure," Zach said. "Footslave! Sniff that foot!" The guy on the couch was extending his meaty size 10, and soon the toes were practically walking on Todd's face, the foot slithering its way up to Todd's nose. Todd didn't even hesitate: his instincts mad him take a deep, amorous sniff of the guy's foot, and it smelled glorious. Sweaty, cheesy, and honestly just downright tasty. His hips moved in accordance, and suddenly Todd could feel the eyes of a dozen or so guys all focused on his crotch. He didn't have time to get embarrassed -- he just whiffed again. And again. And thrusted both times, subconsciously. He was immediately turned on.

"Wow," started Zach, "I think you might have it even worse than I do." Todd heard this through yet another sniff. He could then feel another random foot starting to play with his third leg ...

"Fuck, I love feet," Todd blurted out, without thinking. "Wow," started Gregg "This guy is a *total* footbitch. This is sensational! Hey Evan, start worshiping his soles."

Suddenly, the still-sniffing Todd felt some guy's mouth encompassing his pinkie toe on his left bound foot, and then working its way to the others. That foot on his crotch was having fun, and before long he found himself sucking really, really hard on the toes he was smelling just seconds ago. More feet landed on his chest and just began moving around. Some guys got down to the floor and began lightly tickling him on his ribs, legs, and crotch. Todd was going into pleasure overload, as everything he could ever want was happening right then and there. Todd could feel the rising tension inside of him, the tingles at the tip of his cock just too overwhelming to ignore, and before long his ticklish body soon turned into one big orgasm. "Fuck!!" Todd screamed, his hips trying to thrust upward but a few pairs of feet were keeping him down, just forcing his member to spew rockets upon rockets of hot manseed all over the place, some landing on the guys in his cock's immediate vicinity.

As he thrust his last burst out, splaying the room, he could feel the heat in the room escalate, and some of the couch guys getting down on their knees with their fingers drawn. "Guys, I'm ... I'm too sensitive. Give me a breather, please," Todd gently mewed, falling on deaf ears. Soon, everything was becoming a blur -- there was lots of tickling, lots of feet, lots of worshiping, all while the frat boys gradually began feeding the newfound slave nothing but beer and bong hits. Todd's body was exhausted beyond belief, but he was still horny, and the guys just couldn't stop using him. They were entranced.

Todd was soon licking feet in sandals, answering embarrassing fetish related questions, and kept catching the glimpses of camera flashes coming from unknowing directions. It was like a druggy haze, fantastic and confusing all at once. All he knew was that prior to passing out, he had actually lost track of how many times he came in front of his captors ...

+ + +

5. Light was peaking through the window of the room -- daybreak. All the guys around him were now passed out on the floor or on the couches, some with each others' feet in their open, sleeping mouths. Todd was still awake, still underneath Zach's chair, sucking on his master's toes like the world's best lollipop, all while Zach was gradually edging himself towards a climax. When he came (and Todd could feel Zach's toes clench in his warm mouth as he did so), Zach soon sighed, and just froze for a bit. Even Todd stopped worshiping his classmates' perfect soles, and just laid there, still bound (the zip-ties no doubt having made an impression on his wrists and ankles from all the struggling), and soon hearing Zach's voice saying "c'mon -- get dressed." Scissor snip. Scissor snip. The bonds were undone. Zach threw Todd's clothes -- flips included -- right at his face, and demanded again he get dressed. Todd did so at an exhausted snails pace, but Zach didn't rush him. When Todd looked up at him, he had a look of acknowledgment from Zach: saying that "yeah, I beat you, but I was in your place once." Todd felt better, somehow.

Next thing he knew, Zach was slowly helping Todd walk back to his dorm. No words were said -- the slap of their sandals against their heels in the damp morning air said enough. Todd reached into his pocket and pulled out his cell phone -- he had signed up for Facebook Mobile, and had discovered that he had just been tagged in 44 new photos. There was absolutely no going back at this point.

As Todd got back to his dorm, Zach turned to him and smiled. "You did great, mate," he started. "Really -- you're awesome." "Thanks," whispered back Todd, weakly. "Any questions?", asked Zach. Todd thought, and could only come up with one: "Yeah ... when's the next meeting?" Zach leaned and whispered into his ear "the date and time is written all over your chest." Todd really didn't remember, but knew Zach wasn't lying.

Todd opened the door to his room, aware of the sound of Doug's snoring. He sat down at his computer, and just reeled over all that happened. The he looked up -- the TV was still roaring quietly, but Doug's feet were propped up on the footrest of their couch ... and they were bared.

They were prefect. Todd drew closer. Size 10. Softest soles in the world. He brought his nose to the base of the toes, inhaled, and felt himself spring to life all over again. He tried to remember all the feet that he had worshiped in the past six hours, but nothing hit him as hard as this. This is what he had wanted to see for months, and now that those perfect feet were in front of him, and they were everything he could imagine and more. He listened. Doug was still snoring. After all he had just gone through -- Todd's inhibitions were gone.

Without thinking, he went and began lightly sucking on Doug's perfect, glorious toes. He felt great. He was alive again, his rod hardening into a kind of invincible steel. In a matter of seconds, his worshiping went from simple to passionate, and was soon engulfing the feet with his mouth, savoring every salty molecule. He was so engaged, he didn't even notice that Doug stopped snoring. He did notice this, though:

"Dude ... what are you doing?"

Todd looked at Doug -- he was wide awake. His tone was more curious than vindictive, but here Todd was: caught red-handed in his horny pursuit of the perfect foot to worship. "I ... I'm sorry, Doug. I just ... I have a foot fetish and I've been wanting to see your feet for so long and I would've given anything to worship them and just acted. I'm really, really sorry."

There was a pause. Doug cocked his eyebrow, and asked "*Anything*?"

And Todd was found out, his greatest weakness suddenly exposed at the moment he least expected it, realizing now that he would be a perpetual footslave to the person who he thought would least control him ... and there was nothing he could do about it.

Perhaps this is why it was the start to the greatest day of his life.

STONED INDIFFERENCE
(originally appeared in *How to Be a Tickle Slave*)

+ + +

I'm not going to advocate any sort of drug-use whatsoever here, but the use of ganja can certainly make you open to more "exciting" experiences. Your body's sensitivity and reception towards pleasure, for example, is heightened to an unfathomable degree. As such, stoned tickling (hell, even stoned foot-worship) is mind-blowing. This was a story that explored this notion to its logical conclusion, and, well, let's just say I wouldn't be envious if I was one of my own characters in this one ...

Lee's flip-flops were about to fall off. This wasn't a good thing.

Elevated about a solid foot off of the ground, Lee was being pressed up against the wall outside his college cafeteria by a bulky, buzz-cut young jock named Andy. Andy's forearm was pressing right up into Lee's chest. Lee, being the geeky English major that he was, could do nothing but play puppet to his overly-aggressive handler.

"Gimme the goddamn card, Nerdlinger!"

"C'mon -- these last meals are for me!" said Lee as best as he could through his presently-squished face. His left flip dropped to the floor.

"Do you want to look good for your online girlfriend or not?" bellowed Andy, his two jock friends behind him snickering at the remark.

Reluctantly, and without much choice, Lee handed over his meal card to Andy. Andy released the shy freshman, who immediately dropped to the ground. Gasping for air, Lee could hear Andy make some snidely stupid remark as he entered the cafeteria with his meal card: "Dropped your sandal, Nerdlinger." Almost on cue, Lee could feel his stomach rumble. He was going to be hungry tonight ... again.

Angrily walking back to his room, Lee thought about how this whole predicament started. Writing for his college's student paper during his first term, Lee secretly had journalistic dreams, wanting to become a pro music critic -- unfortunately, there already was a music columnist at his campus paper named Evan; he had a goofy whiteboy fro but the kid knew what he was talking about, so Lee knew best to stay off. Wanting to break into the journalism clique by any means necessary, Lee talked to the paper's editors (seniors, naturally) willing to take on any story available. Wanting to test him out with a high profile piece his first time out, the seniors had him cover the big homecoming football game. Lee prosed his coverage up to make it as dramatic as possible, but what he failed to realize (as did his copyeditors, who just took him at his word) was that there were two Andy's on the team: Andy Fitzpatrick and Andy Holmes. In his article, Lee wrote that Holmes had completed the game-winning touchdown ... when it was in fact Fitzpatrick (putting Holmes' name in the headline certainly didn't help either). Though the captain of the team fired off a very angry letter to the paper, it was Fitzpatrick himself who would up giving Lee the hardest time: calling him names in passing between classes, writing embarrassing remarks on Lee's Facebook wall, and -- as of recent -- bullying him into giving him his meal card so that Andy could swipe himself in to the cafeteria. Either Andy lived off-campus or he was just being a dick to Lee ... either way, it annoyed him.

Storming into his room, Lee kicked off his flips and jumped right into his bed, burrowing his head into his pillow. His roommate Brandon, who was on his computer, looked over to see his roommate's chest heaving mightily: these were angry breaths. The dark-haired Brandon turned to Lee and asked what any good friend would ask in such a situation:

"What the fuck, man?"

"God, I fucking hate Andy." said Lee, angrily, through his pillow.

"Well, that's not too out of the ordinary. What'd he do this time?"

Lee sat up and faced his roommate: "He took my meal card. *Again*. This is the fifth time he's done it! I practically had to beg him to get it back from him last time around. He's used up so many that I don't think I'm going to have enough meals to finish out the term. I mean ... Christ, it was one typo, man!"

"Well, in his defense, it was a pretty big typo."

"You're not helping, Brandon."

"Sorry dude. I'm just saying."

Lee went face down into his pillow again. Brandon walked over to his roommate and placed his hand on Lee's back.

"Dude, he may be an asshole, but you can't let this stuff get to you. Why don't you go out tonight? Have some fun? Huh? I hear Cindy Dorffman is going to be holding a kickass party at her house tonight. You should go. It's off-campus so you know shit's gonna get wild."

"Are you going?"

"Nah, man. I'm heading back to the city to see my 'rents this weekend. They want to 'restructure my student loan payments' this weekend, whatever that means. I figure I can get some free meals out of it as well, so I figured what the hell."

"When do you leave?"

"Tonight. Why?"

"I dunno," said Lee, facing his handsome roommate again. "Just nice to not be alone sometimes, you know?"

"I know man. Hey -- why don't you jack it to one of your tickle videos? That always seems to cheer you up."

"Dude, it's called having a tickle fetish, and sometimes videos just don't match to the real thing, ya know?"

"Well, whatever. I'm just offering suggestions."

There was a pregnant pause. Lee started: "You know, my offer still stands ..."

"Ha!" laughed Brandon. "Dude, again, I'm not gay, and even if I were to let you tie me up and tickle me, it'd have to be for more than $100. Though I dunno, we'll see how this whole 'loan restructuring' thing goes, ha ha." Lee was stunned: he actually said "ha ha."

Brandon looked at the clock on his cell phone. "Oh shit dude, I gotta go!" He ran to his drawer to get a fresh pair of socks and began putting them on. He turned to Lee: "Ya know, man, if you want that frozen pizza in my mini-fridge, you can have it, dude."

"Really?"

"Pfft, why not. I'll be gone all weekend anyways. 'sides -- you're a lot more fun when you're not starving or pissed off."

Lee smiled. "Thanks, roomie."

"Seriously, Lee: have a good time tonight. You can even steal one of my joints if that'll help."

Lee smirked. "You do know you're a good guy, you know that?"

"You're damn right, dude. And don't you forget it." Brandon said that last bit with a smile. Slinging his backpack over his shoulder, he headed for the door. "Catch ya later, Lee."

"Later, man."

The door shut behind Brandon as he dashed out. Lee took a heavy sigh, and laid back into his bed. Before long, he was sleeping.

+ + +

When Lee woke up, it was well past 9PM. Distraught, he popped Brandon's frozen pizza in the kitchen in his common area, and took a shower while it cooked. When Lee was all dressed again (button T-shirt, jeans, and flips -- his favorite look), he helped himself to some pizza, checked his e-mail, some foot and tickle sites, and then his Facebook. His friend Lisa (from AP Lit) did a Facebook invite, asking him to Cindy's crazy party. At least one of his friends would be there if he went. Maybe going would be a good idea, he thought. He finished his third slice of greasy pepperoni pizza, placed the remaining slices in Brandon's mini-fridge, and then made up his mind: he was going to this party. He called Lisa and was soon heading out the door in no time flat.

Meeting the stunning, blonde girl that was Lisa over at her dorm entrance, Lee walked with her as he told her of his latest run-ins with Andy and she told him of how things are getting mixed up with two guys in her poetry class who are best friends but both kinda like her. They had a great understanding. When arriving at the somewhat decrepit house that Cindy lived it, it was obvious that the party was well under way: music was blaring out from the windows, a bunch of guys were casually swigging Bud Lite on the front porch, a girl was already throwing up by the side of the house, etc. Though reluctant, Lee went in, and it wasn't long before Lisa found some other friends and soon branched off, leaving Lee by his lonesome. He made his way upstairs, where it was surprisingly dark. Looking about the open-door rooms, he eventually found a room that was filled with had to be 20, 25 people. A bunch of people were watching *The Dark Knight* in Blu-ray, and on a big HD TV as well -- no wonder the lights were darkened. Most everyone had a beer, but Lee was OK for the time being. He hugged the back wall and just watched with everyone else (some people hadn't seen it yet, so the pencil scene was a great surprise -- Lee smiled at their horrified reactions).

Some 20 minutes later, a voice cried out "Hey, I'm hot-boxin' in the bathroom if anyone wants to join." Lee knew what that meant, and yeah, he wanted to smoke up too -- this was a night to forget about his worries. He made his way into the cramped little bathroom on the second floor of this house and closed the door behind him. He turned and saw who that voice belonged to: Andy (Fitzpatrick).

"Oh, Nerdlinger."

Lee paused. "Do I have to beg to get my card back this time?"

"Nah," said Andy, who seemed to be in usually good spirits. "Here ya go man." Andy handed Lee his meal card back, as if it were no big deal. This was unusual. Andy looked around the cramped room. "Just you, Nerdlinger?"

"Um, yeah, I guess."

"Man ... I thought more people would want to smoke up, I guess. This is kinda disappointing."

All Lee could do was stare at his sometimes-nemesis. He was decked in a red T-shirt, backwards Yankees cap, cargo shorts, and tennis shoes with ankle socks -- he was ... kind of attractive for the moment. Andy was acting as if all the bullying over the past couple of months was no big deal. In fact, it seemed like Andy hardly knew him at all. Lee wondered if Andy had already had a bowl or two prior.

"Well, hey," said Lee, somewhat nervously, "if people don't want to join in, that just means more grass for us, right?"

Andy laughed a bit. "You're damn right, Nerdlinger. Why spread the wealth, ya know?" Lee actually didn't know, but nodded in agreement anyway. Andy reached to the apple on the small little sink, which, Lee noticed, had been carved out into a makeshift bong. There was a healthy amount of weed on the top, and before long Andy grabbed a lighter and began smoking. He inhaled a deep breath ... and then handed it to Lee. Given that the bathroom was, in fact, pretty small, the smoke was accumulating and genuinely "hotboxing", meaning the guys were getting second-hand inhales as well. Lee was going to stop as soon as Andy did, but Andy kept passing the apple back and forth -- they must've had ten hits between them! Around the final one, Lee began to feel the effects that the grass was having on him ... and this was some potent stuff. Lee began laughing for no reason. Andy turned to him with that goofy stoner grin slapped upon his face.

"What's so funny, man?"

Lee giggled. "I don't know, man!"

"Awesome." The boys laughed and suddenly felt good about ... well, everything. Lee started at himself in the bathroom mirror. Then at the door handle for no reason. Then to Andy, who was looking down on the floor for some reason. Lee tried to focus in on what Andy was so intently viewing ... and ... no. It couldn't be.

Andy was looking at Lee's own toes.

There wasn't a doubt that they looked good in cheap flip-flops and draped in blue jeans as they did now, but Andy looked positively hypnotized by then. Lee wanted to test his theory: he wiggled his toes, and it had a visible effect on Andy: his mouth dropped open, agape in wonder. Lee wiggled again, and Andy took a deep, unconscious breath. Lee wondered if it was true, so tried to -- in the stoned haze of his mind -- be very careful with what he was going to say.

"Andy ... what are you looking at?"

"Oh, um ... nothing, man."

"Were you looking at my feet, dude?"

"... no."

"It's OK to say that you were, man."

Andy paused, still staring downward. "OK, I totally was."

"You like 'em?"

"Oh god yes." Andy stared up. "I mean ... no I ... I don't know."

Lee grinned. "Andy ... do you have a foot fetish?"

Andy's face went beat-red. "... maybe."

Lee couldn't stop grinning. "I think you do, Andy."

"Oh god, dude! Please, don't tell anyone! The guys would hate me if they knew I was staring at their feet in the locker room. Promise me you won't tell them, dude!"

Wow, Andy's paranoia was really taking over in record time. Lee, suddenly, had an ingenious idea.

"Sit down." he instructed the jock. Obediently, Andy sat down on the toilet seat. Lee sat down on the edge of the cheap little bathtub installed in this bathroom. Lee raised his sandaled foot and placed it right Andy's lap.

"OK, Andy -- I'll keep your secret ... but only if you worship my foot."

Andy, stoned out of his gourd, got an excited look on his face. "Really?" Somewhere in the back of his mind, Lee knew that were they not as baked as they were, this wouldn't even be happening. Right now, however, it was turning into a fantastic, erotic dream.

"Yes, Andy -- really."

Andy cupped Lee's foot in his hands, and slowly, carefully, removed Lee's sandal and let it slap against the tile floor. Lee looked up: pot smoke was still circling the horny young men. Cautiously, Andy elevated Lee's foot up to his nose, and inserted his nostrils right at the base of his big toe. Andy inhaled, and Lee could see it was affecting him deeply. While one hand held onto Lee's foot, Andy's other hand immediately clutched his own crotch area, feeling for some sort of erection lost in cargo-short jungle. Lee was blown away: Andy got a hardon simply by smelling his foot. Slowly, Andy's tongue darted out to Lee's toe-pad, and it felt glorious. First the tongue was licking the ends of Lee's toes, almost cautiously, but a few moments later, the jock's big, moist, meaty tongue was darting in-between Lee's small forest of blonde toehair, slithering in-between the spaces between his toes. Lee leaned back, and tried his hardest not to think of his own instant boner ... but being as high as he was, that hardon was about all he could think of. His toebath felt like the best thing he had ever felt in his life, and giving how Andy's free hand was continually adjusting something underneath his shorts, Lee surmised that Andy was enjoying himself as well. Then it call came to a grinding halt.

There were three sharp rasps on the bathroom door. "Hey, is someone in there? I need to go!"

Andy's face shot up. He immediately dropped Lee's foot and ran the apple-bong underneath the sink to try and get all the residue out. Lee slid his moist foot into his flip again, and soon both boys exited the bathroom while some other guy rushed in and closed (and locked) the door behind him. Standing in the dim hallway, Lee noticed an erection making itself known in Andy's shorts. Lee looked at Andy and, without any hesitation, said simply: "Back to my place?" Still stupidly grinning, Andy nodded. If Lee wasn't as stoned as he was, he'd be amazed by how easy it was to convince his nemesis to do such wonderful things ...

+ + +

When they got back to Lee's room, only the glow of Lee & Brandon's dual screensavers was illuminating the small dorm that Lee called home. As soon as Andy entered and Lee locked the door behind the both of them, Andy -- stupid, stoned, and very horny -- turned to the small geek and asked simply "OK -- how do we do this?"

Lee, enjoying the slight roleplay from earlier, clumsily said whatever came out of his mouth.

"Well, first off, how can a slave worship the feet of his master if the slave himself is not barefoot?"

"Of course, master!" said Andy, who kneeled down and was able to slide both his sneakers and his ankle socks off in one go. Were Lee sober, he would've noticed a few things already: 1> Andy jumped right in by calling him "master." 2> Back in Cindy's house, Lee said "worship" and Andy knew exactly what it meant. And 3> holy shit, Andy Fitzpatrick had a goddamn foot fetish and had already given his toes a tonguebath! Andy, now nursing his own rod of steel, wanted to see just how far he could go.

Andy looked eager: "May I worship master's feet now?"

Lee was severely enjoying this roleplay. "No! First, you must answer me ... what do you want to do to my feet?"

"Oh man" started Andy a stoned, horned-up monologue, "what wouldn't I want to do to them? I want to lick them and kiss them and suck on your toes and lick them and tie you up and tickle you and have your feet sticking out over the edge of your bed while still in jeans and rub my cock along the tops of your feet just so that your foothair stimulates it just enough and then cum all over you and then lick your num-nums all over again!"

4> Andy just called Lee's toes 'num-nums'.

"OK," started Lee, "you may do so, but *first!* Tell me ... how ticklish are you?"

Andy yelped, completely out of character. "Oh god, very."

"Well then, how much tickling will you be willing to endure to live out your fantasy?"

"Oh man, I dunno ..."

Lee jumped on his bed, his legs hanging off the side, facing Andy. He let his flips drop to the floor. He purposely rolled his feet around in the air just to see how hypnotized his stoned little jock friend was. Andy's tone was changing:

"Well, god ... they're just so goddamn beautiful. I dunno ... I'd do anything just to get to taste 'em again."

"That's all you want to do? To taste them?"

"To taste them and worship them and fuck them and lick them all over again, yes master."

"Then take your shirt off and lay on my bed, slave. You need to be tied up first."

"Yes, master."

5> Andy was letting himself get tied up for tickling just so he could taste Lee's feet. Fucking wow.

6> Andy automatically put his arms over his head, as if he knew what position to be tied and tickled in.

Lee went into his dresser and found the longest dress ties he could find. He soon began securing Andy's arms to the bed's frame, and then moved over to Andy's feet. Lee had to stop for a moment -- he was glaring at the tops of Andy's feet, and they were glorious.

Huge, size 12 monsters with wonderful-looking toes, and just the perfect amount of hair on the tops. Lee was getting turned on all over again, as if there was an erection inside his erection (which was now threatening to rip a hole in his jeans at the moment). After he secured the anxious jockboy, Lee pulled out one other tie and began to blindfold his newfound footslave.

"Oh, c'mon, man! I can't see!"

"That's kind of the point" said Lee, who -- now that Andy was blindfolded, began stripping down to his boxers. Lee jumped up on his bed and straddled Andy right at his midsection. Already the jock was struggling. Lee began asking a series of questions to which he already knew the answer to.

"Do you like being tickled, my slave? I bet you love being tickled. Where are your ticklish spots?"

Grinning, Andy yelled "I'm not telling you!"

"Well we'll just have to find out now won't we?" And like an eager miner, Lee's index finger slowly descended into Andy's belly button. When their skin made contact, Andy screamed.

"DON'T!"

"Oh, it's too late, tickle slave!"

Lee's finger began twisting and contorting within that belly button, like a hungry tickle worm searching for subterranean wells of tickle juice. Lee was relishing the moment: with each move of his finger, he could see Andy's body writhe in accordance. Soon, the finger exited the belly region and both hands began lightly spider-tickling the jock's stomach, sending Andy into giggle convulsions. As the hands slowly, carefully worked their way up his ribcage like a ladder made of laughter, Lee began saying diminutive, simple things to make his stoned acquaintance feel even more powerless:

"Who's my tickle toy? Who likes being tickled? Hey everyone -- laugh if you want to be tickled!" (Andy's jaw looked almost unhinged. His midsection began thrusting in horny desperation as tickle victim.) "Sounds like we have someone who wants to be tickled! Don't worry, Andy: we got bags and bags of tickles here for you, and we're going to use each and every one on you! So much tickling! Tickle tickle tickle tickle! You're such a good tickle toy. I'm just gonna keep on tickling you until you stop laughing ... which is going to be a long, long time, Tickle Toy."

Sweat began collecting in Andy's damp armpits. His toes began twisting and contorting, as if trying to physically release all the tickles from his body. Though still pretty gone in a daze of horny bongwater, Lee was inhaling these small details, saving them for later. Lee's hands found their way onto Andy's hairy thighs, and they squeezed as if tickle juice would come out. Andy yelped and laughed some more. As far as the blindfolded Andy was concerned, Lee's hands turned back into the dreaded Tickle Spiders, and they were ... going up the legs of victim's shorts! They were now under his shorts -- he couldn't take it anymore!

Lee looked on -- the tentpole was so pronounced Andy could hold a circus under there. As caught up as he was in it, Lee suddenly stopped tickling his victim, and collapsed right next to his bound side, his nose dangerously close to Andy's exposed armpit. Even though he wasn't being tickled, these laughter aftershocks kept coming in waves, and Lee was enjoying each and every one. Lee's devious finger reached over and scratched the top of Andy's tent pole, the sensation felt between a layer of both cargo and boxer fabric. Andy's midsection contracted as much as it could, but it couldn't escape. Lee grinned again, his finger now circling the top of Andy's cockhead:

"Tell me, slave ... what do you want to have happen now?"

"Oh god ... I need to cum!"

"What was that?"

"I need to cum, master! Oh god I need to cum!"

Positioned parallel to him, Lee's barefeet now began rubbing against Andy's bound feet, almost polishing them.

"Oh, you need to cum, do you? I thought you wanted to worship my feet ... "

"I want to do both!"

"Well, you can have both, but only under one condition."

"What's that?" said Andy, desperate, pleadingly.

"You gotta suffer through more tickling."

"Noooooooo!"

"No? Well no cumming or toe-sucking for you ..."

"No no -- it's OK! You can tickle me! Tickle me to your hearts content ... but goddammit let me cum!"

Lee noted what he was doing: maybe the foot-foot rub and the cockhead circling was too much ... especially at the same time. He whispered to Andy "OK, Tickle Toy. Walk me through what you want me to do." The finger was still circling. Both were still horny and fantastically stoned.

"OK OK OK OK OK ... stop circling for a second. OK. Now. Undo my shorts button. OK. Now pull the zipper down ... slowly. Oh yeah. That feels so goddamn good. OK. Pull the shorts down. No, further. OK. Now ... god ... pull my shorts down. Yeah. Oh god. OH GOD my cock feels free."

Lee's hands tweaked Andy's nipples slightly.

"OH god no! OK OK ... now ... um ... rub your big toe along my shaft."

Lee's finger instead lightly circled the massive, meaty cut cockhead of Mr. Fitzpatrick. "Are you sure about that? Looks like you could burst right about now."

"I'm about to!!"

Lee's finger stopped. He swung his feet over so they were now facing the still-blind Andy. He placed both feet right near the jock's face.

"Sniff."

Andy did, and his hips rose with his inhale. Andy's cock was even harder now. Lee readjusted himself and took his big toe and placed it right at the base of Andy's cock ... and began dragging it up ... slowly ... centimeters at a time ... and, just like that, Andy came. Hard. Gushing. Shot after shot. Lee got off his bed, his own hardon straining through his boxers. He stood on the other side of his room and evaluated what was going on: this horny young jock boy who had tormented him so frequently as of late just came after hours of tickle torture and a single toe against his cock. This was, unreal. In fact, the joyous stoner haze he had on before was starting to fade.

Suddenly, Lee was a bit scared, as if he was starting to get sober, then surely the post-orgasm Andy was starting to feel that same way as well ... and Christ, what would he do if he suddenly realized that he was tied to a bed in a room he didn't know, covered in cum and Nerdlinger staring at him with a hardon in his shorts? Lee thought about running or untying or ... no.

Lee caught a glimpse of Andy's soles, perfect & glorious, in the light of his screensaver. They looked ... godlike. Lee's hardon was still raging, and he had to satisfy it. He hadn't even pleasured himself to Andy's feet yet! Then, suddenly, he remembered what Brandon had said. Reaching down in Brandon's cigar box that was off to the side of his desk, he pulled out a perfectly rolled joint, and just grinned.

He walked over to his still-bound, still-blind victim, placed the joint to his lips, held up the lighter, and said "inhale." Andy did as he was told, and he took a massive, massive hit. Lee smoked even more. He was buzzing again, and no doubt Andy was as well. Tired, blindfolded, and completely helpless, Andy's face turned to where (he thought) Lee was, and said "Can I worship your feet now?"

Lee grinned, setting the spliff down in Brandon's ashtray on his desk. He turned to Andy, staring at those size 12 monsters, and simply said "Ya know, I hear you get more ticklish after cumming."

+ + +

The "Noooo" that followed would echo in Lee's life forever -- he heard nothing louder, nothing more desperate, and nothing as satisfying. Lee was loving being a 'Ler ...

MY TICKLISH REVENGE

(originally appeared in *How to Be a Tickle Slave*)

+ + +

In the life of just about any kinky person, there will be awkward moments, no doubt, whether it be saying the wrong thing to the person you thought was on your wavelength or just perhaps misjudging how you could trust a certain person. That assuredly happened to me in my post-college years, trusting a dear friend with personal information only to have that spat back in my face later on. It was fairly dramatic situation and one that took me a long time to let go of the anger from. Thus, as part of the healing, I wound up writing a story about it. Of course, the whole thing is pure fantasy and conjecture (as all my stories are), but it was more pointed and bitter than anything I had written to that point, but it definitely needed to happen, and the resulting story makes me glad I did in the end ...

Doug was smoking a cigarette outside. No, scratch that: Doug was angrily smoking a cigarette outside.

He was sitting right in front of his parking space in front of his apartment. It was around 1AM, the moon was out and lighting the night sky, while the 26-year old sat there in exile. A great drunken night of sex with his girlfriend had turned into a great big drunken post-sex argument with his girlfriend. They fought, she broke his glasses, and then proceeded to kick him out of the very apartment they rented together. The night sky was chill, and Doug was shivering: he only had on his ratty old black The Who T-shirt, his light-blue jeans with big knee holes, and his long cotton socks and black Chuck Taylors. This is how I've come to see Doug more than once. This wasn't the first time I had been called over to be mediator to this troubled couple's arguments. This isn't the first time I've seen the young guy locked out of his apartment by his psychotic partner. This isn't the first time he's reached out for help. This will be the first time I don't help him, however.

Doug and I were insanely good friends. Unbelievably so. Thought-predictingly, sentence-finishingly good. That is until that one night. That one, drunken night. The night when I got candid with him, told him about my foot fetish. He was very nice about, not fully understanding but certainly responding well to the news, asking a few questions but generally humoring me about the only real secret I was hiding from him. Of course, he didn't know I had always fantasized about his feet: his size 9, soft-as-hell, slightly furry on top feet that just drove me up the fucking wall. Doug always had a well-kept beard that he maintained, and it was usually that and his lightly hairy hands that always reminded me of those perfect-looking podicial treasures. I say "reminded" because he was always "self-conscious" about his feet. He rarely, if ever, went barefoot. He owned sandals but pretty much never donned them. He was a shoe guy, by and large. As such, his soles were kept in mint condition: soft, clean, and so fucking unbelievably ticklish.

Yet I didn't tell him all this. His girlfriend, however, was eavesdropping: listening in. She misunderstood so much, burst into the room, called me "faggot" and the top of her lungs, and demanded I leave her house. This news surprised the both of us, and an argument soon ensued. Bitch then broke my cell phone just because. Everyone walked away bitterly. When I finally saw Doug a week later, he was cold, distant. For some truly inexplicable reason, he had taken her side on everything. He felt "betrayed" for some reason, and I couldn't figure out why. That distance turned into bitterness, and I still didn't understand why I had just lost my best friend. He continued on as nothing happened. To say I was resentful would be an understatement.

Which leads us to why tonight was so weird. He called me up to inform me he got locked out (again) and needed to find a place to crash. I recommended my place (which he stayed at before), but he felt "uncomfortable" around me. "So why did you call?" I asked. "'cos I have no one else to talk to" he replied. I didn't understand it. Positively none of this made sense. Yet even with everything, I still considered him a friend. I drove out to help him. I let him into my car. He put out his cigarette and got in, still shivering somewhat. We started driving off -- with no particular destination in mind -- and I was trying to figure out what happened. He and his girlfriend were fighting again (nothing new), but this time it was about me for some reason. His explanation soon turned into a tirade: he kept on asking why I had to fuck everything up for him, to which I sat there dumbfounded and confused. Apparently he hadn't gotten over the alleged "incident," despite the fact that nothing had happened. I did my best to contain my anger, but he kept badgering me without any legitimate basis.

I had enough, pulled over the side of the road, and got out. He got out too, and continued yelling at me, asking why I had to even get involved in his life. I reminded him that we used to be good friends and it was just as much his deal as it was mine but apparently that wasn't a good-enough explanation from him. He then started mocking me, and I began to really question why I was called in the first place. The hate that was spewing out of his mouth -- I couldn't stand it. I selfishly thought of all the good times we shared, all the bars we used to drink at, all the movies we had rented and drunkenly mocked. He had developed a selective memory about all of that, apparently. I was not only a stranger to him: I was point of hatred.

At that point, I had had enough. While he stood next to the passenger-side door extolling his hate-speech, I popped open the trunk, and grabbed a bottle of chloroform that was on loan to me by a noted area kinkster. I took a breath in -- taking in full understanding of everything that was about to happen -- and then released. I opened up the bottle of chloroform, pulled a dusty rag from the trunk space, dipped just the right amount in it, sealed up the bottle, and closed the trunk, rag in hand. I walked right over to Doug -- still talking for some reason -- and pressed the rag right up to his mouth in mid-sentence. He struggled for a moment, but things happened too quickly. Within five seconds, he was out. He collapsed on the ground by the side of the road. Fortunately at this hour, there weren't many cars around, and I suspect the ones that were just thought he was drunk. I hoisted him back into the car, and strapped him. I couldn't believe it: I was getting a tear in my eye. God, I really hated that I was doing this, but I had to be honest: one can only take so much abuse for so long before one snaps. I had been Mr. Nice Guy long enough, jerked around by his faulty logic and accusatory tone to an absurd degree. Now, it was time for him to feel alone and isolated -- at my hands, of course ...

+ + +

When Doug woke up, the first thing he noticed was the taste: slightly smelly, very colorful, and very strange. Textured. Cotton-y. Oh yes: I only hope that he would realize that it was my work socks from that very day that were jammed into his mouth. He tried moving his tongue, but all he did was just lick more toe sweat. The sock had then been taped over his mouth, so he couldn't do jack about it. The second thing he noticed was that he couldn't move. His hands were tied very tightly behind his back. Very tightly. He wasn't feeling rope-burn, but he sure as hell couldn't move his hands. Then, of course, were his legs. Dude was still fully clothed -- he even still had his shoes on! -- but his jeans were providing nice cover: his ankles were tightly duct-taped , and even the area just above his knees was restrained as well. He couldn't spread his legs apart even if he wanted to and his life depended on it. Nope: instead, he was belly down on my big futon in my own apartment, helpless as a baby seal. He could move his legs up and down if he wanted. He could even do The Worm. That was about it. He tried making muffled noises, but all he was greeted with was silent. He looked around. It was obviously my apartment, but everything was dark. He tried screaming through his gag, he tried struggling against his bonds, but it was totally useless: he was helpless. He was mine.

After about 10 minutes of fear-induced hysteria, I turned out a small lamp near the foot of the futon (and where his feet were). He tried looking, but the belly-down position didn't give his neck much arc. He tried to see what he could, but that's when I spoke up. "Hey there Doug. It's me." He struggled some more. "Yeah, I know. I'm sorry buddy, but you're home now. And, well, you're gonna be here for awhile." Struggling again. I sat on the futon, my lap about a foot away from his writhing legs. Those somewhat-worn shoes not even knowing where they'd end up in a bit.

Doug was obviously a bit angry, but I let him have his moment. "Listen up, dumbass," I said in a somewhat-menacing tone, "Do you want to know what's going to happen to you?" His neck arced as much as it could and he glared at me. I smiled. "You see Doug, I've been patient with you. I've been patient as hell, really. When you and your girlfriend decided to shaft me for virtually no reason whatsoever, I took it in stride. I know some friendships cannot last forever, and I obviously hit a button with you. I'd apologize, but I don't really know what apologize for. For being myself? For treating you like the good guy that I know you are? It's hard to say, really. Yet when I get this call out of the blue after dealing with you ignoring me for months, when I pick you up -- yourself obviously still liquored up as hell -- and have to deal with nonsense, accusations, and lies flying out of your mouth, what am I supposed to do, Doug? Smile? Thank you for the favor? Need I remind you of my broken phone? Of being called 'faggot'? Of all the isolation and loneliness you forced upon me? All I wanted was an explanation and I never got one, despite reaching out to you. And now you want me to house you again but you can't trust me enough to stay with me? Well I had it, good friend. I've gone way beyond the limit of casual generosity for you. Right now, I get to be jealous. I get to be selfish. I get to ... teach you a lesson." More struggling, take six. "And oh yes, Doug, it's going to involve your ... feet."

The neck arced again: now his eyes were wide -- with terror.

I grabbed his jeans by the belt loops, and used that to toss him around, the boy now belly-up. I stood up and got more duct-tape. I grabbed him by the ankles and pulled his body down so that his legs were just barely over the wooden edge of the futon. I looped the tape through the gap between his ankle-tape and knee-tape to the armrest, essentially isolating his feet to just barely be sticking out over the edge of the futon. I taped and taped -- Doug was not going anywhere tonight. He still tried struggling on occasion, but already his energy was starting to waver. I was becoming alarmingly pleased with how things were going. I pulled over a chair, and sat right in front of his feet. He tried wavering them around from the ankles, but his movement was extremely limited. I knew just what it'd take to put him over the edge ...

I gripped his left shoe with my hand. He got panicked. My grip tightened. I could feel the foot inside trying to break my hold -- like a moth trapped inside a mason jar -- but it was no use. I was owning this boy tonight. I grabbed his right one now, and he fidgeted and panicked like any good victim should. All I did was hold those shoes in place until the fluttering feet inside calmed down. Once they did, I simply ran my hands up and down the tops of his shoes, just to make his own feet feel like they're objects: like they're not even his anymore. He struggled so more, but, again, to no avail. Also, not as much struggling this time: this was all a good thing. It was almost as if he was resigning to his fate.

Both my hands made their way to his laces, and began slowly pulling those knots undone. I talked as I did so. "So, as you know Doug, I have a male foot fetish. It's huge. It's gigantic. If this were real life, I would be paying you hundreds of dollars just to do what I'm doing right now for free. Yeah, a foot fetish is homoerotic -- I'm not going to deny that -- but 'faggot'? No, not as much so. I know you're 'self-conscious' about your feet being unshod, but Christ man -- you can't hide those things from me forever. They're just too fucking amazing. I think after all the shit I've been through, I deserve a little treat, don't you?" He tried screaming through his gag. It was beautifully muffled. The undone laces now dangled downward. I loosed up the tongues on both of them. "Look at me, Doug." He didn't. "*Look at me*!" I yelled in a threatening baritone. He stopped ... and craned his head upwards. Our eyes met.

"Think about everything I've been through. Think of all the isolation that you put me through. Think of everything I lost because of you. Think about how you called me tonight, and think about everything that you said." A moment passed. I then very quietly said to him "Doug, if our roles were reversed, wouldn't you do the same?"

The look that he gave me wasn't one of acknowledgment or resentment. He probably wouldn't do the same if our roles were reversed, but he knew that he wasn't a completely blameless creature at this moment. He just gave me the slightest of nods. He knew. He understood. He didn't condone, but he understood. In truth, that took me by surprise. He didn't have to. He should've been angry still. I stepped away for a moment, and then came back with an sleeping eye-mask. I placed it over his eyes. "You don't need to see what happens next, buddy."

He muffled some things but I sure as hell couldn't understand (nor did I care to hear). I unzipped and pulled off my own jeans at this point: I had been sporting a hardon ever since he woke up. I didn't take off my boxers just yet -- I wanted to play with my toy, first. I went to his left shoe, wrapped my hands around it, and pulled it off very, very slowly. This was deliberate: I wanted to make each moment unbearable for him. Molasses was faster than this. I just wanted him to feel his meager protection slipping away from him. Past the ankle, the sole, the toes -- it was off. The socked foot in front of me wiggled a bit -- it was breathing. I did the same to the other foot, and then boom: I had two socked Dougfeet right in front of me. Oh boy. This was fun. I examined the soles of his socks: there foot impressions. Right around the toes and the arch and heel: he had been wearing these socks all day today (even during sex earlier? who knew!). I went and placed my nose just an inch away from his soles, and could just feel the sweaty warmth radiating from them. I then took a big sniff inward. A symphony of erotic flavors had entered my brain. I got drunk off those feet in mere seconds. I was excited. I was in ecstasy. Yet this wasn't enough. I then pressed my nose right into his toes and inhaled. I had become a smell hound, and he was the prey. By physically pressing myself into his feet, he couldn't help but feel a bit violated, but that was the point: these weren't his feet anymore -- they were mine.

I sniffed and sniffed and even lightly jerked myself while doing so. This was heaven. He muffled and struggled, but to no effect: my hunt for his footstink was just too great. Perhaps it even smelled better knowing how desperate he felt: maybe there was some fear sweat creeping in as well. Then I sat back on the chair again. I prepped my index finger. It inched closer to the ball of his left foot. Then, I scratched it.

His whole body lurched. The wonderful thing about keeping your feet in shoes all the time: they become soft -- and sensitive. Even with that thin layer of cotton between his skin and my fingernail, he could still feel the tickle running through him like a bolt of electricity. It returned again. He jumped again. Then I prepped all 10 nails to start lightly scratching at the balls of his feet. Within seconds, his whole body was writhing again. Holy fuck: he was even more ticklish than I was. Scratchy scratchy scratchy went the nails. The feet tried to cross in front of each other to prevent the attack, but it was no use: the Tickle Spiders were winning. Slowly they moved up his soles, right to the base of his does, still lightly scratching back and forth, back and forth. I could make out deep-throated laughter even through the gag. Oh, I was getting to him. Yet the Spiders were in no hurry: my hands took their time dishing out Doug's tickle punishment. Next thing he knew, they were playing with his toes. They weren't tickling as much as they were just playing: dancing up and around, poking in-between (even with the socks in the way), and then quickly scampering down to his ankle again. Then back up. Then down. Then more tickly scratches. This continued for about 20 minutes. It went by like 30 seconds for me ... I can't imagine how long it felt for him.

"Awww," I said as I turned to him taking a pause. He was breathing heavily through his nose. "I think you put up with a lot already, haven't you Doug?" He nodded in panicked agreement. "I think we should reward you, shouldn't you?" His head shook vigorously. "Well, I know you pretty well," I started, "and if I'm not mistaken, you just love ... being ..." I stretched each pause out longer. He was sweating with anticipation. "Bare ..." His eyes widened. "... foot."

He screamed so hard. I could almost hear it through the gag this time! I knew each second was slowing down into a torturous minute with him, and I fucking loved it. I was going to break Doug's spirit, and I hadn't even gotten started yet. I sat down again -- he was still moaning -- and I pinched the little bit of sock between his index and big toe. I did this for both socks. "Ready for liftoff?" He screamed "Noooooooooo!", and I laughed. With firm grip, those socks were coming off slowly. The sock rims sliding down his leg ... then around his ankle and heel ... and up the sole. His feet were pointed upwards, so by the time the sock rims were just above the toe base (and totally not touching any Dougfoot at all), I just let them dangle there, like a cotton bell, around his toes. They weren't on his feet, technically, but the socks still covered up his toes just dangling there. I wanted him to feel his last big of protection just barely, barely within reach. I just let the socks dangle for well over a minute, tempting and teasing him. And then, I threw them aside. Doug was now barefoot. Barefoot. Barefoot.

Oh god what a sight.

The toes stretched like how your arms do when you first get out of bed in the morning. They were only covered by air now. Those hairs on the tops of his feet -- god, so sexy. And those soles: so perfectly shaped. So beautiful to look at. And they were here, in front of me. They were here, ready to be ... tickled.

Without warning, my hands had become insane Tickle Spiders again, and the lightly whipped along the soles of his feet. Then the sides of his feet. Then the tops of his feet (my favorite part). Then, I cupped both ankles in my hands, freed up my index finger for each, and just let that finger scratch and scratch and scratch. It was like a Scratch-and-Sniff lotto ticket in a way: I scratched 'em, then sniffed his toes. He must've felt so used right about now, but that was kind of the point. My hardon was now raging like a maniac at this point. The index-finger kept scratching and I could hear him chortling and giggling through his gag. I looked over, and saw the biggest smile stretch across his face, and I smiled myself. He had no control over his emotions anymore: I did, and right now I felt like Doug should be laughing. I stuck my nose right next to that big toe on his right foot and inhaled. Then his left. Then his right again. Then his left again. Man, I could keep this up for hours.

"Feel used yet?" I asked. He gave me a "Mm-hmm" that was almost through tears. God this was fun.

I went over to a nearby drawer and pulled out some bird feathers. Nothing much, but just something fun to tease him with. I began feathering the sides of his ankles, and kept that up for five solid minutes. I know what that feels like: it almost tickles but not really but still kinda does. It's almost like tickle foreplay, your senses getting mad before finally crying out "*Just tickle me already*!" The feathers then messed with his toe hairs, then in-between his fun boytoes, then up and down his soles. He kept laughing and his body (low on energy) still had a spastic twitch here and there. Doug was being worn down into tickle putty. The feathers did their dance, the victim just laid back and laughed.

I stopped, finally, to give him a breather. Every single nerve ending on his feet must've felt on fire. Even though I wasn't tickling him, he was still laughing. Almost like waves upon waves of aftershocks still hitting him. I went to the kitchen and grabbed two water bottles: one for me and one for him. I kneeled down next to the side of the futon and pulled of the tape. Then I slowly pulled my socks out of his mouth. His voice was hoarse. "You ... you bastard."

"Have some water" I insisted. Though he still couldn't see, his open mouth eventually found the plastic salvation. He took the water without hesitation, practically draining the entire thing like a hamster in a cage. "Good boy" I told him. I drank some myself. "Please ..." he beckoned, all scratchy-sounding. "I give up. Please let me go." It sounded so delightfully pathetic. "Oh but Doug ..." I started, "we haven't even got around to lubing your feet yet."

"Noooooo!" said the scratchy, almost non-existent voice.

I went back to my chair near his beautiful Dougfeet. "But wait Doug -- I'm all out of lube. Well, you know what I'm going to have to do then, right?" I didn't hear any response. I smirked. I kneeled down next to him so his feet were at face-level. I licked my chops, and planted my moist tongue right at the ball of his left foot, left it there, and slowly drug it upwards. "Noooooooo!" he cried, but it was too late: the worship had begun.

My slow tongue was giving his helpless soles their much-needed saliva. My tongue flickered a bit when it got to his toes. Then it started at the bottom again -- on his other foot. I went back and forth licking his Dougsoles, my tongue as Huck Finn's paintbrush and his feet as that endless picket fence in need of a fresh coat. I then went and licked the sides of his feet, his insteps, and then slithered my greedy tongue in-between his toes, savoring every flavor. God this was heaven. His hips thrusted a bit involuntarily, but mostly, Doug was laughing. He's no doubt been tickled before, but not like this. Never like this. He was in pure tickle hell. Plus, the new moisture on his feet was making his skin sensitive to the air around him, the bit of wind in the room occasionally rolling past his sensitive dogs and giving them an extra, bonus tickle. I like bonus tickles.

When I got to his toes, though, god I had a ball. I sucked those things like lollipops, spending extra time flickering his toehairs. Sometimes I'd even scratch his feet while doing so. He was laughing and hating me and probably secretly loving all of this at once. His mind didn't know anymore: it was all confused and irrational. I was controlling it now. I kept sucking and sucking and sucking his toes for well over 20 minutes. Then stopped. I laid down a bit. I looked up at his bound feet. Even through the window, there was a sliver of moonlight bouncing off of his saliva-coated toes now, and it was one of the hottest fucking images I've ever seen. Only now was it time to have fun.

I grabbed some scissors and cut his legs free from the futon armrest. His legs were still bound, but he was no longer in one place. I picked up his body and laid him on the ground face down. I then walked about 15 feet away to the entrance of my apartment. I opened the front door wide open. I put my jeans back on (hardon be damned), kneeled in front of him, and pulled off his eyemask. I pointed to the front door. "Alright Doug, I gotta use the restroom, but let's be fair. If you can make your entire body out that door by the time I get back, I'll let you go. How does that sound?" He didn't respond, but I didn't wait up. "Go!" I said. I really did have to use the restroom, so I did.

When I stepped back out, I knew exactly what had happened: Doug, only able to really move his legs, had "wormed" his way 4 feet closer to the door. His head was still about 10 feet away. It was so demeaning to crawl on his belly towards freedom, but I liked it that way. I snuck up behind him and without warning began licking his soles while they were moving. "Noooo!" he cried, and tried to escape as quickly as he could. I kept following and licking. Of course, this was all part of my plan: I wanted him to use up every last remaining reserve of mental and physical energy towards this task that I knew was impossible for him to do. And even if he did, make it out, what was he going to do? Go down whole flights of stairs by himself? Stand up and use a phone with his nose? I had merely created the illusion of freedom for him. In his delirious state of mind, the illusion was real enough for him.

As I (quite literally) nipped at his heels, his chin had finally made it out the door. At this point, I then put his legs in an armlock, and then just proceeded to tickle his feet with vigor. Oh, how they squirmed still. Like little creatures. Little bits of life gasping for freedom. And he tried moving, but I was holding him immobile. "Oops, times up!" I cried. Still holding his legs, I simply stood up and dragged his bound body allllllll the way back to the base of the futon. "Noooooo!" he cried (again -- it was becoming his catch-phrase for the night!). I casually walked over to the door and locked it, trying to make the clicking door lock sound as loud as possible.

Now that he was completely on my carpeted floor, I swung him around so that his face was next to the lamp I turned on earlier. I put the eyemask on again, but he was too tired to say ... anything. I pulled my chair over and pulled out my cell phone. "OK Doug, do you really want to get out of here?" "Yes," he whimpered, in near tears. "Do you now know how shitty you made me feel?" "Yes" he said. "Why did you do that to me?" His fevered mind couldn't think of anything, which is what I was counting on. "I don't know," he said in desperation. Just the answer I was looking for. "You don't know? Then why did you even do it if you don't know?" A pause. All he could think of: "I don't know." "Well, it's almost all over soon. I just want you to return me the favor that I did for you tonight ... and lick my feet."

His face grimaced for a moment, but he knew he had no choice. "OK" he sighed. Even though he was blind and on the floor like a worm, I inched my socked feet ever-closer to his face. "Now take my socks off." Once his face felt the shape of my feet, his mouth bit down on a bit of sock tip, and I pulled my left foot out. Then he did the other one. "Do you like taking the socks off my feet, Doug?" "Yes," he blindly bemoaned, knowing no other answer would've worked. "Now suck on my toes," I ordered. His mouth felt around, and then he engulfed my big left toe. His mouth sucked on it smoothly, simply, steadily. He went around to other toes and licked and sucked them with equal precision. Even for faking this gesture just for me, I would've mistook him for a guy with his own foot fetish any other night of the week. He simply sucked and sucked my digits. I was fucking loving it. I kept badgering him with questions. "Do you like my toes?" "Yes." "Do you love sucking on them?" "Yes, sir." "Say it to me!" "I ... I love ... sucking on your toes ... sir." "Will you do it anytime I ask?" "Yes, sir."

CLICK. His mouth stopped. "What was that?" he asked. "Hold on a second" I said. A few digits were pressed in my phone, and boom -- it was sending to my e-mail inbox. I rewound the minutes-long video I had just been filming, and then held up the playback to his ear: "Do you like taking the socks off my feet, Doug?" "Yes." I stopped it. I could see he was crying a bit. I broke him.

As tears streamed down his face, I grabbed the scissors and unbound him everywhere. His weak, depleted body just lay there. I sat down and nursed his head, stroking it gently. "It'll be alright, Doug. It'll be alright." Within moments he had passed out.

I don't know when he woke up, but I know where he woke up: a cheap motel not too far from his house. He didn't know what transpired, but I checked out a cheap room after he passed out, and basically flopped his barefooted body onto the bed. When he awoke, he would've found the shoes he was wearing last night (but no socks -- I kept those), and a cheap pair of purple plastic flip-flops with a note, indicating that if he truly was sorry and wanted to give a chance at restarting everything again between us -- with full understanding that if it doesn't work, it doesn't work -- he should wear those cheap flip-flops into work the next day.

Of course, he and I worked in the same office: that's where we became friends. They had a very strict dress code. Admittedly, he didn't have to change into "shoes" until he clocked in, which is what I was banking on. I was sitting in a manger's office the next day, barely finishing out my opening shift when I glanced out and saw Doug standing in the doorway, himself on a closing shift. His shoes were in his hands. The cheap flip-flops were on his gorgeous feet. We exchanged glances. He nodded. I smiled. He walked off to change.

I had a good feeling about this ...

THE BELT
(originally appeared in *My, What Ticklish Feet You Have*)

+ + +

The thing about fetishes that not many people really seem to acknowledge is that they actively evolve over time. Aside from the sheer type of fetishes that people can have and adopt over time, the way people engage with them also changes. What makes you horny about a foot one day may be completely different in a month's time, and sometimes through poppers or inebriation or a visit to a dungeon or whatever, you begin pushing the erotic nature of the fetish to even newer horny highs. For some people, the mere use of chastity can help to achieve that. By denying yourself the power to even have a hardon, the buildup of erotic excitement in someone is parallel to nothing, as the hornier you get, the more it siphons off your IQ, sometimes to glorious results, which is why I wrote this story here: to see just how far that erotic breaking point can be ...

"Fuck man, I'm gonna cum!" moaned out Michael, almost desperately, bathed in nothing but the glow of his computer monitor.

He stood there, jerking off furiously to the image that stood before him: a webcam screen that was filled with the soles of Benjamin, his long-time net friend and owner of the most glorious pair of soles he had ever seen, lightly toned and massive in their size 13 stature. All Ben had done was simply prop his big bare feet in front of the webcam on his desk, and slowly began rubbing his feet together. Michael -- thin frame, lightly shaggy brown hair, and owner of an unbelievably intense male foot fetish -- was in sheer ecstasy, about to cum merely from the sight of Ben's perfect feet. Ben somewhat unconsciously twitched his toes, and that was enough to set Michael off: that intense electric feeling at the very tip of his cock manifested itself in a furious stream of cum; so intense that Michael -- not expecting for that toe twitch to do what it did -- jizzed all over his desk, some even getting on his keyboard. As embarrassed as he was going to feel in a few moments, his cock -- hell, his whole body! -- radiated a tingle of pleasure that he had not felt in some time.

Of course, Michael's webcam was on, too, and Ben saw everything. Ben took his feet down from his computer desk and watched from his own computer window as Michael took a few moments to gather his thoughts -- his cock gradually deflating as Michael appeared, well, dumbstruck. Michael spoke into his mic: "I'll be right back. Let me clean up."
"No problem," said Ben, slyly. He watched as Michael grabbed some paper towels from his apartment bathroom, and soon cleaned everything up. Ben spoke to Michael as he did so:
"Quite the load this time, man."
"That toe twitch near the end ... that's what did me in. I don't really know it just ... gah, it was so fucking sexy."
"Man, I *love* how deep your foot fetish is. It's pretty intense."
"That *cumshot* was pretty intense, dude." Michael threw the paper towel away and sat down in front of his desk, his face now in perfect frame for the webcam. It was night out, so the only thing that was illuminating him was a lamp off to the side.

Michael sat there, looking at the large, heavy cardboard box that was next to his chair on the ground. He asked Ben upfront: "Can I open it?"
"In a moment," said the dusty-haired hunk on the other end. "But first, let me ask you: you love my feet, right?"
"Yes."
"And ... just using your best guess ... how many times have you cum to my feet? Including our little webchat tonight?"
"Geez ... dozens, easy. Maybe even close to a hundred, even."
"That's good, Michael. I hope you know that I *love* how horny my feet make you."
Michael smiled a bit, genuinely pleased with that statement. "Thanks, Ben."

"Now, here's the question: what is *my* fetish?"

"You have a male tickle fetish sir."

"Now, how many times have I tickled you?"

"Well, none, really. I know you want to tickle me, but I ... I hate being tickled."

"And what have I asked of you before?"

"To ... to fly out for a tickle session?"

"Well," clarified Ben, "a tickle *and* foot session. You'd get to worship my dogs in person, you lucky devil you."

Michael smiled again. "Well, yes, but you know me -- I work at a friggin' KFC. You're at an architecture firm now. You, naturally have a bit more cash than me."

"And I've offered to fly you out."

"I know, but, well, it's kind of hard to plan these things."

"But!", started Ben. "I think I have a way to fix it."

"Oh you do?" asked Michael, genuinely curious.

"And it's in that box."

"Can ... can I open it now?"

Ben smirked. "Yes, yes you can, Michael -- but put it in your lap. I want to see your reaction as you open it.

Michael smiled, and then lifted the too-heavy cardboard cube onto his lap. He got out his scissors and cut open the taped flaps at the top. He flipped the flaps down, tossed a ton of packing peanuts onto the floor, and then stared at it ... confused.

"What is it?" asked the 23-year-old lad.

Ben -- only one year older than him -- smirked back. "Take it out."

Michael did -- and it was some sort of, well, belt thing. It was hard plastic, and appeared to be something you place on your junk. Yet, what scared Michael was the most obvious thing, really: a hard plastic sort of pocket that seemed perfectly shaped to house ... his junk. This whole thing looked very professionally tailored but it also seemed like it could lock very easily as well. There was a small metal lock that came with it as well, although no key as far as Michael could tell.

Michael looked blankly into the webcam and asked quite simply: "What is it?"

Ben smiled back: "It's a chastity belt."

"Why ... why would you get me a chastity belt."

Ben smiled, and coyly lied to his online friend: "Well, I thought it could make things more exciting."

"What do you mean?"

"My feet are the hottest you've seen, right?"

"No question."

"Well, think of it as a loyalty thing. This orgasm tonight was the best yet, right?"

Michael blushed a little. "Well, ... yeah."

"Then put it on, and in three days, I'll send you the key. We'll see how horny you get after two days of not being able to jerk it."

Michael thought for a moment ... and liked the idea. The idea of "saving himself" for his secret foot master, his dick being owned only by him, begging for release after two days of not being able to do it. Michael didn't have anything else really going for him, thought, *why not?*

"Sure." He said. Looking at the screen, he saw Ben light up with a gigantic smile.
Ben responded: "I want to see you put it on over the cam and lock it."
"Alright!" said Michael, a bit excited by the possibility.

With that, Michael dropped his pants and shorts, but still kept on his solid-red hoodie. Ben had previously remarked how much he liked Michael in that hoodie, which is why Michael made sure to wear it every time they cammed together. With body half-naked, he got out the semi-complicated interlocking network of plastic rings and hard shells and pins but after some wrangling and looking at the included instructions (complete with pictures!) he was able to put it together, a bit of lube on his junk used to help slide his flaccid member into its new cage.

"Wow ... this thing is snug, Ben. Like ... it fits almost perfectly."
"Well I once asked for your measurements. I'm not sure if you remember, but I certainly did. This thing has been custom made to fit you."
"Well ... well thanks, man."
"Don't worry about it. Now, here's the important part: when putting your junk in the front, make sure it fits comfortably."

Michael heeded this advice as he adjusted and maneuvered his balls in place. Finally, it felt pretty cozy.

"Alright. I think I'm good."
"Excellent," said Ben. "Now, turn it so that your right side is facing the cam, and let me see you lock it in place."
Michael did so. With the pin sticking out right where the cock "cylinder" was, he affixed the included lock and clicked that motherfucker into place.

"I think it's ready to roll, Ben!"
"Alright -- now try to take it off."
Michael arched his eyebrow. "Um ... OK."

Michael tried pulling it down ... but it was no go. The thing was locked above his hipbones, so he was now pretty secure. He tried a few different angles, but ... nothing.

"Nope, locked in pretty securely, Ben."

"Alright," said his smiling friend. "I'll catch you later then."

And then their chat was disconnected.

Michael sat there -- in nothing but his hoodie and chastity belt -- and was a bit shocked by the suddenness of Ben's disappearance. After a few moments, he realized that his friend meant nothing personal by his sudden disappearance, and that in a few days time, they'd cam again, and Michael would be as horny as ever, and the resulting orgasm would be nothing short of spectacular. Having already drained himself quite exhaustively, Michael went to bed feel pretty pleased that night. Took a bit for him to get used to the belt, but after about an hour, all was good.

Although showering was a bit weird, Michael was slowly getting used to the belt. Within the first hour of his KFC shift, behind the register while the smell of refried chicken permeated behind him, Michael felt a bit ... naughty. He kind of smiled a bit, knowing that he was keeping a secret that no one else knew. The idea kind of got him a little horny for the first time since his cam session last night but ... it wasn't going. His hardon wasn't materializing. In fact, it kind of hurt that his cock was being pressed up against the hard plastic shell that contained his junk. Michael stepped away from the register for a second -- prompting one bucket-ordering soccer mom to ask if he was OK -- but after a bit, he got his grip on things, and was able to continue his job as per usual. He didn't realize that a sharp pain like that was all it would take for his erection to go away. He had one more "erotic wave" hit him like that near the end of his shift, but for the most part, his chastity belt was still a pretty fun idea.

That night, after getting back to his small apartment and working on his long-gestating children's book (which he's rewritten about 10 times now), he started feeling a bit needy. He opened up his folder containing all of the hot foot worship picks he had gotten off the web, and began browsing through them, his finger unconsciously tapping his plastic cock cage. After a bit, he got a bit horny, but then came the pressing plastic pain, and he very much wasn't anymore. Suddenly, Michael realized that he was experiencing true sexual frustration. Not just that he wasn't getting blown or anything, but that when he wanted to jerk himself off -- which he did twice daily, usually -- he wasn't able to. He was getting a little mad that he wasn't able to, but, hey, Ben said he'd be online in a day or two anyways. No big deal. Having not cum, it was a bit harder for Michael to sleep that night, but he did so anyways.

On his third day, Michael was getting a little bit flustered. Although day two saw him kind of at the limits of what he was capable of experiencing, this was now getting kind of crazy. He hadn't cum in at least three days, and, for him, that was some new sort of record. Around his co-workers he got kind of testy, but he was still in control. That night, upon getting home, he loaded up his webcam first thing and just waited. Ben was going to come on any second now. He looked at some pictures in his folder just to get himself ready, and -- to taper off his frustration -- he began walking around the apartment just to burn off some energy. An hour passed with nothing. Ben popped in a DVD into his computer (boy did he love *The Office*), and watched one episode in a reduced screen, one eye always lingering on his webcam just to see if Ben was online and connecting. One episode turned into two, then two into three. After Michael had watched an entire disc, he broke out his cell phone and sent a text to Ben, asking where he was. Ten minutes passed, and no response.

Michael popped in another disc of that same season of *The Office*, and barely even watched the entire thing, as he kept glancing at his phone every twenty seconds, followed by his webcam at every other interval. Nothing. After the third episode on the second disc, suddenly his phone vibrated! "*It was Ben!*" he giddily thought. He flipped open the phone, and it was ... a message from Tim, his best friend. He was asking if Michael was up for another pub crawl tomorrow night (that night being Friday). Michael and Tim *always* hit a new bar on Friday, but ... what if he missed a session from Ben? Michael texted back saying that he'll "play it by ear" ... but that's all he could promise now. A whole third disc of that same *Office* season was watched, but by the end, Michael knew his fate: Ben wasn't going to be on tonight -- and he wasn't going to get to cum.

Michael took an extra-long shower that night, his body tingling with a certain kind of frustration that he hadn't known. Cumming was just about all he could think about right now, regardless of what the stimulus was. Hell, he'd have sex with a woman, even! As long as he got that thing off. His head swimming with horny ideas, Michael only got two hours of sleep that night.

The next night, after another frustrating day at work and having sent off at least *three* texts to Ben (all unanswered), Michael finally consented to a pub crawl with Tim. It was the start of April, after all -- what could a little drink hurt? Maybe he'd even get so drunk that he'd forget about his horny predicament ... at least for one night.

Michael eventually found his way to a downtown place called McGuillicuddy's, a pseudo-Irish place that seemed to have a bunch of barflys wearing trucker caps. He awaited by a small table next to the jukebox, and after a minute, his buddy Tim walked in: white ball cap, white T-shirt (which, suitably showed off his muscled arms), ratty blue jeans and ... flip-flops. Tim had never, ever, ever worn flip-flops. Michael almost gasped as Tim walked over to hug him in that frat-brotherly way.

"What's going on, George Michael?"
"Oh," started Michael, meekly, "Nothing. Just a long, long day at work."
"Hell, I hear ya man," said Tim, sitting down. "Let's get some beers and forget about it,

OK?"

Michael nodded, but couldn't help and glance under the table. Tim's feet were ... fantastic. They were gloriously pale, thin and veiny, which contrasted nicely to Michael's too-rich memory of Ben's, which were rich and meaty. That said, Tim's feet still had an incredible charm to them. The more Michael delved into his fetish, the more he found certain unique pleasures to be found in the shape of each and every foot he came across. The fact that he had never seen Tim's before only intrigued him further, and now that he was staring at them, he felt awash in a certain kind of lust for them, something which was making his wearing of his chastity belt all the more inconvenient.

Then, Tim's hand was under the table, and it formed a finger pointing up. Oh shit -- Michael had just been found out.

He arched his head back topside, and Tim was staring at him with one of his eyebrows prominently arched. "Um ... what were you doing, Michael?"
"I ... I couldn't help but notice you were wearing flip-flops."
"Well, yeah."
"You ... never worn them before."
"I know, man. I went to the store with Donna just a few days ago, and figured 'why the hell not?' ya know? Worth trying something new. They're pretty fun to wear, actually."
"Yeah, they look good on you."
" ... 'they look good on me'?"
"Well ... I kinda ... just ..."
"What kind of statement is that?"

Michael got flustered and was definitely feeling cornered. This was his friend for several years, but ... maybe it was time to be honest with him about it.

"Well, I'm sorry dude, but ... I got a bit of a ... foot fetish."
Tim's eyebrow arched again. "A foot fetish?"
"Yeah."
"For like, all feet or just ... guys feet."
"Guys feet."

Suddenly a waitress came over and handed off a round of beers. Tim thanked her and Michael barely had the strength to lift his arm to grab his, his whole body racked with guilt over this confession. Tim took a swig of his beer, and leaned in a bit, making a gesture for Michael to lean in as well. Tim spoke softly: "So ... what would you want to do them?"
Now Michael was the one with the quixotic look on his face. "Pardon?"
"If we were alone right now and you could, I dunno, 'indulge' -- what would you want to do to my feet?"
Michael scanned Tim's face for malice -- and there was none. He genuinely wanted to

know. For the first time in days, Michael smiled, and began spilling his guts.

Over the next two hours, the guys consumed about five beers apiece, and Michael told Tim all about his fetish: how it started, whose feet in particular he wanted to worship, and how Michael theorized this all stemmed from a psychological need to be subservient in sexual play, and licking the bared soles of a guy's feet was the ultimate subservient gesture. Tim ate it all up, smiling the whole time and even tossing in some questions of his own. Michael wasn't as much horny as he was happy, and the booze was *definitely* opening up his treasure chest of secrets. The evening bore on, and when the guys -- very tipsy -- turned to look at the football game on the big screen behind the bar, Tim slid his right foot out of his sandal and placed it right in Michael's lap. He turned a bit and simply said "rub it" off the side of his mouth. The guys drank and carried on a conversation just as normal, Michael eagerly rubbing his friend's foot the whole time. It felt ... so damn good.

As the bar began closing up around 1:30AM, Tim admitted that he was kind of feeling a bit kinky from all this open talk, and wondered if they wanted to go back to Michael's place to do something about it. The very mention of it -- a long-standing fantasy of Michael's -- was enough to drive him overboard. His erection was immediate -- and halted just as immediately by his plastic encasement. He admitted to Tim that the offer was "tempting", but it best wait for another time. Tim seemed a bit disappointed with the news, but secretly knew it was for the best. As Tim went off to hail a cab, Michael grew frustrated by the biggest missed opportunity of his life, and stomped his way home.

Jumping right into his e-mail as soon as he got in the door, Michael fired off an angry missive towards Ben, saying how this whole chastity belt thing was not what he signed up for and that the code for unlocking it be given to him now, further explaining of the opp he just missed out on with Tim (the whole document riddled with typos and spelling errors, a mixture of both Michael's rage and drunken state of being). Michael hit Send and felt pretty good ... until about five seconds later when he got a message back. It was from mail.return-sender. Ben's e-mail address no longer existed. Michael checked his screen name on AIM, his webcam service, and everywhere: Ben wasn't online or was simply gone. Michael went to bed in a state of rage and frustration.

Being Saturday, Michael woke up about noon, and staggered around wearing just the belt. He put on some pajama pants and T-shirt so he could go check his mail, and opened the door to his apartment. There was another cube cardboard box simply sitting there. Michael inspected it: it was from Ben.

Frantically, Michael closed the door behind him and brought the cube into his living room area, setting it down on the couch before promptly ripping it open. It felt lighter than the previous package, and then, finally, Michael saw the contents: inside a tightly sealed ziplock bag, there were two pairs of Ben's worn socks. As exciting as the revelation made him, he searched for a note, for a sign, for anything. Nothing. Just a Zip-locked bag filled with the used socks of his favorite footgod. Lacking anything else to do, Michael opened up the bag, and immediately the fumes hit him. They worked right into his nervous system, and right into his pleasure center. Michael was officially turned on. Even as his cock pressed furiously against the plastic of his belt, Michael didn't care for a little while: he was enjoying the moment.

For about an hour, Michael rolled on his bed smelling every inch of Ben's socks, his hand circling his plastic cock cage as he indulged what was essentially a horny feast for the senses. Michael simply couldn't control himself. He had never gone this long without cumming, and was awash in just about any hope he had of getting to PleasureTown. After that hour, though, Michael realized he wasn't going to get off, and got frustrated all over again. He revisited the richly textured socks frequently over the weekend, but to no use. As erotically charged as those playthings were, nothing would come of them.

Another week passed.

Michael finally was getting used to peeing through the little hole in the plastic cock cage, but that was about all he was getting used to. With each passing hour of him not getting off, the longer the days seemed to drag on. Someone at work simply mentioning "feet" -- even if it's just in a sentence like "we got a line of customers 10 feet deep" -- was enough to retrigger his fantasies all over again. Michael even contemplated going to a blacksmith to get the infernal device off, but his lack of funds (and sheer embarrassment over what that would look like) was enough to keep him away from that idea. With each passing day, his anger and frustration turned into defeat and frustration. That next Friday, he wound up crying himself to sleep he was so desperate. He frequently looked up the photos that Ben had sent him, and all they did was stir those romantically horny feelings he had for those massive feet all over again. It was an endless cycle.

On Saturday morning, Michael opened up his door and found another package at it: this time smaller. Opening it up, it was Ben's old, worn, leather flip-flops. Ben said that he had worn them for years -- and it showed. Bit of fringing on the side, a definite worn shape to them, and, dear god, the most perfectly sweatblackened imprints of Ben's feet that Michael had ever seen. Looking at them, he didn't realize just how big Ben's feet were in real life. He brought the sandals to his nose, and inhaled. God, these were even *more* potent than the socks, having locked away almost five whole years of footsweat inside of them. Horny and desperate, Michael licked the area where Ben's soles were, and the taste drove him mad. Despite his inability to get an erection, Michael couldn't help himself and licked both pairs of flips for whole hour-long lengths of time, relishing the taste like he was starved for a month and finally offered a juicy steak. The socks lost their potency, but these bad boys didn't. For yet another horny week, this was all Michael had to hold onto, and he did so with an almost psychotic desire. The belt had broken him, and he was now simply a slave to his own desires.

After what was the longest week of his life, Michael was up at 6AM the following Saturday, bright and early, sitting right next to the door of his apartment, waiting for a package to be dropped off while each second slowly ticked away. Ben's socks and flips were clearly out of sight, lest they trigger another frenzied licking session. At 10:07AM exactly, a package was dropped off. Waiting for the mailman to walk away a bit, Michael finally opened the door and saw that this package ... was the smallest yet. It was a little bigger than an envelope, but it was still a package. With a fury rarely seen in a human being before, Michael opened up the package, and saw ... a plane ticket. A single plane ticket. To Chicago O'Hare. Ben lived in Chicago. Ben had paid for Michael to come out there and visit him ... and possibly unlock that belt once and for all.

Michael careened with joy. This was the best news possible! Finally, after three weeks of frustration, he'd finally get to worship the feet of his master! Wait a second ... Michael was calling Ben his master in his mind. He really *was* broken. No matter. This was big news. Then, Michael actually took a second to read the ticket: the flight took off tomorrow. And there was no return ticket either. Michael flipped out his phone and sent a message to Ben noting that he couldn't get the time off of work for a visit like that (keep in mind, this was a nice change of tone to the last 100 unanswered text messages that Michael had sent out that week, the last two being 'dear fuck you are my god i want to lick your solezz' and 'i will do anything for the chance to worship you, sir'). The message, naturally, went unanswered. He then got dressed and headed down to his KFC to talk to his manager about it.

After not getting a day off to attend a "family emergency", Michael quit right then and there. Perhaps it was a good thing there was no return ticket: Michael would never want to come back here anyways.

The very next day, Michael found himself in mid-flight, staring out at the white fluffy clouds before him and wondering what the hell he was doing. He thought about how he met Ben via an online web chat 'lo those many years ago, when they both were about 17. They both were kind of coming into their fetishes with each other, and though Michael hated being tickled and Ben wasn't as much a fan of worshiping feet (he did, however, like getting *his* feet worshiped), the boys found mutual ground and frequently discussed their victories and failures openly with each other, initially in regards to their fetishes, but increasingly about their lives as well. Ben was a bit unsure when Michael asked if he could see his bare feet for the first time, but upon seeing his reaction, Ben grew to enjoy the power that his toes held over Michael. Then again, Ben was a no-nonsense guy and it made sense that he would enjoy little hints of power. He slept with women, sure, but to tie a guy down and break him, to destroy his mind through the very act of tickling his ribcage ... that was a kind of power that was special. Being who he is, Ben convinced lots of guys (straight ones even) to succumb to his tickling whims, but he always seemed to be on the prowl for the unwilling, the ones who you really had to coarse to get to do something like that. Ben liked challenges, and maybe Michael -- the very first person he spoke to about his fetish -- was the ultimate challenge, this plan years in the making. A college graduate but recently jobless, Michael wasn't sure what he was doing. This was all strange, but all new. He was as scared as he was excited to feel the plane wheels touch down in Chicago, not knowing what would happen next.

After getting his small bit of luggage from a baggage carousel, Michael stood in the airport (still wearing that red hoodie Ben loved so much), facing the glass doors leading out to the streets ... and then realized that Ben didn't specify anything about was to happen now. Was Ben supposed to meet him here? Was he going to sneak up behind him and poke his sides in the airport? What if Ben was wearing flips? All those thoughts caused stirrings in his belt, but it's that very belt which put a stop to those stirrings. Then, suddenly, Michael felt his phone vibrate. He flipped it open -- it was a text message from Ben. It said that there was a cab outside from Blue Taxi, its door open, and it had already been paid with directions right to Ben's loft apartment. Excited, Michael hurriedly called Ben, expecting him to be on the other end of the phone ... but simply got voicemail. Ben was teasing him. Michael stood on the balls of his feet and looked out: there was, in fact, a cab, door open, waiting for him. Within two minutes time, Michael was gone.

He was dropped off in a nice high-rise just out of downtown Chicago. He went into the lobby, dragging his bags, and received another text message: "13th floor, room 1307". Excited and scared, Michael got in an elevator and made his way up. He got out at the 13th floor and ran through the carpeted hallways, looking for 1307. As he ran along, Michael noticed art hung up in certain areas and nice lighting everywhere -- this was a really flashy place. Finally, Michael got to a door with "1307" across the front. He set his bags down, nervous, and knocked on the door. It opened almost instantaneously.

It was Ben. Ben was smiling.

"How goes it, Michael?"

Michael stood there and thought about all the things he could say to Ben right now, about how he's gone an entire month without jerking off, about how he missed out on the greatest worship opportunity ever with his good friend Tim because of the damn belt, and how the socks and sandals that were sent (which, Michael would be loathe to admit, were in his luggage right now) did nothing but drive him up the wall. But when he saw Ben standing there -- short brown hair, firm (but not flashy) build, and (dammit) some blue Chuck Taylors on his feet, coupled with how Michael has been able to trust Ben with virtually all of his secrets and was personally responsible for close to 100 orgasms for him personally -- Michael just felt all that aggression melt away. This guy was his genuine friend ... and he sure as fuck better get him off soon.

"It goes well, Ben." The two guys hugged. Ben motioned him in, and Michael looked around: there was hard wood paneling on the floors, an *island* fireplace, and some real nice couches. Ben had always mentioned that he made a decent hunk of cash from his fresh-out-of-college architecture job, but Michael never realized it was this much. No wonder he could also afford one-off plane tickets, crazy mailing fees, and even a custom-made chastity belt. Michael set his stuff down near the entrance.

"Really nice place you got here, Ben."
"Thank you Michael."

There was a bit of a pause between the boys, somewhat awkward. Michael started ...

"So ..."
"The belt." Ben cut him off. "I've received all your text messages. From what I guess, it's been driving you a little crazy."
Michael immediately dropped to his knees and began pleading "Holy shit you have no idea how insane this has been! I'm horny as I've ever been in my life and will do anything to get off oh please oh please oh please!"
Ben smiled a too-knowing smile at Michael.
"So you'll do anything for me to get that belt off of you?"
"Yes."
"And, I assume ... you would like to worship my feet, is that right?"
"It's the only thing that's gotten me through this past month. I know their smell and their taste so well now -- all I want is just to suck on your toes for hours, days on end."
"Alright. That sounds fair." Michael grinned the biggest grin he had ever donned. "But ..."
"But?"
"You have to do me a favor first. You're going to get me off in exchange for the dozens of times I've gotten you, OK?"
Michael, shocked yet resigned to his fate, simply said "OK. What do you want me to do, sir?"
Ben grinned again: "My bedroom is in the hallway on the right. I'll be in in two minutes, by which point I want you down to your boxers -- and that hoodie of yours. Sound good?"
"Yes sir." said Michael, who marched on off.

Michael stood there and admired Ben's big, comfy bed. You really have to hop on up to get on it, but boy did that mattress look wonderful. As Michael examined, there appeared to be leather cuffs attached to each corner of the bed, but that's just when Ben walked in.

"Admiring those?"

"Well," Michael stammered, "I ..."
"Don't worry. You'll get to know them real soon in a moment anyways. Now lie down in a spread eagle position face-up."

Wordless, Michael did so. Soon, Ben pulled out adjustable leather straps from each corner of the bed, and it wasn't long before Michael's arms were stretched rather wide. Ben tightened the bonds even more, and Michael was even more helpless. He couldn't even move his arms an inch. "Now put your legs together," said Ben. Michael did so, and in a heartbeat, the boxers came sliding off in an instant. All that remained was that chastity belt. The bane of Michael's existence. In less than 30 seconds, Ben pulled out a small metal key -- and the lock opened. Michael felt a wave of joy run all over his body. Slowly, the belt slid off. It was gone. Michael nearly cried in relief. Then, of course, Ben spread Michael's legs apart and fastened them with straps very tightly. Michael was tied to a big bed, completely immobile, naked except for a hoodie. As crazy as it was, Michael felt somewhat at ease. Then, he popped a question:

"So, Ben?"
"Yes, slave?"
"Why the hoodie?"
"Well," snorted Ben, amused, "I like it because it gives you protection. A very thin, pointless protection. If I were to tickle your ribs with my fingers right now, you'd still be tickled, but that little bit of weave fabric will take a very small amount of that tickle away. You'll have the illusion of protection. When I slowly slide it up, and begin tickling your bare ribs, however, you'll feel like it's being stripped away, and you'll be even *more* vulnerable than you were before. With a tickle victim, the more you can 'build' their anxiety, the better payoff you'll receive."
"Ah ... so, you're going to tickle me then."
"Heh, you're a smart one, aren't you, Michael?"
"I figured as much."
"But, my friend, you don't know *how* I'm going to tickle you, do you?"
"No, I guess I don't."
"Michael, I want to try something ..."

Ben leaned over and put his mouth right to the ear of his bound friend. The first word came in, very intimate: "feet." Michael's eye's opened. "My feet." Michael felt a small tingling in his balls. And then ... "I am barefoot right now." Ben wasn't, and Michael knew that (he hadn't heard the sound of any shoes plopping to the floor), but those words alone caused Michael to get a little hard. "You're horny for my *bare feet*, aren't you, Michael?" The way that Ben softly pointed the words "bare feet" was enough to send him off, and, still wearing a hoodie, Ben was spread out, naked, and with a hard cock pointing directly at the ceiling. Then Ben said the words he most dreaded: "Now we're going to have fun ..."

Ben took of his Chuck Taylors but kept his ankle socks on. He sat himself between Michael's bare, exposed legs, and leaned forward. Ben's hands slowly placed a small grip on the base of Michael's hoodie. Then it came: "Tickle."

Ben's fingers slowly kneaded the lowest rib on Michael's body, and Michael -- still somewhat resilient, clenched his mouth tightly. A smirk, half-giggle emerged, but Michael was going to fight it off. The fingers softly but firmly danced in a slow pattern: index middle ring pinkie index middle ring pinkie, over and over. The hands kept this pattern as they slowly moved up the hoodie, kneading the ribcage as it went along. Index middle ring pinkie index middle ring pinkie. Another half-giggle. A snort. A grunt. Michael's mouth was stretched into a horrible, Joker-like grin, but he couldn't do anything about it. He was horny, bound, and ticklish, and through his years of training, Ben knew how to push his buttons. Suddenly Ben's big index fingers jumped to Michael's nipples and began fondling and circling them. That by itself would be a torment, but because they were doing it *through* the red hoodie fabric, the electric sensation just increased. Michael's hardon got harder, but the waves of pleasure started coming. The nips got harder and firmer, and the more protruded they got, the more Ben played with them. Back and forth, round and round, side to side, a slight, soft tug. Michael knew he was going to go insane. And then it was hands at the ribs again: index middle ring pinkie index middlering pinkie indexmiddlering pinkie indexmiddleringpinkie. The hands got faster, and finally the dams broke: Michael let out a chortled laugh, but couldn't even complete it, as the next wave of tickles was coming right after to muffle it.

Yes, Michael's ribcage was a tickler's delight. Ben traced each rib from side to front with his fingernails (through the hoodie, naturally), and tickled the soft spots in-between. Without warning, the hands darted under the hoodie, went right up to Michael's stretched armpits, and then clutched his sides. The index fingers began circling the little patches of armpit hair that Michael had, and they caused delightfully involuntary muscle spasms. They tickled and tickled and tickled. Sexual lightning coursed through Michael's helpless body. His hips flexed without warning. The toes wiggled in their desire to escape. Worst of all, Michael tried to bring his arms down *just a bit* to stop the tickling in his pits, but he was bound so tight he couldn't even do that, straining and laughing and convulsing all at once. Michael was fucked.

The hands came out the hood, and began tickling the ribcage right at the base of the hoodie. They moved up again, but began dragging the hoodie with it, all the way up to his neck. Michael desperately (desperately) begged a "no!!" but it wasn't going to happen: as the index middle ring pinkie motions went up his ribs, it drug that hoodie with it, and Michael was more naked and exposed then ever. "Bare ribs?!" said Ben with a joking sort of relish! "I be they're even *more* ticklish!!" Michael screamed in anguish as Ben's too-powerful hands mined for laughs wherever they could, but unfortunately that's all he could do now: scream and laugh. Even if Michael wanted to stop doing either, the tickling, cunning hands prevented him from having any sort of free will. Ben found it beautiful.

An hour of uncontrollable laughter passed.

Ben stopped, and Michael panted in bucket breaths. Ben looked at his sweaty friend with a mixture of envy, pity, and lust. As Michael panted even more, Ben simply said
"Michael ... would you like some feet?"
Michael weakly yelled "More than anything sir!"
"You got it."

Ben swung his legs around, and suddenly two ankle-socked feet were near Michael's face. Michael looked at the sole of the socks: there was enough of a lightly dirty outline to tell exactly where his curves and toes were. "I've been wearing these for three days straight" Ben interjected. The feet inched closer, and, despite being bound tightly, Michael could already feel the heat from those feet hitting his face. Michael leaned in, placed his nose right at the base of Ben's left big toe, and inhaled. His cock throbbed within seconds. Michael kept on breathing in Ben's foot sweat, and with each inhale, got harder and harder. Michael, already worn down from the tickling, was just a lightning rod of pleasure. There was no filter between his brain and his cock: it was all animal right now, and all Michael wanted to do was smell. As the sniffing got more furious, Michael then used his teeth to pull off each sock, and there they stood: the mighty, meaty, just-perfectly-slightly-damp feet that he had always dreamed of. Michael smelled again, and Ben clearly saw another mighty cock-twitch. Michael liked this. Then, he looked at the left foot, and stuck out his tongue, slowly dragging it from the heel ... to the arch ... to the balls of the feet ... and to the toes. If he was stimulated, he would've cum right then and there. More licks. More licks. Michael lived out his fantasy, and he almost cried from joy. He then finally stuck Ben's big left toe in his mouth, and sucked on it like a flesh lollipop. Back and forth, his tongue lightly tapping the toenail; Michael did so with each of Ben's toes. When Michael caught a glimpse, he saw Ben nursing his own hardon.

In the midst of all this worship, Michael's fate cooking under the feeling of warm bare feet, Ben reached for something he had set aside on his little bedside table which Michael failed to notice when he came in. It was a rag. A soft rag. There was a bottle of oil too. Ben poured some oil into the rag. Then, he placed the small little rag right on Michael's cockhead. Michael gasped a little in the midst of a toesucking, but continued. Slowly, Ben turned the oiled rag back ... and forth ... and back ... and forth, like running half an orange on one of those juicing devices. Michael's pleasure-meter shot into the stratosphere. Although the oil naturally dripped down the length of Michael's cock, so did oodles of precum, all mixing together with Michael's bodysweat to form a horny little cocktail on his balls and cockbase. Michael, getting off while licking some feet, was in total ecstasy. Yet ... something was wrong. Ben was only working his cockhead

... not the shaft at all. As pleasurable as this all was, Michael was approaching a climax ... but not getting the proper nerves touched for him to cum. It was just all cockhead pleasures and footlicking ... his shaft was begging, begging to be touched. After minutes of frustration, Michael stopped his foot tonguing and asked Ben:

"Hey Ben?"
"Master."
"Oh, right. Um, master?"
"Yes?"
"Could you please touch my shaft. I'm ... I'm fucking horny and want to cum, sir."
"You ... you want me to touch your shaft?"
"Yes sir."
"Do you mind if I touch it in ... my way?"
"Um ... yes sir. Just please ... touch it."

Ben grabbed another item from that nightstand. Suddenly, Michael felt it -- it was a big, loose, fluffy feather. There was some firmness to it, but not too much. Slowly, Ben dragged it across the top of Michael's shaft. Michael inhaled as he did so, and, as Ben's feet were close to his face, inhaled some footsweat as he did so, which, in turn, caused his shaft to twitch (again). Then the feather did the same motion across the topside of his shaft. Then on the underside. Then Michael realized that Ben was simply sawing at his cock with a feather, tickling it as he smelled the best feet of his life. Fuck, it was too much. Another saw on his sensitive underside. Another saw on the rim of his cockhead. Another ... oh fuck.

Without warning, Michael's body spasmed, and a whole months worth of sperm buildup came flying out of his cock. Flying towards the ceiling. Then another stream, then another. Then another. Michael let out a moan of pleasure that sounded nothing short of supernatural. His body was filled with electricity. Yet for being as teased as long as he was, Michael soon began begging for his cock to stop, but it kept on cumming against his will. Michael couldn't believe he even had this amount of cum in him. He came again, and again, and again, and it was almost hurting he was cumming so much. Finally, finally, it stopped. Michael's body collapsed, spent. Ben pulled his feet away and adjusted himself so that his mouth was right next to Michael's ear. Michael heard Ben reach for something from the nightstand and something else actually on the bed, but couldn't figure out what it was. Ben whispered in Michael's ear:

"How was that?"
Michael smiled weakly, "You are a god at what you do."
Ben continued: "So, how about this: why don't you live here with me for awhile. I'll go to my job during the day, you can work on that children's book that you've been slaving over for almost a year while I'm gone, and at night, we'll eat some food, watch some movies, and have so much fun together we won't even know when to stop. How does

that sound."

"Ben, that sounds absolutely beautiful."

Ben reached over for a kiss, and got it. Michael's mouth hung open for a second ... and then something was shoved in it.

Ben had attached his worn ankle socks to a gag when Michael wasn't looking, and now tied said gag around Michael's mouth. A blindfold was next. Michael tried screaming ... but just gave in and suckled the sock taste for a bit, enjoying it. Then, Ben revealed a secret:

"Michael, I'm pleased you agree with me, and I know that going through a month without jacking was hard, but the day I sent you that package, I took a vow myself not to cum, and I kept it, not even cheating once. So now, while you just got off for what may actually be the 100th time to my feet, I'm going to indulge in my first cumshot based off of you. Of course, I shouldn't even have to tell you how much more sensitive a body gets after cumming ... especially after a cumshot like that ..."

Michael screamed into his sock gag with his last remaining strength as Ben dug his fingers into his sides. Yet even as he did so, Michael was smiling ... and not just because he was being tickled ...

THE PLEDGE
(originally appeared in *My, What Ticklish Feet You Have*)

+ + +

As have been noted several times before in scientific articles and even in my own books, the reason why a foot fetish is so damn common is that the parts of the brain where "genitals" and "feet" are located are actually right next to each other, which why scientists postulate that the reason foot fetishes account for over 1/3rd of all body fetishes is that there's a simple "cross-wiring" which occurs. Sometimes to a small degree and sometimes to a very large degree (I fall in the latter camp for sure). Thus, the idea of taking a cocky someone who might look down on such a thing and reprogramming them against their will was intensely intriguing to me, because the great thing about fetishes is that it's never too late to start them ...

Aden was about to become invisible. The best part was that he wouldn't even have to try.

Aden was your typical freshman year frat pledge. He barely turned 18, looked fit but had a slight bit of a gut when he lifted up his shirt (which he worked on every day), and short brown hair that -- if combed just the right way -- made him immediately look like he came out of church choir practice. Yet if Aden was good at one thing, it was believing his own hype. If there were people that could party hard, well he could prove that he could party harder. If someone was telling a funny joke, he'd tell one that he just knew in his gut was funnier. He truly felt he was cut from a different cloth, but what he didn't know was that amidst all his projections of himself as the coolest guy in the room, he was actually off-putting and frequently came off as a bit of a dick. Some wondered that even if Aden was aware of this, would he even care?

But here he was, drunk at another mixer at Tau Kappa Lambda, feeling a part of the Fraternity when, in fact, he was a pledge, just like everyone else. Aden always stood out: while the other guys were happy to add to the bro-heavy atmosphere, wearing T-shirts, cargo shorts, and flip-flops like the rest of the known collegiate universe, Aden still wore slacks, socks with his tennis shoes, and a single button-down shirt as he always did. Tonight was another pledge mixer, and, ultimately, people were a little disappointed that Aden showed up. Some were even surprised: he had been somewhat "choosing" which pledge events to go through. Things like the ceremonies and whatnot -- those meant something, and therefore he felt the need to be there. But the obstacle course? The scavenger hunt? That wasn't what it meant to be a part of a Frat. That was just stupid. He could have been expelled from consideration many times over, but Anthony was in charge of Tau Kappa Lambda and frequently gave him the benefit of the doubt -- much to the chagrin of several other senior members of said Frat. Only adding fuel to their fire was Aden's behavior tonight, drunkenly belittling one sorority girl who stopped by who said she was Christian, demanding that someone else change the iPod playlist 'cos this one was boring him, and getting smacked by no less than three different girls who were in attendance for this Friday night event. Aden was striking out, but so drunk on booze and his own sense of entitlement, he didn't seem to notice, in his mind dismissing these girls as sluts who he didn't even want to sleep with anyways.

After getting the cold-shoulder from half the people in attendance, he stumbled his way upstairs and into the bathroom. He washed up, stepped out into the hallway of the huge frat house, and heard some strange rap song from the rooms below (were they saying "skee skee skee"?). *Now* those shots from earlier were hitting him, so he stumbled unknowingly into some frat brother's room. The lights were off. No one was in there. Before he even considered laying down to recover, he tripped backwards into the room's closet, and he sat there next to some shoes and a laundry hamper. It hurt a bit, but ... well, fuck, he didn't want to move now. He was strangely comfortable. He nuzzled his head against the wall of the closet, and began dozing off. With the lack of lights and his obscure position, no, no one would be able to see him even if they looked. Aden had turned temporarily invisible and he didn't even know it.

The door to the room slammed open. Aden opened his eyes -- how long had it been? An hour, maybe? Either way, it was still dark in the room, but he could clearly see two guys entering the room, arms around each other, moving feverently. Were they ... fighting? No, they were ... kissing? Holy shit, they were kissing. Aden squinted a bit more in his haze, and noticed that the two guys were -- some of the Frat members. Not pledges -- full-on brothers. One of them was the dark-haired guy with Italian heritage, Jason, who was a bio major. The other was the blond, frisky Damien, a Chemistry major. Aden frequently dismissed them as eggheads, but couldn't have possibly guessed that they were gay, much less into each other. Amidst their making out -- which, from his intoxicated angle, was just a furious mesh of flesh continually transmogrifying before his eyes -- Jason & Damien eventually made it onto the bed. Suddenly Aden realized: this was Damien's room. He had been in here before. Suddenly, as Jason was laying down with his head on the pillow, Damien turned to him and said "May I?" "Of course," Jason replied, with a grin. Both guys were intoxicated on *something*, but Aden just couldn't tell what it was.

While Jason laid on the bed, Damien had propped his back up against the wall, still sitting on the bed, so Jason's sneakered feet were right in his lap. He slowly ran his fingers down the seams of Jason's blue jeans, which Jason favorably responded to. Eventually, Damien's thin, devious fingers made their way down to Jason's sneakers and began ... to fondle them? That's what it looked like from Aden's angle. Because they didn't turn the light on, it was hard to tell. Yet Damien was definitely feeling those sneakers with relish, his fingers daring in and out of where the laces were, eventually untying them. There was definitely a strong sexual element to what was going on -- it was almost foreplay for them, Aden deduced. Then, Damien *slowly* pulled off Jason's left shoe -- and then the right. Suddenly, Jason's thick white ankle socks were exposed. Jason's socked toes wiggled with their newfound freedom, which only seemed to hypnotize Damien more. "You like that?" Jason quipped. Almost embarrassed but with a hint of excitement at the same time, Damien managed out a "Yeah ..." Both grinned. Aden, as fascinated as he was somewhat repulsed, had no idea what was going to happen next ...

Suddenly Damien's fingers circled the rims of Jason's socks like vultures at their pray, hooking under the rim of the elastic and teasing Jason as to what was going to happen next. Jason's face was awash with a look that said "God I'm so fucking lucky to have this happen to me", while Damien's face was saying "God I'm so fucking lucky I get to do this!" Suddenly, Damien's fingers tightened their grip around the sock, and slowly pulled it off of Jason's foot -- past the heel -- over the arches -- and finally dangling over the toes. And with that, Jason's left foot was bare. His toes stretched a bit. Damien took the sweaty sock right up to his face and his inhaled. His whole body arched and then shuddered with pleasure, which itself put a grin on Jason's face. The routine repeated with Jason's other foot, and suddenly Damien held both socks up and got a double-whiff -- he was in fucking heaven.

Even though Jason's bared feet were now in Damien's lap, Jason began kneading Damien's crotch with his feet, and before long Damien was moaning in pleasure, his cock already hard as steel and straining through the blue denim it was caged in. He tried like hell to be calm, but having Jason's gorgeous, meaty size 11 feet -- with such wonderfully plump toes -- massaging his pleasure stick was causing him to go into overdrive (as he would later describe in a private blog post, Damien's cock was "radiating with pleasure -- every single point of contact with those feet were sending pure electricity through my body -- fuck i was horny"). Yet right before it looked liked his body was about to go into overdrive and cum through his jeans, Damien showed restraint and stopped the foot-fuck that was happening, turning to Jason and saying, "OK, now it's time to try something on you ..."

Aden was practically frozen in the closet. He didn't know what to think. However, he couldn't help but believe that somehow, he could use this to his advantage. He very quietly got out his cell phone and made sure all the screen settings were as dimmed down as possible so he wouldn't be noticed. He broke out the video feature, and began quietly filming what he saw next:

Damien got off the bed and Jason scooched down so that his bared feet were hanging just over the edge of the too-small frat mattress. Damien got on the floor and knelt down. Given the small height of the bed, by being on his knees, Damien was now facing Jason's gorgeous soles, and was in heaven. He quickly undid his pants, pulled out his coated-in-precum cock, and then placed his nose right at the base of Jason's toes. He inhaled, and Aden could clearly see Damien's cock twitch with pleasure. This was getting intense. Then, out came Damien's tongue, and it began to slowly trace the soles of Jason's feet, slightly tickling him along the way but mainly coating that boy with sweet horny pleasure. Before long, one of Damien's hands was jacking himself off furiously, and it didn't take long for Jason to join in as well. Jacking was one thing, but jacking off a pent-up, horny cock while having someone pleasure your toes, sucking on them wholesale -- that was another realm altogether. It didn't take long, because both boys soon came at the exact same time, Jason's toes clenching within Damien's mouth right as Damien was sucking harder than ever. Jason's cumshot flew clear over his shoulder while Damien came hard right into the side of the bed. Both boys were motionless, the only thing moving being their chests as they panted deeply -- it was intense for both of them.

Aden, meanwhile, was trying to hold his breath as best he could. He didn't want to give himself away, but he couldn't wrap his mind around what just happened. These guys got off on ... feet? Smelling and licking and sucking feet? What the fuck was this? Without thinking, Damien picked himself up and crawled into bed with Jason, and both boys simply laid there, content with each other. After a few minutes, they were both snoring heavily.

Aden was ever-so-suspicious, but quietly got up and was as quiet as could be. Every creak in the floor from a sneakered footstep felt louder than a bomb, but the drunk, cum-spent, exhausted boys wouldn't have heard him even if they wanted to. Aden made it out into the hall and back to the main floor of the Frat. The music kept going, but the place was mostly empty -- the party was definitely winding down, if not wound down completely. Some people were making out on the couch, the floor felt sticky from spilled beer out of cheap plastic red cups, and the place had an air of, well, an abandoned frat party. Aden made it back to his room unnoticed.

Opening the keys to his place, Aden was actually able to breathe for once, he felt. Here was his too-gorgeous single that his parents were paying out the nose for: third story of a building, glass "window wall" that gave him a nice overview of the campus (with curtains to close it all, naturally), and a nice art-deco vibe to the place. Aden particularly liked the standing bar he had. That was his favorite thing. He took off his shoes and socks and then got himself a small splash of brandy, wondered for a moment if any of the girls at the party would Facebook friend him tonight, but, alas, it was not to be. He still wondered how anyone could get off on a foot, and looked down at his own -- typical build, well-kept nails, nice meaty toes -- and wondered just how anyone could like this. Oh well. He didn't think much about it. His exhaustion mixed well with his brandy, and before long, he passed out in his bed.

+ + +

Aden woke up around 1PM the next day (a Saturday), and got a strange message in his e-mail inbox.

It was from Jason, who was in charge of Pledge Recruitment. It basically said that after hearing about his behavior from some of the other Pledges and some of the visiting girls at the party, Tau Kappa Lambda decided that he did not have a place in the Frat, ending by wishing him luck in the coming school year. The e-mail included everyone's name in the signature, including Anthony. That last one is what stung the most.

If Aden had a glass of brandy in his hand, he'd throw it against the wall right now.

How *dare* they! After attending their stupid events, going to their parties with douchebags and stuck-up girls all around and dealing with all their hypocrisy and whatnot, he had to deal with this? This was bullshit. Aden actually began pacing around his apartment in a bit of a rage, and would've broken something were it not for the fact that most of his stuff -- the Japanese-only James Bond DVD box set, the cherished

Disney animation cells -- was actually worth money. After a bit of pacing and trying to calm down, he decided to pick up his phone and text a friend back home about this BS predicament ... and then remembered something. Oh that's right ... he got a video last night. A very, very incriminating video. A smirk creeped its way across Aden's face. "This ... this will show them not to fuck with me," he thought.

He sent back an e-mail to Jason, saying that they should reconsider kicking him out, especially after he RE:'s to the rest of the Lambda e-mail list and lets everyone see what he and Damien were doing last night. He dropped the word "fag" in a couple of times just to drive the message home. *Send.*

Two minutes passed. Aden then got an e-mail back from Jason. It was pretty straightforward: "We're sorry about any misunderstanding -- do you mind if we talk this over? Just you me & Damien? Your place?" Heh heh -- they were playing *right* into Aden's trap, getting desperate to the point were they were willing to meet on *his* home turf. Aden simply RE'd with where his single was located, a time (8PM), and a P.S. that said that he had already made copies of the video he got (which was a lie -- but they couldn't check that). Another two minutes passed before Jason responded "see you then."

Aden broke out the N64 for the rest of the day and played some Zelda games to take his mind off of the forthcoming encounter, but eventually microwaved himself some leftover pizza before 7:30PM struck. He put on some Adult Swim reruns he DVR'd, but at 7:55PM, there was a knock at his door. There stood Jason -- in a yellow Ultimate Frisbee T-shirt, cargo shorts, white ankle socks and tennis-shoes, as always -- and Damien -- blue-T-shirt, jeans, and a pair of cheap black Old Navy flip-flops -- at the door, each carrying a grocery bag. Aden could clearly see the liquor bottles sticking out over the top. This was one hell of an olive branch they were offering -- and all Aden had to do was simply catch them engage in fetish play and call them "fag." In Aden's mind, this was about as win-win a situation for him as he could get. Yet he decided to play it smooth, and simply said "Come on in ..."

The boys came in and Aden directed them to the couch in front of the TV, an episode of *Aqua Teen Hunger Force* paused part-way through. They sat down and Aden sat in adjacent chair. Jason began to speak, but Aden cut him off:

"So, you guys, I know why you're here. You don't want to be embarrassed -- I get it. But, seriously: kicking me out of the pledge process? That's pretty low ..."

Not expecting to go on the offensive so soon, Damien casually butted in: "Aden, you got to understand where we're coming from. We don't just allow anyone who's anyone into the Frat. We all go through sacrifices and things we don't want to do. It's not a matter of enduring that stuff though -- it's a matter of becoming Brothers with a capital B. There's a .."

"Yeah yeah yeah, I get it," Aden interrupted. "More accurately, you're backing down after I see you guys play with each other. I mean, that's kind of spineless."

Jason started: "Aden, what Damien and I do is between us, just as how what you do is between you and yourself. We don't pry, because we ..."

Aden injected again: "Seriously? C'mon guys. I know the spiel. Again, you just don't want your secret exposed. Now I see you brought drinks to try and change my mind about releasing the video, so break 'em out why don't ya?"

Jason & Damien tried like hell to bite their tongues -- it was hard. Yet they were civil. Damien looked around. "Mind if I use your bar?" Aden said "Go ahead." Aden liked lording over his domain. Then again, Aden liked being in control. He always did.

While Damien made some drinks (he was a part time bartender, unbeknownst to Aden, who never bothered to ask), Jason got down to business. "So, Aden, there's a reason why we're here. Obviously, we would not like the video to come out, but it's not a matter of reinstating you into the Frat just like that. Again, the girls complained last night directly to Anthony, so, really, this is bigger than the three of us ..."

"What do you mean?" asked Aden. Damien was finishing up and brought over some lemony vodka mixtures that looked great in small cups.

"Well," said Jason, as Damien handed the boys their drinks, "let's say you get in. Let's say that the girls and other brothers complain about your ... um, attitude. You can release the video all you want, but if Anthony still gets complaints, there's little we can do. I mean ..."

"What if I say that this video represents what goes on at Tau Kappa Lambda all the time?"

Damien sat down on the couch. Jason sighed. "Aden, we're trying to extend an olive branch here. So why don't we just take a drink and start things off right, OK?" Aden smiled and said "I can drink to that." The boys clinked their glasses and took a sip.

Aden stopped for a second, and stared at his glass. "Does this taste weird to you guys?" Damien & Jason smirked. Aden was about to run in a panic, but whatever was in the drink just hit him like a hammer -- and his body froze up.

Jason jumped into action and grabbed Aden's body, holding onto it gently. Damien cleared a space on the floor of Aden's apartment, and then got out a pillow right in the center. Aden's body ... wouldn't move. Damien then came over and grabbed Aden's legs. The boys hoisted Aden's body onto the floor and placed his head on the pillow pulled from the couch. They put his body in an X-pattern, and then after checking his mouth, they both sat on the couch, and quietly, calmly finished their drinks.

Aden was freaking out. His body ... wouldn't move. Not a finger, not a toe, not an anything. His heart, though panicked, was still beating. His lungs were still breathing. He could move his eyes and blink his eyelids if he really put his mind to it. But, that's it. He was trapped in his own body. He couldn't move a single fucking thing. What were these bastards doing to him?

"Aden," Jason started, "we're ... sick of you. All of us are. The Frat brothers, the girls who stop by our parties just to have fun, and hell even people who stopped me in passing between classes to let me know that we *shouldn't* let you into the Frat 'cos you're a dick. You're insensitive. You say stupid things and upset people. You think you're the shit when in fact you just act like a shit. People can't stand you, and god help anyone who does. The straw wasn't mocking our fetish or calling us fags -- although your rampant homophobia hurts us too. No, it was threatening to send your supposed video to our other Brothers. Keep in mind: they won't care -- they're our Brothers. But seriously, this is how you respond to being kicked out of our Frat? By threatening us? Being in a Frat isn't about you advancing your career. No, it's about being in a team. And tonight, we're going to teach you *all* about being on a team ..."

Aden tried to scream, but he couldn't.

"You see," started Damien, who Aden deduced was normally the quiet one, "we just paralyzed you. Not permanently, mind you, but being a chemist as long as I have, you learn how to cook up a few things." As Damien talked, Jason got out a pair of scissors and began snipping off Aden's shirt, pants, and boxers, much to his protest. "What we have here is targeted muscle paralysis. Your body muscles can't move, but your heart and lungs can. You're a fully-functional person except for your extremities. Your body can still feel stimuli -- which we're counting on -- but that's it. This is worse than the tightest bondage because you can't fight back even if you tried. Oh, and you can try like hell -- we encourage you, even -- but your body is *our* body for the next eight hours. And boy, are you going to enjoy the ride ..."

SNIP. Suddenly, Aden was naked on his own floor in an X-pattern with only his socks on. The two guys could see his cock exposed to the world. It was beyond humiliating. The guys then began pacing around their prey very slowly.

"Aden, tonight we are going to get you to become a member of our Frat. We really are. But first, we have to get you all initiated and ready to be a real team player. We want you on our team, Aden, but it has to be *our* team. Now, you're a team player, aren't you?"

Aden tried to shake his head no, but ... no avail.

"It's OK, Aden, we're going to have a fun time. But first, you'd agree that your comments were a bit out of line, weren't they?"

Aden's non-existent shaking of the head continued.

"Yeah, I thought so too. So, we're going to have some fun with you, Aden. A *lot* of fun. Because you don't own sandals -- as far as we can tell -- and frequently dress up in long-sleeve, long-panted type outfits, I would guess you don't get much sun or rough tumbles. So, your skin must be soft ... and sensitive, right?"

Aden was a bit scared, but suddenly Aden laid a very thick piece of cloth over his eyes. It wasn't attached or anything -- it just laid there ... and Aden couldn't see. What were they going to do to him? I mean, if they were going to ...

Aden felt something. Across his leg. It was ... soft. Could it have been ...

... then another movement, across his exposed armpit. He tried to rein it in, but ...he couldn't. Then another brush ... across his left nipple. Did the boys break out ... feathers?

OH. FUCK.

Suddenly, feathers began tracing the lines of his arms and ribs, going up and down, up and down, slowly, teasingly. It ... fucking tickled. Shit! Aden was ticklish. Oh god was he ticklish. And these boys ... they knew how to get him. Aden was laughing on the inside ... but he couldn't fucking smile! He was trapped in a tickle chamber known as his own body! Suddenly the feathers concentrated on his pits ... and they circled slowly, touching every single nerve ending. Aden's was screaming with laughter on the inside but quiet as a mouse on the outside. The feather circled the craters of his pits, tickling his hairs, and seemed to dance with an almost evil relish. They were teasing his body, and trying to break his will. Aden tried to resist ... but this was getting hopeless fast.

The feathers danced around his ribs, and scraped the front of his belly, circling the base of his gut all the way to the insides of his belly button. The feathers *loved* the belly button, lapping at it with great intent. Sometimes a feather would jump back to his armpit just for variety, but tickles were being mined *everywhere*. Aden was just so fucking ticklish. He couldn't stand it. His rage towards them was less focused now -- all his mind was filled with was tickle. Tickle tickle tickle. Feather feather tickle. Fucking hell, he was losing it.

Soon the feathers began circling the insides of his thighs. That tickled even more. Slowly, the feathers teased their way upwards, up to his exposed crotch, and then right in the gooch. Oh, the feathers had a fucking party in the gooch, circling and tickling his most sensitive of areas. Around and around and up and down. Then they circled his sensitive balls, and painted every inch of them with feathery torment. Perhaps that's what got Aden the most: not the tickling itself, but the *teasing* tickles, the *almost* tickles, the playful tickles that were having such fun and delight while he was suffering through hell. Complete hell, made of tickles and feathers.

Yet the ball tickling was upping the ante. Jason & Damien weren't as much using the edges of the feathers as much as the very very very tips of them, and they were teasing the base of Aden's cock -- and, suddenly, it twitched. WHAT?! Aden's cock was twitching and moving and ... slowly becoming erect. Had the potion worn off? Aden tried to move his left arm with all of his might, but nothing happened. So why was his cock suddenly coming to full HOLY SHIT A FEATHER WAS MOVING ALONG HIS SHAFT!

Aden had never felt anything like it. It felt *so* fucking good! Tickled along his radiating member ... it was a rush he wanted to bathe in and lean in towards, but, alas, there was nothing he could do. It was a dirty tickle: he didn't want to like it but he kind of wished they wouldn't stop. He was being manipulated by two guys, but, fuck, a girl had never made him this horny since ever. Every single feather stroke made his dick feel like it was tingling with horniness, and then the feather stroke after pushed his horniness into the next level. His mind was focused entirely on his throbbing cock right now, and a very small dribble of precum was emerging from it -- and his arms still hadn't moved in some time. Or his legs. Or anything. He was motionless save for his erection.

The feathers circled and teased and tickled his cock, and then finally he wanted to cum ... but he couldn't. The throb was there, but there was no push from his body. It just ... throbbed. Throbbed with anticipation -- but that push over the edge never, ever came. FUCK HE WANTED TO ORGASM AND FEEL SPERM SHOOTING OUT OF HIS COCK ... but instead, the feathers just circled some more. And more. And were driving him bananas. Then, suddenly, Jason said "Get a whiff of this ..." Jason's dirty socked foot was shoved right into Aden's nose, and Aden had no choice but to inhale. That foot funk. That odor. It was so ... off-putting. Suddenly the erection subsided, much to Aden's frustration -- but the foot remained there, looming over his face and teasing him. All Aden was smelling was Jason foot sweat and he wanted to gag. It wasn't uber-rank or anything, but it was enough. Then Jason removed his foot, and let Aden's sweat-riddled body just lay there -- motionless as before.

Then the feathers attacked the nipples, circling and tickling Aden's pleasure-centers. They teased so softly and so quietly that Aden again wanted to scream. Yet then the feathers moved to the armpits and biceps for some more feather-light tickle teasing ...

and then into the cavernous tickle pits again ... and then to the nipples. The cycle began again.

Then the feathers stopped, and something else touched Aden -- two eager tongues, descending onto his nipples. They slurped slowly, every single microscopic tongue bump dragging across Aden's nips at an incredibly slow pace. Then, the tongue flicking started across his nips. Flick after flick after flick. The boys' saliva began dripping and pooling all over them. Suddenly, Aden's dick was hard again. Then the tickling went back into his pits. Then the frustration ... just escalated.

After ten more minutes of non-stop teasing, Damien went over and began lightly licking and slowly sucking on Aden's cock. Aden has had his cock sucked before -- mostly by freshmen girls who didn't know any better -- but fuck, Damien was a pro. Aden went immediately into that realm hovering over a brain-busting climax. The faint slurping, sucking sound in the distance only turned Aden on all the more. Jason sat down and gently put Aden's nipples between his fingers and began lightly rubbing them back and forth and back and forth. Aden -- mentally exhausted -- was in heaven, his body a pleasure playtoy for two horny Frat guys. Continuing the nipple teasing, Jason finally spoke:

"You know what's great about a formula that freezes all your body muscles, Aden? It freezes all of your body *muscles*. Your cock, however, is all tissue. We can make that do whatever we want it to for as long as we want. We're going to tease and torment the bejezus out of it. You'll be spewing an endless stream of precum in anticipation, enough for a fuckin' river, my friend. Yet ... there's one catch. You see, you can't climax unless you get a push from your muscles. That's how the body works. I'm a bio major, and human anatomy is one of my favorite areas of study. What we have here is a nightmare scenario. Damien can suck you off literally for hours. Your near-climax can get bigger and bigger ... but it's never going to come." Jason grinned with evil glee. "Welcome to hell. Now have some feet ..."

Jason's sweaty socked feet -- both of them this time, with clear outlines of Jason's toes visible from where Aden was laying -- were now occupying all of Aden's face. The smell was forced and unmistakable ... but Damien's cocksucking was like a goddamn miracle machine, hitting every one of Aden's pleasure buttons without even trying, that warm mouth hitting every gorgeous sensitive spot it could fine. All Aden tried to focus on was the horny, not the foot smell, but as much as he tried, that foot funk was still there in his face, tormenting him. After about 10 minutes of fighting the urge to be horny while sniffing a genuine jockfoot, both Damien and Jason stopped. Aden didn't climax. Again. The erection went down. Aden's frustration knew no bounds.

+ + +

This process continued eight more times.

+ + +

It was around 4AM when it began again. Aden's nipples were almost caked with dried saliva now. The sucking on his nips began yet again. His erection almost immediately shot up after frustrated anticipation (practically screaming "give me something -- *anything*!!"), but seeing this, Jason & Damien stopped, and awaited for Aden's frisky, ticklish cock to go down. When it did, Damien turned to Jason and said, "I think it's time." Jason agreed, and with obvious relish, Jason stuck that big sweaty socked foot of his right in Aden's face one more time.

Aden's cock immediately shot up. It was throbbing. Each inhalation drove him further up the wall. Then ... Aden realized it. Jason, perhaps even knowing what Aden was thinking, said "That's right. You're one of us now." As Aden sniffed, the internal screams came back ...

... he was Pavlov's dog. No wait: he was Pavlov's bitch.

They got him hard time after time, but always made sure to stick Jason's footsweat right in his face as they did so. Given how broken his mind was after all the tickling, of course Aden's brain would start connecting footsweat with horny. Now, it had gotten to the point where all Jason had to do with his foot was stick it in his face and Aden got instantly hard. The connection was made. Male foot sweat got him horny. And what Aden didn't know at the time was that once a foot fetish is formed in the brain, it's nearly impossible to shake. The boys had given him a taste of what teamwork was all about -- he was on the team whether he liked it or not.

Suddenly, broken, battered, and humbled, Aden conceded. He knew the lesson they were trying to teach him -- and he got the message. He was pulling a lot of shit over something so small, willing to humiliate his would-be brothers over placement in something as simple as a Frat. Maybe these guys *were* in the right. Even if they weren't, Aden had no idea how much longer the teasing of his sensitive skin would continue -- even though it already felt like a fucking eternity.

A single tear went down his face -- which Jason noticed. He pulled his socked foot away, and looked at the naked, helpless, ticklish boy in front of him. "You learned your lesson, didn't you?" Aden -- still blindfolded -- would've nodded in agreement if he could. "Good boy," said Jason. "Now we just have to take one quick thing for ourselves and go ..."

Suddenly Aden felt a tugging on his socks. They were on the whole time. They had been sweated into the whole time. All along, they were slowly being transformed into personal fetish objects for the two devious Frat brothers. Jason & Damien slowly peeled them off Aden's moist feet, held them up to their noses while kneeling in front of Aden's immobile body, and began to jack it, moaning while they indulged in flavor of Adenfoot smells. Eventually they came at the same time (how do they always do that?), spraying gobs of hot cum all over Aden's chest. Since each boy was on a different side of him, the cum streams formed a bit of an X-pattern over Aden's completely immobile chest. Fuck, even the cum streams felt ticklish, even as they slowly melted down his ribs, Aden totally unable to do anything about his liquid torture ...

The boys began packing up, and Damien got some sort of drink out in the glasses. Jason simply sat down between Aden's legs and began running his fingernails up and down Aden's bared soles ... and Aden -- horny, helpless, and more ticklish than ever -- couldn't do jack shit. The laughing inside of him was worse than before -- he was almost manic. Tickle Hell, again.

Eventually Damien mumbled something about the drink being ready. Crouching down next to Aden even as Jason lightly ran his fingers over Aden's soft soles, Damien said "Aden, we know how you feel. We really do. All we can hope is that you come out of this a better person. There are consequences for your actions, and it's a shame that we had to teach you ... but we only hope that something like this will only make you stronger. It is for this reason we want you a part of the Frat. We'll give you a quick drink that'll knock you out, and by the time you wake up, you'll be right as rain." There was a grin behind that last line. "Talk to us tomorrow, and think about what you want to do, OK?"

If Aden could've nodded in submission, he would've. Damien tilted his head up, a splash of a drink dribbled down Aden's too-dry throat, and before long, Aden was out like a light.

Aden woke up, groggy -- but mobile. He stretched for what felt like the first time in years, and fuck it felt good. He looked around -- he was still naked, but on his couch. He couldn't remember exactly how he got there. Then, he suddenly flashed back to last night, and one image after another jumped into his mind -- and Aden felt that he had never been so humiliated in his life. A little bit of anger came back, but it soon faded. Those kids got him good. He groggily stepped over to his computer, loaded it up, and saw there were ... friend requests on Facebook. Even after all of that, Jason & Damien were making an effort to reach out to him. Aden thought about one thing ... and got out his phone. Yes, he still had that video file from the night he spotted Damien & Jason doing their thing. He opened it up, ready to upload onto his computer, but ... wait. It was different. Same file name but, no ... it was a shot of him getting horny at the first sniff of Jason's foot. Just like that -- instantaneously. It was ... degrading to even look at. He checked his phone message outbox -- looks like Jason already e-mailed it to himself. For the first time in his life, Aden felt that he had gotten his comeuppance.

Maybe it was time, he thought. Maybe he *had* hurt some people before. Were ... were they right? No, they couldn't be! *He* was always right ... or maybe Aden was just full of shit. He had never thought of himself in that way, but what if what they said was true? What if people really did complain that much? Maybe his hubris had even hurt some of his friends back home?

Aden wandered over to his bedroom to get some clothes on ... and saw that Jason's dirty socks were left there on a pillow on his bed. There was a single notecard underneath that simply said "Welcome." Nothing else. Aden ... no, he couldn't -- or could he? Aden put his nose to the sock and inhaled. The erection returned within an instant.

After eight hours of pent-up sexual frustration, the 15 minutes that followed were some of the happiest of his life. If only Aden knew that his adventures were just beginning ...

HAPPY
(originally appeared in *My, What Ticklish Feet You Have*)

+++

Ask the experts: no tickle fiction anthology is complete without one story of a semi-sentient robot that manages to commit acts of sexual torment on an unsuspecting astronaut without even a hint of mercy ... obviously.

"Why aren't you smiling, David?"

The camera adjusted, gaining focus. Slowly David's face came into view: lean and muscular, a thin layer of fuzz covering his chin and neck from days of not having shaved. It was an almost-beard. Dark-haired and sullen-eyed, David was staring at the monitor in front of him. The computerized voice repeated:

"David, why aren't you smiling?"

David let out a dejected sigh: "'cos I'm not happy, CAIRO. I thought that even you could figure that out." David hesitated for a moment, and then stood up to walk down the corridors. CAIRO adjusted its camera yet again to get a glimpse of its subject walking away. CAIRO had no emotion, but could sense that the health of its subject was in question.

David went back to his sleeping quarters. He saw the date and grimaced a little. David has been on NASA's first moon base for well over 17 months now, which was a record by itself, but made even more impressive by the fact that he was the youngest astronaut (28) to ever go on a mission of this magnitude. This was to be his last month on the base, but got word just two days ago that his mission had been extended by a whole month. He was stuck here on this station with CAIRO -- the automated astronaut-maintenance system -- as his only company. CAIRO resembled HAL 9000 a little too close for David's comfort, but what else could he do? CAIRO still made him macaroni & cheese for dinner, gauged his heart rate while jogging on the treadmill, and warned him of debris storms when he was outside, doing maintenance or conducting experiments. CAIRO was an immaculately well-constructed mechanical system, and its purpose was to make any and all astronauts in its care as lively and at-ease as possible. All these months later, David was coming around to liking the damn thing, but upon hearing news of his extension, talking to an emotion-free series of circuits like CAIRO was the last thing he needed right now.

Back in his quarters, David -- dressed in a loose white maintenance suit but without shoes or socks -- tapped on the video screen right above his bed. He loaded up his log of the last few video transmissions he received from back on Earth -- these were the things that he treasured the most during his time on the station. Three of them were from Aly, his fiancée. Aly was a sweet young red-headed girl who thought the world of David. She was into scrapbooking and was looking to start up her own arts & crafts store -- easy to do when sharing in on the salary of an astronaut. Since they could only transmit or receive one video at a time, each entry was like its own video blog, and Aly would update him on what she was doing this week, any newspaper articles that mentioned his name, and -- of course -- how much she (and her three cats) missed him. Each entry was sweet, yet repetitive. Being on a moon base for a year and a half had given David a lot of time to think about their relationship. Watching these videos always reminded him of why he fell for her in the first place, yet since arriving at the station, David's thoughts began thinking of someone else ...

The night before he left before his weeklong detox and prep at the NASA center, David was out having drinks with his friend Brian. Although many friends were out with them, they all petered out pretty early, and soon Brian & David were alone, drunk off of a ton of Blue Moons (they lost count of how many they had, but were confident they had breached the double-digits). Brian was 26, blond, handsome, and had a great career at a large PR firm. He had a special bond with David, as the two could talk about just about anything to each other: their embarrassing moments, their secret desires, everything. Now, drunk at a downtown bar on a Tuesday night with virtually no one else around, Brian & David were getting in a bit of sentimental mood: they were really going to miss each other. Brian was finishing up some thoughts:

"Oh, and before I forget," he said before slamming his beer on the table with a bit of clumsy force, "I really wanted to wish you and Aly a really good time."

"What good time? I'm only going to be video-messaging her for 18 months. That's about as long as a long-distance relationship gets!"

"Well, you know what I mean. Seriously: she's a lucky lady."

David paused for a second and stared at Brian. "What do you mean 'she's a lucky lady'? You make it sound like you've been pining for her yourself ..."

"Well, I have been pining for someone, David."

"Who?"

The air was thick with silence. Brian simply stared back, obviously emboldened by the drink, and looked at his long friend with a warm smile: "... you."

David stared at his younger friend with intent: was he serious? Was this some elaborate going away gag or something? But no. It was clear that Brian was really, truly pining for his good friend David, and the vulnerability shone through his eyes: that confession really took it out of him, and his fate now lived and died by David's words.

"Well," started David, "this is ... unexpected to say the least."

"Pfft, tell me about it." Brian seemed to be very nonchalant about David's reaction. "You don't know how hard it is to secretly want to be around your smart, funny, and sexy friend all the time ..."

"Sexy?"

"David," started Brian, "I'd worship your body 100 times over if you'd let me."

David's brain, a bit hazy from booze, was processing all of this -- and was unsure of what to feel. At first, yes, being the object of desire of one of your good friends for years on end was a bit much to take in. However, "sexy"? No one had ever called him sexy. In college, girls called him hot, and Aly never went beyond calling his body "nice", but "sexy"? Being called that -- with genuine sincerity -- made David feel really, really good. He kind of liked the idea of being an idealized sexual object, lusted upon from afar. David wasn't an egoist; he just found such a compliment very flattering and ... kind of hot. His brain was instantly making all sorts of connections, and thought about Brian -- and how kind he was ... and how nice he looked ... and -- wait, how nice he looked?

"When you say worship," David started without thinking, "what do you mean?"

A spark went off in Brian's eyes.

"I mean ... well, have you ever had anything besides your cock sucked on?"

David thought for a second. "No."

"Well come here," started Brian, motioning for David to lean in.

Brian's mouth was at David's neck, and he could feel Brian's warm breath bouncing off of his skin. A light kiss was planted -- intimate but not romantic nor sexual. Just ... nice. Suddenly Brian's hands began moving slowly up David's arms and into his armpits -- David giggled just a bit, and laughed. This kind of playful prodding -- was nice. It was fun. It was ... turning him on a bit. Then the fingers began slowly tracing down David's ribs as the warm breathing continued on his neck. Then the fingers went for the kill and squeezed David's thigh. David jumped and squeaked a bit, but upon smiling, said, "Go on."

The fingers felt down the seams of David's jeans, and eventually pulled up David's ankle into Brian's lap. The fingers circled the outside of David's tennis shoes with a playful kind of stroking, up and down like the feet themselves were sexual objects. The fingers then began untying the laces and slowly slipped the shoe off. Weirdly enough, David was totally digging this. Not that the sex he had with Aly or any other girl in college wasn't fun, but fetish play was suddenly opening up whole new doors to him. The shoe came off, and then the fingers worked their way up the socks. David was uncontrollably smiling with pleasure once again. This was actually *really* fun. Feeling Brian's fingers run across the soles of his socks, lightly scratching the bare, ticklish feet contained within -- it was too much. Then the sock got ripped off, and -- all underneath the table of this dinky little bar -- David was receiving his first real foot massage of his life. Perhaps it was the booze or perhaps it was the stress of leaving for a year and a half, but fuck if this didn't feel like bliss. It was like the best kind of foreplay he had ever experienced. Occasionally the nails would tickle the soles, but for the most part the skin-on-skin rubbing contact was sending the drunken astronaut into the stratosphere of sheer ecstasy. Of course, they couldn't go any further without being detected by the bar staff, but after about ten minutes of non-stop drunken fun, Brian handed David back his sock and leaned over to say "You think you enjoyed that? That was just the beginning my friend." Brian left a quick kiss on the nape of David's neck and whispered "We'll talk more when you get back. You will be missed." Brian then departed and David was left alone in this bar, drunk off his ass, his right foot bared, and his mind flooded with a ton of thoughts that were totally new and totally alien to him.

The next week of detox and last-minute training occupied virtually all of his time, but the thought of Brian and fondling and playing like that -- they were on the backburner of his mind. They echoed in his late night thoughts on the space station and in his dreams sometimes. Now, he was looking to see which one of Brian's messages was in the video cue. David loaded it up as he usually does, and watched the whole thing. Of course, since every incoming and outgoing call was screened by NASA (and CAIRO for that matter), Brian's update was basic: he talked about some big clients he was working for, shared some good celebrity run-in stories, and mentioned what David's other friends were up to (Heather had a baby!). Yet it was that goodbye with the wink at the end that kept David wondering. His updates from Brian were every two months or so (which was unlike Aly, who sent a new video every week), but strangely, David watched the Brian videos more. Even though at this moment they were not helping his state of mind (staying another month meant that he couldn't see Brian for another month as well), it brought him a little assurance: there were people from all sides awaiting his return, with a mixture of warmth and lust, envy and delight. If it weren't for those feelings, David thought he would go insane out here in the dark nothingness.

Yet this warmth was temporary. David put on his sneakers without socks and went to the small gym area. One of CAIRO's robotic arms greeted him with a towel, which he then wrapped around the top of his treadmill. He just began running like hell, exhausting his body so that his mind couldn't stray too far, the TV ahead playing the latest crappy sitcoms that he liked so much (NASA could beam them up to him, but it took well over a week for him to get anything new). As sweat started pouring down his face, the physical anguish soon triggered his emotional pain, and soon violent tears were mixing in with his sweat, one indistinguishable from the other. His mind began thinking in pointed sentences: "How DARE they keep me here another goddamn month! Away from my family! Away from my friends! And, worst of all, away from Brian!" He thought about that wink from Brian at the end of that last transmission, and that did it. David screamed as loud as he possibly could in an unbridled fury, and then walked right off of the treadmill, lying down on the floor in anguish, as unhappy as he's ever been.

Tears were still going, as one of CAIRO's mobile cameras managed to extend down to right where David was laying. All David could see was a giant, unemotional camera eye staring back at him. He really didn't want to deal with a robot right now, but he didn't really have much of a choice.

"What's wrong, David?" it asked in its measured, warm tone.

"What the fuck do you think is wrong?"

"You don't appear to be your regular self today."

"*Well of course not*!" he yelled. "Can your fuckin' motherboard even process emotion? Even a fuckin' ounce of it? I'm pretty damn upset right now. I feel ... alone."

"But I'm here, David."

"Yeah, but you can't make me happy."

There was a bit of a pause as CAIRO processed its thoughts.

"I can try."

David, frustrated, stood up and looked right into the robotic arm camera that was hovering over him. "You can try to make me happy? Do you even know what happiness is to a guy like me?"

CAIRO was curious. "What physical attributes do you exhibit while being happy?"

David snorted a bit. The dumb robot didn't even fuckin' know.

"I'd be smiling, CAIRO. I'd be grinning from ear to ear so much that I couldn't even think about anything else. That's when I'm happy. I'd fuckin' love to see you try."

"But David, my main mission is to make sure your health and functions are sustainable for service."

David took off his sweaty sneakers and began to make his way back to his quarters. Soon tossing off one last, fatal remark: "Well you got a new mission now, CAIRO. Your goal is to try and make me the happiest goddamn person in the world. I really can't wait to see what the fuck you come up with." The slaps of Dave's bare skin across the floor echoed in the white, perpetually-clean hallway. The camera gained focus on its subject as he turned the corner into his room. Quietly, its processors began churning away -- it had a new task at hand.

The "night lights" went on, simulating some vague sense of late evening so that David could maintain something closely resembling a sleep schedule. There were now just a small, faint florescent over his bed that David could turn off at will. Here he was, re-reading James Joyce's Ulysses for the umpteenth time, feeling painfully, terribly alone. He shut the lights off and curled up in his bed, facing the spotless wall right next to it. Wrapped in his blanket, he felt somewhat comforted -- but not a whole lot.

After napping for a few hours, he woke up to see -- his room in the evening light setting. This was odd. He didn't normally get up before CAIRO reset the lights to daytime. He looked at the time on a nearby monitor -- yes, it was 10AM, definitely when sunlight should be out. "CAIRO?" he shouted. David waited. Nothing. Something was definitely wrong now. David walked out into the main hallway -- still barefoot, wearing just his space jumper -- and noticed everything was in night mode -- only a faint row of lights overhead illuminated his pathway. He kept on walking until he saw that a light was on in the Isolation Room. That was even stranger -- the isolation room only had drop-down monitors for emergencies, but for the most part was simply used when an astronaut needed to concentrate on something and needed no distractions to speak of. To have that room and only that room have its lights on, as if someone was in there -- was actually a bit terrifying.

David slowly creaked the door open, and saw that there was a chair simply sitting in the middle of the room, facing the door. David looked around -- and saw nothing. He slowly walked in, one cautious step after another.

"Hello there, David. Why don't you take a seat."

David looked around -- wasn't this supposed to be the Isolation Room? Did CAIRO really have access here as well? David looked around, and could see a camera arm in the corner -- apparently the corners of the wall were removable, which means that CAIRO pretty much had free reign. This was ... unsettling.

"CAIRO, what's going on?"

"Have a seat, David. I'll soon tell you everything you need to know."

David sat down cautiously. His toes kind of felt around the floor a bit, exhibiting his nervousness and anxiety.

"Alright, CAIRO: what the hell is this about?"

"David, last night you tasked me with a very important charge: to make you happy.

When you are happy, this usually physically manifests itself in the form of a smile. Can we agree upon these simple principles?"

Dave was a bit flustered. "Um ... I guess."

"Good. Now David ..."

"Ya know, you can just call me Dave. It's OK, CAIRO. It's not like you've been saying 'David' for a year-and-a-fuckin'-half."

"Noted. Now Dave, what would you say makes you happy?"

"Going home would make happy right now."

"That is something that will make you happy in the short-term, but I'm wondering about something that makes you happy in general."

"Well fuck, I don't know. A cold beer. A beautiful day in the spring. Taking off your work socks after a long 12-hour shift. A sweaty, efficient evening of fucking. I don't know CAIRO. Probably best would be ..." David realized he was dipping a bit into sentimentality -- possibly even schmaltz -- but didn't care, "to simply be in an evening where you're in the arms of someone you love dearly."

"And who would that be, Dave?"

"Aly, naturally."

The response was instantaneous: "Not Brian?"

A flint of anger surged through David's body. "... what?"

"Well Dave," CAIRO started, "I've been watching your habits in the past while. You mention Aly as being important in your life, yet you've watched the transmissions from Brian more times than all of the transmissions from Aly together. You seem to like replaying that moment when he winks at you over and over again ..."

"OK, I've had enough of this shit, CAIRO!"

Suddenly, the automated door for the Isolation Room closed and locked in front of David.

"Dave, we need to get this taken care of. My goal is to make you happy before you even leave this room -- and presently, I feel that all I've done is upset you. We'll find what makes you tick before too long."

David stood up in a rage. "CAIRO, now is not the time to fuck around with me! Let me go!"

The faint hum of mechanics was all that filled the pregnant pause between the two sentient beings.

"OK, Dave, but I'm still doing the weekly infection sweep of the halls. I'm going to need to sanitize you before you go back out there. I'm sorry for not tending to you before."

David cocked an eyebrow, knowing that such a thing was very unlike CAIRO's usually-organized, to-the-point behavior -- but who was he to question? David raised his hands in the air, and just like every time that had happened prior, two sleek robotic arms extended down from the ceiling (so there was some stuff up there!), the rounded fingertips moving in closer to David's hips so that it could start removing the jumpsuit. Without even thinking, though, David -- somewhat already distrusting of CAIRO, backed to his left side somewhat subconsciously as the arms went to remove the jumpsuit. He accidentally ran into the soft, rounded robotic fingers which were kneading into David's sides, and he laughed a bit. "Hey, watch it!"

The camera zoomed in.

"Dave ... were you smiling?"

"Um, yeah, sorry. The fingers just tickled me a bit."

"Tick-le?"

"Yeah," David replied, non-chalantly.

There was silence. Suddenly the robotic fingers begin tickling the air in front of them, slowly moving towards David, menacingly.

"Tick-le," the voice coldly repeated.

"Wha ... ?"

David instinctively backed up, but the arms descended far too quickly, and soon were placed perfectly in his sides. The fingers began to oscillate, and boy did those perfectly smoothed and rounded robofingers tickle! David's mouth stretched into a grotesque distortion of its former self, as a laugh simply tore its way out of his body. It was violent, sudden, and unexpected. David's eyes shot open wide in surprise.

"WHAT THE FUCK, CAI ..."

He didn't even had time to finish the sentence: the robofingers managed to sneak their way right up into David's armpits, kneading the soft patch of flesh right next to the top parts of his ribcage, just tapping it repeatedly like a telegraph -- awaiting a response from the tickles on the other end. David drew his arms in as close as he could to escape the torment, but the arms were deep in there, and there wasn't a moment when they weren't moving, twisting David's armpit hairs slowly, pinching and poking and tormenting his flesh without stopping for a second.

David fell on the floor but the arms continued to tickle and tickle and tickle. His bare heels began grinding into the floor and pushing his way back into the wall, but arms remained there, like they were glued to his sensitive areas, just tickling and teasing more and more. David was choking on his uncontrollable laughter. As his eyes clenched shut and the smiles tumbled out, David failed to see a second pair of robotic arms had come down from the ceiling and proceeded to grab his ankles, turning his body around in the process. David looked up and yelled profanities, but as he did so, the finger in his pits suddenly pulled out and wrapped their way around his wrists, soon lifting his whole body up off the ground.

"Oh no you fuckin' don't!"

David struggled as much as his strength would allow, but before long, his arms and legs were stretched out like a piñata, belly to the floor, his whole body stretched and suspended about ten feet in the air. His hands were held in front of him, his legs held behind him, his body sagging helplessly in between. David fought as much as he perceptibly could, but it was obvious that CAIRO's grip on him was way too tight -- he was his caretaker's own fuckin' puppet, and the show was just getting started.

A camera attached to a robotic arm careened down and stared at David in the face. CAIRO's unemotional voice spoke as if nothing was happening.

"Are you ready, Dave?"

"Hey fucktard! Do you see what kind of position I'm in?"

"Yes -- I am the one putting you in it."

"That's not what I meant, jag-off! What the literal fuck are you doing?"

"Dave, I'm making you happy."

"By what, tickling me? You're not making me happy -- you're pissing me off!"

"I disagree, Dave. You said that you were happy when you were smiling. And by performing tick-le on you, your smile grows wider than anything I have seen in my video archive. I think tick-le is quite effective."

"That's not how it works, CAIRO."

"I have concluded that the wider the smile gets, and the higher the pitch of your voice goes, the happier you are. All I'm trying to do is to make you happy."

"CAIRO, I ..."

Two additional cybernetic arms -- which had emerged with no warning -- suddenly jabbed fingers into David's ribcage, and they fuckin' tickled.

"Gah-ha-had stop it! Pl-e-e-ase!"

"I have to override your request Dave. You obviously struggle against tick-le, so I have to force you to receive it, much how I'm programmed to make sure you reach your daily amount of nutritional supplements. It's for your own good."

David tried to formulate a response, but it was drowned out in the stunted, sputtering laughter that he was spewing forth.

The round robotic fingers were having quite a bit of fun dancing in David's ribs, moving a bit closer to the nipples and then gradually making their way back to his spine, still tickling the whole time, kneading his flesh, playfully poking the spaces in between his ribs. However CAIRO was figuring out ways to tickle, it was working damn well.

Slowly, fingers teased the area right underneath David's ribcage, playfully poking and scratching the front of David's tummy, curious as to what kind of reaction it would produce. When something caused David's synapses to fire off the scale, like when CAIRO found that by doing the "pinching" motion of tickling across his belly his voice shot up two octaves, CAIRO learned the technique and began finding variations on it. CAIRO was learning that one particular "style" of tickling didn't work when prolonged: it had to switch things up, trying unexpected angles at off-beat times, constantly moving and changing so that the laughter pouring out of David's mouth was constant -- and entirely against his will.

David's lungs began heaving and panting perceptibly. CAIRO was monitoring his heart rate and health, and decided to give him a break. As David caught more bucket breaths to try and regain at least some of his strength, CAIRO had one of those smoothed robofingers trace along David's spine, scratching rather softly at different points just to test reactions. Sometimes it'd tease a muscle on his back, other times glide along the curve of his neck, occasionally circling around to his armpits just because it would definitely produce a laugh -- his armpits always did. The arms then moved around to David's securely bound feet -- those toes had been flexing and wiggling the whole time. David felt like passing out, and then he felt it: that small, barely noticeable scratching along his heel. It was on both feet, and it almost felt like a hummingbird wing was continually flapping against his the thickest part of his heel. It tickled a bit, sure -- but it wasn't stopping. Those fingers were barely scratching his heels, but they weren't stopping, like a pair of tickle-crazed insects were just feeding off of those heels alone. Sure, his feet tried moving sideways and flexed and curled, but the goddamn tickling wasn't stopping.

David's hesitant giggles were starting to choke out as full-blown laughs. The grimace on his face was intense: he was doing everything he could to fight it, but CAIRO was pushing buttons he didn't even know he had. That perpetual, constant, unstoppable feathering of his heel was driving him up the wall. His bare feet were practically having seizures of agony, doing every miniscule thing they could to fight the overwhelming power of tickle that was assaulting them -- but all these efforts were in vain. David had limits, barriers, and exhaustion walls that he was hitting. CAIRO didn't have any of these.

Once the heel feathering started getting David's vocal chords regurgitating laughs in the most painful of ways, those tickling fingers began moving toeward. They started scratching right in that sweet spot where heel and sole meet, and it felt like David was being teased in a place he had never even been touched before. Scratchy scratchy scratchy. It didn't stop. Although the toes flexed and screamed to try and get away, it was obvious their fates were sealed. The fingers kept moving up, scratching those too-sensitive soles, and it was like they were having a field day. Once again, David's voice shot up an octave, his laughing became even more pathetic than before. David was practically pleading with CAIRO now, but certainly not in any language resembling English. The robofingers scratched upward slowly, slowly, soon attacking the balls of David's feet and then the base of the toes, alternating between scratching them and then simply poking David's foot right in the center and then wiggling that finger around. The corners of his mouth almost hurting from the ridiculous strain they were being put through. CAIRO, meanwhile, was simply watching. Observing. And worst of all, it was learning.

The more the toes splayed and tried to escape their inevitable fate, the more CAIRO learned what tickle techniques were working best. The scratching worked great, especially when followed by a nice stroking. Done with David's helpless feet, the fingers began to lightly pinch his flesh through his jumpsuit around his ankles, and then up the calves, and then lightly fingering the back of his knees. Once it discovered that the back of his knees were producing whole chokes of laughter, the arms that were restraining his legs pulled his body taught -- there was now no way those knees would be able to bend even a fraction of an inch to escape their tickle torture. David's mind, so far gone already, was snapping now -- his body had already enjoyed the spasms his nerves put him through, largely because it gave him a brief, fleeting moment of release, but CAIRO was preventing him from even enjoying that.

The robofingers almost bounced in that soft spot on the back of his knees, poking that sensitive, fleshy patch before scratching a bit on the outside. David's laughs mutated into whines during this, as CAIRO's devious itches proved to be the thing that worked him into overdrive. Then, without pause, the hands began pinching David's inner thighs, and his voice reached full on soprano heights. "FUCCCCCK!" he cried out, before drowning in a sea of laughter. CAIRO took this in. The pinching slowly went up his thighs, closer and closer to his hanging balls, and David's last bit of fight emerged, trying to prevent the robot from toying with his junk.

Yet it was all in vain. Soon, the robotic arms were reaching around and merely poking around his pelvis: slightly below the belly button, an inch away from his balls on his thighs, square on each side of his hips, merely teasing the area around his genitals. David was sweating.

A flash of lasers suddenly appeared and disappeared, and David wondered if any hit him. Then, he found out that they did: in an instant, his jumpsuit fell off his body in tatters. Being how he was belly-parallel with the floor, the roboarms restraining his arms and legs proceeded to lightly tip him upwards, and the pieces that remained on his back simply slid off his bum onto the floor. He was still suspended in air, but practically in a standing position now, feet nearly parallel with the floor. He was fucked.

He would've screamed at the robot. He would've asked how the hell nudity was going to help this "experiment", but the connection between his conscious thoughts and his mouth was severed long ago. David merely panted. That was pretty much all he could do now: pant and laugh for his new robot master.

Another robotic arm had extended down from the ceiling -- David didn't even want to look so looked down at himself and -- he was half-erect. He almost didn't even notice it -- that poking around his crotch was enough to tease him to half-mast. Fuck. Even as he stared at his junk in amazement, the new arm slowly craned into view: it was the brush-scrubbing arm from the shower. With small, wispy bristles along its rounded head, it sometimes could whirl around at high speeds -- which now made David absolutely terrified about the fact that it was positioning itself right underneath his balls.

He weakly struggled in his bonds, but he knew better than CAIRO did that it was useless. The little wispy bristles made contact with the undersides of his testicles, and he nearly wanted to jump out of his skin. Fuck was he sensitive, and fuck were those sagging sacks of sensitivity not ready for such a goddamn sensation. CAIRO's arm merely moved around a bit, lightly teasing his flesh, and David wanted to cry -- it tickled *so much*! Little, devious lightning flecks murdering his synapses with each passing nano-second. David was laughing so hard, which, in many ways, was his reality right now: he lived in a realm of ticklish laughter -- and that is all that he knew.

Then, David heard that whirring mechanical sound that he had so gotten used to over the past year and a half: the scrubber's head was beginning to rotate ... slowly. Gradually, those soft little bristles began to circle David's most sensitive of areas, and his body began to spasm violently. A whole new world of tickle suddenly broke wide open. The whirling brush was only so lightly touching the back of David's balls, but, then, gradually began to rotate, going from the back of his balls to the bottom of them, slowly working their way to the front, attacking his glands like they were marked by an assassin. Full-blown tears were now streaming from David's eyes, and all of this tickling of his privates was causing his erection to get just a little bit more engorged than before.

This wasn't news to CAIRO, however, which had been watching David the entire time he's been here -- which meant that, of course, it even observed him masturbating. CAIRO had determined that humans like having their genitals played with in a pleasurable way, although each was different in its approach. David never liked to leave a huge cumshot for whatever reason, and instead just wound up teasing himself to the edge before backing off, time and time again. However, merely repeating the exact same thing wasn't going to work for CAIRO. Given that David's smile had already mutated several times since this "session" began, CAIRO was certain that an orgasm was the only way to get David's smile as wide as it could possibly be.

The whirling brush was slowing to a stop. As it did so, it removed itself entirely from David's balls. Panting, sweating, and trying not to cry from this merciless tickle abuse, David imagined in his mind a place that wasn't in this room, much less on this orbiting satellite rock. He envisioned himself lying safely in his bed at home, the morning sun peaking in through the window to wake him up, hearing a softly whispered "good morning" come from the other side of the bed, turning his own body around to see Brian's sweet face looking back at ...

Wait, Brian? What the hell did Brian have to do with this? Could it ...

"OK, Dave -- I have a surprise for you."

CAIRO's intonation was as far from sympathetic as you could possibly imagine.

"CAIRO," whispered David, weakly, "Please, let me go. My voice is hoarse, and I don't know if I can ..."

David heard the sound of another compartment opening from overhead, and down came another arm, but, wait, this was a tube. A blue tube that -- oh no, it couldn't be.

"CAIRO ... is that the ..."

"Yes, Dave: it is liquid transportation cable used on this station base."

David's eyes opened as widely as they could -- he was looking terror in the eyes.

After all, David knew exactly what that cable could do. It was like a space hose: if CAIRO had to transfer a part of the water supply from one part of the base to another, remote part of the base, it couldn't simply carry a bucket. Instead, this special tube was used as a direct link from one water supply to another. Of course, hooking up a hose by itself wasn't going to do the job (the gravity was too low for that), so scientists developed this special cable wherein a small electrical impulse could cause the cable to pulse in one direction or another. Instead of the water merely floating in the air, it would be "squeezed along" the tube because the tube itself was pulsating towards one direction. It was a very cost-effective breakthrough that no doubt had made millions of dollars for the inventor that came up with it. For David, however, it was a whole new nightmare.

"CAIRO, I BEG OF YOU PLEASE DON'T DO THIS!"

"It's for your own good, Dave. You wanted to be happy, right?"

And with that, the mouth of this blue hose began to swallow the head of David's penis, soon encompassing the rim, then the shaft, and somehow working its way straight down to the base. There was Dave: suspended in the air by four robotic arms, completely naked, and with a giant blue hose attached to his dick. Humiliation didn't even begin to describe it ...

David's eyes cringed as much as they could: he was simply waiting for that first, dreaded pulse. He waited ... and waited ... and ... well, maybe it wasn't going to ...

SUCK. The first pulse was incredible. The interior of this space hose was remarkably soft, and to suddenly feel it gently grab a hold the base of his cock and suddenly work it was up the shaft, past the rim of the head and finally give the head a bit of a squeeze itself -- well, it felt incredible. David wouldn't admit it to anyone ever, but ...

SUCK. There it went again. It wasn't as much pleasurable, though, as it was completely overwhelming. Sure, it felt good, but David didn't really have a say, the machine merely SUCKed when it wanted to, which already SUCK holy crap it was increasing. It seemed that each time it did it, David's train of thought was SUCK goddammit, CAIRO!

David seriously tried to struggle but that vile space hose was latched on firmly to his manhood, and it was thoroughly enjoying torturing him. The frequency of the pulses was increasing ever so slowly, and David began to make all sorts of moans to accompany each one. He wasn't proud of it, but the feeling of the soft hose against his penis was proving to be too much -- it was, in a sense, winning the battle of his senses, and there was almost nothing he could do.

David's face twisted into a grimace, now trying his best to fight off the machine. It doesn't matter how good it felt -- he just didn't want a space hose to determine when he had an orgasm. Each SUCK that happened made David's thoughts of "fight this monstrosity!" get a little quieter each time. He eventually just abandoned the whole thing, because devil be damned, this felt amazing. Having some outside force control his cock was a bit terrifying, but also turning out to be a bit exciting, because he truly didn't know what was going to happen next. His body was drained of all of its energy, so to have one single (diabolical) pump bring him closer and closer to the orgasm of his life -- well, it was more than worth it.

The pumps were getting more rapid, and CAIRO could see that David's heart rate was increasing: a climax was just around the corner. The big dumb smile of his was certainly widening the closer he got, though. Seeing this as an opportunity, the robofingers placed themselves right outside of David's armpits, and right as his voice starting getting into that high-pitched "I'm gonna cum!" threshold, the fingers dived right into those flesh patches, lightly teasing his ticklish armpits just as his cock was tingling with excitement and oozing precum. Not expecting the sharp sensation, David's body jolted a bit, and that's all that needed to happen: David shot a monstrous, threatening load of cum. His entire cock quaked with gooey spasms of joy, his body flexing as much as it could while restrained, each pump feeling like it was draining a gallons of energy out of the boy. The cock shots were getting smaller as they went, but boy were there a ton of them. David, now with his mind completely empty of thought, tilted his head back and pleasantly sighed. He had never felt this good in his life.

A good 15 minutes had passed, and nothing happened. David was just blissfully alone his thoughts, his balls completely drained, his body barely able to move an inch. When his groggy head did try to readjust itself, the ever-present CAIRO camera eye made its way down to make eye-contact with the boy.

"How do you feel, Dave?"

"I ... I hate ... you."

"But Dave, I was only helping. Your smile was wider than I have ever seen it. It appears that you were truly happy."

"CAIRO, just let me go."

"But why Dave?"

"'cos ... well c'mon, 'cos you're done with your ... fun."

"Dave, I thought you wanted to be constantly happy."

"CAIRO, there is only one way that I could be truly happy, and that's if ..."

"I think I understand, Dave."

"... understand what?"

"You want to see him."

"Who?"

"Brian."

"No, CAIRO, what I meant was ..."

"It will take some time to get him here, Dave. Placing a decoy file with Brian's information into NASA's database takes time, but I should be able to do it. There is a flight already scheduled to bring in your replacement in a month's time."

"CAIRO, that's not what I ..."

"If that is what will truly make you happy, Dave, I will make sure it gets done. It is, after all, my new priority to make you happy."

"CAIRO! LISTEN TO ME!"

"Now, according to my instruments, your skin has become rather sensitive following orgasm. Do you think a tick-le would work well on you now?"

"CAIRO PLEASE I BEG OF YOU TO ..."

David still tried to fight, even though he was still hopelessly bound. The first robofinger traced a line up his sole, and David found out that in space, no one could hear you scream.

THE ROOMMATE
(originally appeared in *My, What Ticklish Feet You Have*)

+ + +

One of my favorite things in the universe is working my way into the minds of straightboys, the more stereotypically alpha the better. Playing around with a guy's own heteroflexibility is something I divinely love, just seeing how far I can press into their sexuality without them even being conscious of the fact. This here is an adaptation of the true life story of me and my junior year college roommate. He was a nice, talented guy, but also more stereotypically alpha than I initially thought. When things got a little more physical/roughhouse-y between us, I wound up putting myself in positions wherein he was able to exert his dominance, and, slowly, crafted him into one absolutely devious foot and tickle dominant unlike the world had ever seen. While several real-world details are used for this story, there's a good fictional element as well, and the end of it is something completely made up, but makes sense in the course of the narrative of it all. Also, it's just damn great horny fun ...

A single drop of water was all it took to change Cody's life forever.

This drop had landed on his forehead, and Cody slowly woke up, wondering what the hell was dripping water on his forehead. Right there, in the middle of the night, Cody's dormroom pipes were extracting revenge on him once again. For while Cody did have his bed right next to the window, his bed was also directly underneath a run of metal pipes (painted, of course, to match the bland walls of the room), and even after calling it in to campus maintenance, here he was, once again, awoken by a single drop of water, right in the dead of the night.

As Cody turned to his side, however, he noticed there was a light still on in the room. That was strange, he thought, given that when he & Alan went to bed, everything was completely turned off. Alan was one year older than Cody, but the two had become friends through various literary classes, as both shared a wicked sense of humor that soon bled over into movie nights, drinking nights, and much more. Alan, with his slight Italian heritage, bowl-cut black hair, and somewhat athletic inclination (well, if you consider Ultimate Frisbee supremely athletic), certainly had an attractive charm, less so his build, although he was still a catch for the ladies on campus. Cody, meanwhile, with his short, straight blonde hair and gawky frame, was less so a catch, even though he radiated creativity in virtually every class and endeavor he participated in. Perhaps Cody & Alan's friendship looked slightly odd on the outside, but on the inside, things were bubbling: while Cody was Alan's trusted confidant, it was Cody himself who actually harbored a bit of a crush on his older friend -- and had an intense male foot fetish to boot.

Living with his object of desire and foot-lust was nothing short of heaven for Cody. When his roommate was gone, he could raid through Alan's laundry basket and find the dirtiest pair of socks he could possibly find, laying back in his bed (window blinds very obviously drawn) and inhaling every single molecule of foot stink there was, which, in turn, caused his hardon to rage like it never had before. Unlike most people in such a position though, Cody felt guilty about his urges taking over during those alone times, as he felt like he was being dishonest to his friend. Every once in awhile, a paranoid delusion would race through his brain, like the one time he was licking the sweatblackened insoles of Alan's leather sandals, tasting each and every bit of Alanfoot that he could, before hearing the door to their dorm room be slowly unlocked, causing Cody to scramble back to his computer, wondering if Alan "figured it out" a few minutes later when he put his foot right in the sandal that Cody had just finished tonguing the living hell out of. Anytime a "close call" like this would happen, Cody would stop doing anything fetish-related for a few days (well, except maybe jack off to some of the images he had stored on his computer), out of both his fear of losing his friendship and for the fact that he couldn't help but feel that he might be slightly in over his head. Yet after a few days, Alan would come back from a brief jog, toss those white ankle-socks into the laundry hamper before taking a shower, and Cody's curiosity got the better of him. It wasn't his fault that the smell/taste of Alan's feet seemed to only get better and more pungent with each and every passing day ...

Which brings us back to Cody and the Case of the Mysterious Light. After quietly looking around, Cody could see where the light was coming from. In their room, Alan & Cody's desks were placed together, creating a slight bit of a wall/private area for each roommate. Being standard-issue for a college campus, there was a backing to these desks, but not underneath where the students' legs were supposed to go: this was designed to make it so that they could more easily feed computer/printer/speaker cables through. Yet, when placed back to back, these desks allowed someone a perfect view of everything that was happening waist-down on the other side, like Cody for example. At this moment, what he was seeing was the dim blue light of Alan's laptop reflect across the young man's naked, horny body.

Yes indeed, at around 3AM that evening, Alan was sitting there at his computer, pantsless, slowly teasing and jerking his cock to who-knows-what. Although this didn't necessarily fit into Cody's "interests", he was nonetheless fascinated by what his roommate was doing. So confident in his own quick-jerk habits, it was fascinating to not only see someone else take his tender time in getting off, but also to see his closest friend do something so base -- it cast him in a different light. His object of lust was no unintentional foot god -- he was just another guy at a college who was horny like all the rest. Alan had some sort of lotion with him, and slowly, carefully worked his cock over, moistening it up every few minutes for maximum effect. Every once in awhile it would involuntarily twitch, no doubt excited by something it had seen. Over 20 minutes, in the faintest of lights, Cody watched with absolute fascination, unable to tear his eyes away. When it came time to climaxing, a few quick sheets of tissue were brought out, and Alan's mighty shaft pumped away on its own, oozing out cum, undoubtedly satisfied with its accomplishment. Cody simply lay there awe-struck -- he couldn't believe what he had just seen. He remained motionless as Alan went to the restroom to clean himself off, having just seen the most private of command performances.

As the weeks rolled on, Cody came to realize that this was actually a fairly regular event, and each one seemed to be more fascinating than the last. Cody always wondered why Alan took showers at night, but now that he was watching these too-private shows at night, he began to understand: ain't nothing like walking into your room with a bathrobe on, opening the front, and feeling like you're truly a king in your chair. One night, Alan even jerked it while still wearing his ankle socks, which fascinated Cody even further, seeing those toes stretch and wiggle while hidden in a thin sheet of white fabric -- it was proving hard for Cody to not jerk it in tandem. Of course, those very socks became even more fantastic jerking material for Cody later ...

Gradually, Cody's own behavior was changing. He was staying up later, feigning sleep just in case Alan decided to attend to his more primal needs. Some nights this gambit paid off, sometimes he was up for hours on end for no reason. He still did his schoolwork and hung out with friends, but still couldn't help but wonder what new Alan-oriented fetish treats awaited him at home. One night, Cody got back from a friend's downtown birthday celebration (see: drinking), and stumbled in around 2AM, trying his darndest to be quiet. He got to his bed without turning on the lights in the room and quietly slipped into his pajama bottoms, but not before he began to register something he hadn't heard before: the sound of Alan snoring. Alan almost never snored, so he must've been hella out of it. Cody looked around the dark room, his head still swimming a bit, but his inhibitions largely ... gone. He, being as drunk as he was, thought that crawling across the room would make less noise, and proceeded to get on all fours and walk slowly towards the foot of Alan's college-regulation bed. Being how it was the spring, there wasn't much need for covers, and lo and behold, sticking out barely over the edge of the bed (and right out of the one thin white cover that Alan used to cover himself with) was Alan's glorious bare right foot. In his kneeling position, Alan's foot was about eye-level with Cody. The snoring continued, almost echoing in Cody's mind. So Cody, feeling a bit more daring than usual, placed his nose just an inch away from the base of Alan's toes. He sniffed. Already, he could get a sense of Alan's delicious foot scent, and he had an instantaneous hardon. This was exactly, exactly what he wanted ...

Emboldened and unquestionably horny, Cody decided to take things a step further. He leaned forward and pressed his nose right onto the base of those toes, and inhaled deeply. Within seconds, a newfound sexual energy surged through the horny college boy, and if he hadn't been dripping precum before, he certainly was now. His left hand unconsciously began stroking his cock through his pajama fabric, knowing full well that he was in a state of total wrongdoing and total ecstasy all mixed together. That left hand began to start jerking his cock through the fabric, and before he knew it, Cody's soft mouth reached out for Alan's unconscious, helpless toes; starting by lightly sucking on Alan's pinkie toe, and then the one right next to that, and onward until he was simply sucking on Alan's big toes in an very passionate fashion. The taste of Alan's footsweat positively delighted Cody's tastebuds, which, in turn, seemed to be connected directly to his raging rock, which twitched in approval. Cody took one more wet slurp of Alan's toes, and just like that, rockets of cum shot out his cock, making the entire front of pajama pants moist with hot sperm. Even after the final shot, tingles of pleasure continued to dance around Cody's entire body, and he could even feel this event get burned into his memory -- this was an event he wouldn't forget anytime soon.

Once his body came down from its horny high, the kneeling Cody suddenly felt even more exhausted than before. He took one last glance at Alan's saliva-coated foot sticking out from the bedsheet, and after he heard one more deep snore, drunkenly crawled on all fours once again back to his bed, where he promptly passed out.

When Cody awoke, it was around 2PM, and he realized it was Saturday. This upset Cody, as that was the day that he & Alan had mutually agreed would be their "dorm room cleaning day." It was a bother (especially for Cody, who wasn't the cleanest of undergrads), but needed to be done for the sake of Mutual Roommate Sanity (or, as they oft referred to it, "MRS"). A quick look around showed that Alan was not around -- perhaps he was studying or at a rehearsal for something -- Cody could never remember which. So, after having a small bit of cereal from the duo's shared mini-fridge and changing into a dirty old T-shirt & his shin-high white socks (he kept his long pajama pants on though -- they were just too comfy), Cody got to work wiping the dust off of their computer monitors and TV, doing a quick wash of the inside of their window (lord knows he wasn't going to go outside), and after checking his e-mail, went back to bed wondering what movie he'd lay back and watch this evening, soon dozing off while getting lost in his own thoughts.

Cody could hear faint bits of voices as he woke up, only to realize that it was yet another *Family Guy* DVD that Alan had put in the TV (that seemed to be what the TV was used for about 80% of the time). The 'mates chatted about their respective days with a relative lack of interesting detail -- it was typically droll behavior for two guys who had been living together for all of four months. Alan asked how it was taking care of the "MRS", and Cody said it was fine -- he got his cleaning done. Alan -- in dirty white cotton ankle socks, cargo shorts, and green T-shirt from his Ultimate Frisbee team -- kneeled to the ground for a split-second, looking across the room towards Cody's bed.

"Well, from here, I can even see some dust bunnies underneath your bed."

Cody, still on his bed, groaned. "Oh, but I did everything else!"

"A rule's a rule, man. I'm doin' my part tonight."

"But Alan ..."

"Jeez! You could've done it by now instead of just yammering at me!"

Cody knew it had to be done, but conceived of the laziest way possible to do it. Without getting up from his bed, he reached over to his desk to grab some Swiffer wipes he had, and then rolled over on his stomach, squeezing his arm between the side of his bed and the wall, blindly using the Swiffer to grab whatever bunnies might be hopping around under his bed. During this process, his right leg was also seeping into that crack between the bed and the wall. No, this was not the most efficient position for cleaning things, but Cody didn't really care at this point -- at least he didn't have to get out of bed. Well, technically, his feet were beyond the foot of his bed, but whatever: he was horizontal, and that was all that mattered.

Then, just as he was reaching for something he thought seemed like significant bunny, the weight of his leg and arm seeping between that crease between the bed and the wall gave way, and the bed pushed out from the wall just a bit, causing Cody to fall through the crack. It was very sudden and very loud.

Alan called over: "Are you OK, man?"

"Yeah," said the grounded Cody, figuring out what just happened. The bed only gave way a bit, but the rest of his body slipped through the crack between the bed and the wall (having an unbelievably gawky frame no doubt helped with this). His right foot, however, was still wedged in pretty tight between the foot of his bed and the wall -- trapping it. He tried maneuvering his socked foot in every which way, but nothing happened.

"Hey Alan?"

"Yes?"

"Could you help me out?"

"What happened?"

"I'm ... I'm stuck."

This warranted Alan getting up from his bed and walking over to his roommate's bed, and as soon as he saw Cody's predicament, he began to laugh wildly: Cody was completely trapped under his own bed, with one foot trapped between the wall and the bed. This ... was comedy gold for him. Cody was less amused.

"How stupid are you?!" bellowed Alan, laughing hysterically.

"Alright, alright," started his trapped roommate. "Can you please just help push the bed to the side so that I can get out?"

"Aww, but how else can I play with your trapped foot like that?"

"OK dude," started a visibly panicked Cody, "no time for games. Just move the fuckin' thing, OK?"

Alan nodded, and said, "Sure ... but I just got to do one thing first ..."

With that, Alan walked over to the foot of Cody's bed and plopped himself down, cross-legged, in front of Cody's trapped foot.

"Hey Cody."

"Yes?"

"Are you ticklish?"

Cody's eyes widened considerably.

"DON'T FUCKING TOUCH MY FOOT FOR A SINGLE GODDAMN SECOND."

"Oh, you mean like this?"

Alan ran his index finger from socked heel to socked toes, just seeing what kind of reaction it would elicit out from his roommate. Cody, trapped, watched his body quickly convulse and scream. "FUCK!" he cried, "I'm very ticklish there!"

"Oh, really?" said Alan with a shit-eating grin. One more swipe of that index finger from heel to toe -- Cody convulsed again. This made Alan smile quite a bit -- he was enjoying this.

"Please," started Cody, "just stop. You had your fun, I just ... please stop. I am so ticklish."

"Oh I know," said Alan. "That's what I'm enjoying the most. I'm just curious about what other reactions we can elicit out of you ..."

Alan took all the fingernails of his right hand and began scratching up and down on the part of Cody's foot where the sole meets the heel, and Cody proceeded to fly into more of a hysterical fit than before. Laughter shook out of him, sometimes in cut-off bits and pieces. He tried protesting, but his words were choked by laughter, and so all that emerged from his mouth was a stream of delirious nonsense. All Alan had to do was scratch that foot just a bit, and it sent his roommate up the wall. He then grabbed the rim of Cody's sock and pulled it down and straight off. "Now, let's see if you're any more ticklish without the sock ..."

Cody was about to scream but Alan's too-perfect fingernails were already at work on the base of Cody's toes, scratching and poking and prodding Cody's footflesh. What should also be noted about Cody is that this is a guy who, despite his own fetish, does not really find much fun or joy in being barefoot himself, so houses his dogs in shoes and socks almost perpetually. What that means, however, is that his feet are unbelievably soft, so while fingernails across bare soles would be torture for some people, it was a living hell for Cody, and Alan's fingernails were practically ripping his nerve system in half with their ticklish touch. Some people describe certain sensations in a way that they're going to "jump out of their skin", but for Cody, it wasn't a metaphor: he honest to goodness felt like that was what was going to happen to him as Alan deviously played with his foot.

Twenty minutes passed.

There was Alan, tickling Cody's bare foot with the same effort and vigor as twenty minutes ago, and there was Cody, trapped under his own bed, sweating, weak, and leaking out rambling half-laughs all while Alan used his fingers to trace the sides of Cody's foot, which was making him blather even more. Finally, after what felt like three hours for Cody, the tickling stopped. Alan stood up and moved Cody's bed a bit so that he could free his tortured foot. Almost instinctively, Cody curled himself up into a ball, his barefoot rubbing next to his socked one, as if one was comforting the other. His ordeal was over, and all he wanted to do was pass out into unconsciousness right then and there.

He then felt Alan grab his leg and begin to pull him out from under the bed. "C'mon boy, we ain't done yet." In any other circumstances, Cody would resist and fight, but here, exhausted from excessive tickle torture, he couldn't do a thing. Alan pulled the boy's full body out and splayed him facedown on the floor, but positioned Cody's feet on either side of the corner post of his bed. Alan then grabbed one of his belts and tied those feet together behind the post very tightly. Even though Cody had no strength to do anything, things were obviously about to get very real ...

Alan then helped Cody get to his knees, which was tough given his feet were bound behind the bed post. Once he was fully rigid though, Alan then took Cody's hands straight up over his head, like a prayer that turned into a backbend, and once his hands were past the wooden bar that kept both bedposts together, Alan used another belt he had to tie Cody's hands together. He then stood back to look at his masterpiece of bondage: there was Cody, kneeling, hands tied above and behind him, leaving his ribs and armpits perilously exposed.

What's worse, Alan then pulled over the chair from his desk and placed himself just inches away from Cody's bound body. Cody, still exhausted, thought that perhaps this was all just one big nightmare he was going through.

Alan really enjoyed seeing his prey all-helpless like this. "It's kind of cute, actually."

"What?"

"You all tied up and ticklish like this."

"Fine, just get it over with," started Cody, hoping some reverse-psychology would do the trick.

"Oh no, we're going to do something even better than that, Cody."

"Um ..."

Slowly, Alan's wiggling fingers descended towards Cody's ribs.

"Tell me Cody ... what's the password for your computer?"

"YOU'RE NOT GETTING MY PASSWORD!"

"Oh, but I think I am, Cody ..."

The first few fingers fell right onto Cody's left side, and then his right shortly after. Cody's face grimaced and turned, doing everything it could to not break out into a smile.

"Tickle tickle ..." Alan was saying this in the most teasingly evil voice Cody could imagine, and it was weirdly making him even more ticklish, enhancing the feeling of those fingernails poking and dragging across each and every rib, setting his nervous system on fire and driving nothing but tickles into his brain. Tickles was all he could think about and yet he was doing everything he could to stop them. The corners of his mouth drew up as if operated by strings and yet he couldn't stop. Bits of giggles emerged here and there, but this -- coupled with the way that Cody's eyes were so firmly closed -- it was obvious that his twisted face was holding back an ocean of laughter. This egged Alan on even more, as he felt that this was a new challenge for him. He alternated his strokes; he wiggled his finger around in Cody's belly button, and then did something new: his fingers dived right into the center of Cody's armpits, wiggling and tickling the whole way.

Cody practically exploded in laughter. He couldn't stop. The pits tickled like all fuckout. These were deep, wildly unhinged laughs. While tickling obviously causes involuntary laughter, these new pit tickles were causing said laughter to be wildly unhinged, as is if Alan was conjuring up some sort of great tickle spirit and Cody was the unwilling vessel. Cody couldn't even think straight -- his brain was just nothing but tickles.

"Tickle tickle, Cody. Tickle tickle!" Alan loved the taunting almost as much as the tickling itself. "What's the password?" he'd ask on occasion, and just as Cody began forming the words "fuck you", his pits would be tickle-assaulted again, as Alan was single-minded in getting an answer from his newfound victim.

Finally, the tickling stopped. Cody's body sagged, slight aftershocks of laughter emerging every few seconds. Alan leaned back in his chair, content.

"OK, Cody, let's try this again. I am going to ask you for your password for your computer. You will tell me your password. Failure to tell me your password will result in a non-stop 20 minute tickle session. Even if you tell me your password during it, I won't stop. If you cannot say the password after that's over, then I'll give you yet another 20-minute tickle session. I'll keep doing this for as long as it takes to get your password. So, let me ask you one more time: what's your computer password?"

"Please," panted Cody, "Please don't make me say it ..."

"Alright," started Alan, fingers primed for tickling, here we go again ...

"NO! I'LL SAY IT! PLEASE DON'T TICKLE ME!"

"What is it, Cody?"

"It's ... it's ... "

"Yes?"

"alantoes."

"... what?"

"The password is 'alantoes'."

Alan's eyebrow cocked, and looked real hard at his roommate, searching his face for answers. Silently, Alan stood up and went over to Cody's computer, sitting down and typing in the password. Windows made it's little "welcome sound", and Cody, who couldn't see what Alan was looking out due to his position, still knew he was screwed. Alan began narrating his thought process out loud:

"You see Cody, I don't know about you. I see you getting drunk at parties and things but I never see you ask a girl out or even go on a date -- and we've been living together for months. I don't see you flirting with guys, though, either, so -- oh yes, right click -- so I've just always been curious as to what porn *do* you look at. I mean, if we're really going to ..."

Alan was silent. All Cody could here was Alan clicking his mouse over and over and over again. A few minutes passed, but they felt like an eternity to Cody.

Alan then stood up and went over the chair that was placed right in front of the immobile Cody, sitting down and tapping his fingers on his knees.

"So ... you got a foot fetish do you?"

"Well, it's not that simple, you see ..."

"Oh no, I disagree Cody, I think it is that simple. Why else would there be close to a dozen photos of me barefoot in there? Some were even obviously taken while I was sleeping, one foot sticking out barely over the covers. Come to think of it, I think perhaps that is the reason that I sometimes am missing socks from my laundry. Maybe the machine isn't eating them -- maybe you are."

"Alan, please, let me exp--"

"Oh no, that's fine, Cody, I think I can figured it out. Your password is 'alantoes' after all. You think my feet are goddamn sexy, don't you?"

"I ... I don't want to ..."

"Oh no, I think it's hilarious, Cody. Here, have a sample ..."

With that, sitting in the chair, Alan raised up his socked feet and placed them square on Cody's face, the two feet practically enveloping him like a mask. "Sniff," Alan ordered. Cody didn't need any direction. Hell, he could practically smell them the second those socked feet were an inch from his face. In a few short moments those, those feet became Cody's entire world, and feeling them wiggle and move underneath a layer of cotton-sock fabric pressed to his face -- it was bliss.

"This turn you on, Cody?"

Cody was unsure of what to answer in this case. "Well, I mean, it's a fetish, but ..."

"Well I'm going to have to try harder, won't I?"

With that, Alan quickly slipped of his ankle socks and placed the base of his toes right underneath Cody's nose. "Sniff again."

"No ..."

"Oh, you'll be kicking yourself later if you don't do this now, Cody. C'mon ... give in ... give in to the power of my feet ..."

Cody struggled, trying not to show how much this was turning him on, but to feel that most foot flesh right against his upper lip, those feet radiating warmth as those toes wiggled -- it was too much. A hardon began to form and began to press through his pajama pants.

"Well, well, well, looks like we have someone who wants to play."

Cody was beet-red with embarrassment, but there was nothing he could do: Alan, tormentor supreme, had found a secret way into Cody's horny fantasies, and there was not much he could do about it. All the while, Alan's meaty toes continued to wiggle on Cody's face, and his hardon twitched slightly underneath those pajama pants.

"Well Cody, it looks like you're obviously enjoying this. You've no doubt enjoyed looking at and playing with and taking pictures of my feet without my knowledge, so I think it's time I return the favor, don't you? Let's see just how embarrassed and horny you can get ..."

With that, Alan took his feet off of Cody's face and grabbed the elastic edge of both Cody's pajama pants and the boxers underneath. In one swift move, he brought them right down to Cody's knees, exposing Cody's rock-hard, extremely red, precum-dripping circumcised cock, leaving it out in the open air of the duo's dorm room. Alan was living up to his promise: Cody had never felt more embarrassed in his life. Alan placed one of his feet right underneath Cody's balls, so he could feel this toes wiggle down there, and then placed the other foot right in front of his mouth, saying simply "Suck."

Cody had never been more of a slave to his own desires than right then and there. He slowly took Alan's toes into his mouth, and slathered his moist tongue around them, sucking on each one with relish, savoring every molecule of taste and every wiggle Alan could muster. All while this was happening, Alan was wiggling his toes gently underneath Cody's balls, and the two sensations together made for a delirious, insanely horny combination. In between toe-sucks, however, Cody caught a glance of Alan leaning back in his chair, eyes closed, stroking his cock through his shorts. It was a brief glance, but whatever Cody was doing to Alan's toes, it was obviously something very, very enjoyable ...

Then, in one swift motion, Alan pressed his foot a bit further into Cody's mouth, allowing another toe to slowly sneak in to the warm, moist maw, and that was enough to send the boy off: Cody's cock shot off a gigantic cum rocket, landing almost entirely on Alan's hairy shin, which was then followed by another shot, and then a lesser one, and then a lesser one. Alan removed his foot from the boy's mouth and watched as Cody's body slowly came down from its horny high. Alan reached over and grabbed a new Swiffer cloth from Cody's desk to clean his shin with. He then got off the chair and kneeled down so that he was eye-level with Cody.

"Did you enjoy that?"

Cody was almost too weak to answer, but mustered out a faint "Yes."

"Good. Now, I have an unbelievably embarrassing story to tell about you."

"OK." Cody literally couldn't think of anything else to say.

Alan was shifting some thoughts around in his mind, and, surprising even himself, said, "Would you like to suck on my toes once a week?"

Cody felt it was a trap, but had to be honest: "Yes."

"OK. I will let you go, and you can suck on my tasty Alantoes for an entire hour every week .. as long as you submit to an hour of bound tickle torture."

"Oh god, no!"

"No, you say? You would turn down the thought of my manly, tasty, tender toes dancing around your tongue just because you can't stand a little bit of tickling?"

"I ... I ..."

"This is a one-time offer, Cody ..."

"Fine! I'll do it!"

"Good boy. Now rest up." Alan very unceremoniously undid the belts that were binding the boy to his bed, and as soon as they were gone, Cody simply fell to the carpeted dorm room floor and was asleep in seconds.

In the days that followed, he began running over the experience again and again in his head, and since the two carried on as if nothing happened, wondered if Alan was really going to live up to his end of the bargain ...

... then again, it wasn't until a few days later that Cody accidentally stumbled upon the porn that Alan was jerking off to every other night. Cody's eyes went wide when he discovered the sheer number of tickle vids that Alan had stored on his laptop ...

THE GALLERY

(originally appeared in *Getting Off on the Wrong Foot*)

+ + +

As mentioned in the intro of this anthology, while I do enjoy writing these stories and I have been told by more than one person that they're not terrible, I have some very clear influences here, and one of them, without a doubt, is Eddie, who used to be active on Jack's Male Tickling Rack, which is housed in some web archives and is worth scrolling through every single inch of. It was an incredible site, and an early beacon for tickle enthusiasts the world over, and boy howdy the stories it housed. Devious, brilliant, evil, sexy, well-written, and undeniably hot stories of every style and subject relating to M/M tickling. Yet there was one author who simply went by the name of Eddie who just outshone everyone. Aside from the fact that his prose was intensely well-detailed and his commitment to story and character absolute, he just had a knack for conceiving some of the horniest, most devious, most delightful scenarios in all of erotic history. They were devious but never grotesque, nor did they cross any "lines" as it were: they were just downright evil in conception and execution. "The Fiend" is a stone cold classic, but "The Wall" is the most direct influence out here to this very story right here, taking foot fetish deviousness up to the next level ...

Jonathan returned from the restroom, drying his hands on his jeans as he walked, and looked back at the computer where his friend Ryan was sitting. Ryan, a thin guy with penchant for plaid short-sleeve button-down shirts to go with his thin pencil frame, wasn't turning around to acknowledge his approach, though. As the rugged twenty-something Jonathan pulled forward, he saw an image on the screen. A private image. A horribly, horribly private image buried deep in his hard drive that Ryan had discovered. As Jonathan drew closer, his sense of embarrassment and personal horror grew and grew.

There, on the screen, wasn't just a picture of Ryan's bare soles, no. It was far worse: it was a collage. A series of digital photos taken of Ryan's feet in various state of dress: sock-footed, donning flip-flops, his toes peaking out from the covers of Jonathan's futon during one of the drunken nights he must've passed out at Jonathan's place -- a whole litany of foot fetish glory. The collage, however, didn't end with multiple images of Ryan's feet digitally duplicated and splayed out in a quasi-creative fashion, no. In the middle of this art, there were big printed letters saying "You like these feet, don't you? Go ahead and tickle them ...", as if taunting the person who made it. This was 100% genuine jackoff material, and, assuredly, something Ryan wasn't supposed to see.

Once Jonathan was standing next to the computer -- where the friends had been watching stupid YouTube videos earlier -- Ryan turned around, his look of horror complementing Jonathan's blushing face quite well. While Jonathan wanted to call out his friend out for digging through his private picture folders on his computer, he kind of knew that Ryan had the upper hand no matter what.

"What the fuck is this, man?!" shouted Ryan, angry and mortified all at once.

"Dude," started Jonathan, "let me explain ..."

Ryan stood up. "What's there to explain man? I know you've had a male foot fetish -- that's fine, I don't care about that -- but you've been taking pictures of my feet when I wasn't looking? When I was sleeping here? And you've been jacking off to them? Holy shit dude, this is getting into, like, tuber-creepy territory ..."

"Ryan, I ..."

"Did you do anything to my feet while I was sleeping?"

"No!" exclaimed Jonathan, defiant.

"Did you want to?"

A painful pause filled the air. Jonathan stuttered a bit: "I ... I mean, I'd want to, but there are certain lines between friends that shouldn't ..."

"Jesus Christ, man!" Ryan was angry now, still walking around with his faux-leather almost-work-friendly sports shoes on. "I mean ... god. This is just too weird. I'm too freaked out man, I ... I just can't be around you right now."

"Ryan, don't go ..."

"Did you send those pictures around to anyone?"

"No!" exclaimed Jonathan, again. Jonathan really meant it, too, as he would never do something as tuber-creepy as sharing those photos online with others. They were for his own personal use, and that's it -- not like it justified his actions, of course.

"Why do I get the sense that you're lying?" Ryan was really twisting the knife in at this point.

"Ryan, I'm not lying. I never shared those pictures with anyone?"

"Well I feel humiliated ... and, and kind of terrified."

"Ryan, I understand that. I really do. If you'd just let me ..."

"And your ultimate goal is to tickle them? Tickling my feet would get you horny and get you off? Is that right?"

Jonathan stuttered again, "It's ... you just got to give me a second to ..."

Ryan grabbed his gray hoodie and began heading from the door of his friend's apartment. "You know what? I can't stand this. You went too far, man. Seriously, this is ... sick. I'm telling everyone we know. Yeah. Yeah, that'll show ya!" Ryan was delirious with anger at this point. "Now let me get out of here."

Ryan unlocked the apartment door and left without saying anything else. Jonathan tried to run after him and plead for his return ... but it was pointless. If Ryan really did do what he was going to say, then yeah, he'd be ruined. The two friends went to the same high school. They work at the same place now that they both have Bachelor's degrees. There is, in short, a lot of fallout that could happen from this, and Jonathan, in a word, would be screwed.

The next 30 minutes had Jonathan pacing around his apartment frantically, his hand trembling with nervous tension. All he did was go use the restroom as he usually does. What made Ryan decide to start snooping around on his computer, much less find a folder that far buried in his hard drive? Nothing was making any sense right now. Jonathan wondered if he should call Ryan or text him or ... no. He was pissed off and there was nothing that was going to change his mind, and if there's anything that Jonathan knew, it was that it took a *lot* to piss off Ryan.

Jonathan really didn't want to do it. He didn't want to open up that can of worms, but, really, in a case like this, he had no choice. He picked up his cell phone, and called a number he's called many times before, but this time with a sense of urgency he's never had. A voice on the other end picked up, and Jonathan began to speak: "Hey ... I got a crisis situation here. I ... yep. Ryan, the one I've told you about. I know it'd be a last-minute addition to ... I know. It ... oh trust me, he'll win it. Easy. I'd be more than happy to bet on that but right now I just need some containment. I ... OK, yes, let me give you his address ..."

+ + +

Ryan was sitting on his bed, barefoot. Although his TV was on (turned to one of those "World's Scariest Police Chases" shows, with the volume way down), Ryan wasn't paying attention to it. He was focusing on his feet, and trying to figure out what about them made them appear "sexy" to his now-former friend. He didn't get it: his size 11s were thin, his toes were long, his arches were pretty well curved, and his skin was pasty-white (except on the base of the toes and the heel, as those were a shade red due to constant contact with his shoes/the ground) -- how is that sexually appealing? Here he was, 26 years old, living with his parents still, albeit with a hot girlfriend and now dealing with the fact that his best friend had been taking pictures of his exposed feet for what may very well have been years on end. It was a strange conundrum, and he didn't really want to think about it anymore. He still felt very violated by what he saw on Jonathan's computer. He'd known for years about Jonathan's foot fetish, but he just never thought his own toes would factor into the equation. This still made Ryan feel angry and exposed, and he was about to expose his friend in return. He put his dark gray socks back on and headed for his computer to start posting some stuff on the interwebs when he couldn't help but notice a flashing blue light on the evening street below. Ryan stuck his head out the window and saw a police car pulling up ... to the front of his house.

After a few minutes of those red and blue lights jutting in to his room, sockwalked down to the front door to see what it was all about. His mother stood at the open door speaking to two police officers.

"What's going on, mom?"

She turned to her son with a look of worry on her face. The two officers' faces were practically expressionless.

"Oh honey, it looks like someone may have gone missing and the last place they were seen was at work. The officers here are wondering if you wouldn't mind coming down to the station to view some footage and see if you can't help find this per-- I'm sorry, am I speaking out of turn, officers?"

"No ma'am. You're doing a fine job," said the taller, slightly older one.

"Listen," started Ryan, "I don't really think that ..."

"It'll just be for an hour or so sir. Put some shoes on please and come with us."

Ryan was a bit flabbergasted by the suddenness of this whole thing, and was about to protest, but saw the look on his mom's face -- that look that implied he might be the key to this whole thing -- and couldn't say no. "I'll be right back," he told the officers, grabbing those shoes once more.

The officers were using a standard police car, with a fenced partition between the front and the back seats of the car. When Ryan got in the back with those same work shoes slipped on, the other officer -- shorter, stockier, ethnic but in a way that Ryan couldn't immediately identify -- got in the back with him. Ryan thought this was unusual for sure but didn't say anything of it. The car slowly drove away into the nighttime streets.

The shorter officer sitting next to Ryan began to speak to him while appearing to reach for something under the passenger seat in front of him.

"We thank you for your cooperation, sir. We'll have you home in a few hours."

"I thought you said one hour."

"There's been a change of plans."

"But, we just barely ..."

And in a lightning-fast motion, the officer took a chloroformed rag and placed it right over Ryan's mouth. Before Ryan's brain even comprehended what was going on, it was too late: this too-strong sensation took over his brain, his eyelids seemed to get extremely heavy all of a sudden, and just like that, he plunged into a deep unconscious sleep. All was black.

+ + +

Ryan awoke, groggy. He felt like he was awaking from a sleep so deep that everything felt very dreamlike, surreal, slow motion-y. A strange blue hue of light was penetrating his vision, and everything was all fuzzy. He tried rubbing his eyes ... but couldn't. His arms were stretched out to either side of him, but they were strapped down. Not very hard, mind you, but still within some of those big leather straps that he's seen in insane asylums in films, making sure no harm came to him no matter how hard he struggled. Ryan was still laying down, comfortably, but his arms just wouldn't go. He cussed out loud, but it was to no effect. He stared up and that glowing hue above him, and discovered that, in fact, there were a series of TV monitors positioned directly above him. Each monitor seemed to be tapped into some sort of CCTV, and he was looking at a ... gallery, of some sort. Everything was in black and white, but it looked like a series of hallways painted red. One monitor seemed to be zoomed in on something unusually specific: a piece of smooshed gum. Well, wait, maybe it was ... yeah, smooshed gum on the sole of a shoe. There was a matching shoe right next to it. Well that's weird. Ryan tried propping himself up to get a better view, but ... his legs were also bound. Ryan looked down at this feet and couldn't even see them. Although he was tied down in some sort of room where he couldn't move his arms, his feet seemed to be not just in a set of stocks: they were stuck inside a gigantic black wall. Ryan couldn't see anything outside of the glow of the overhead monitors, but his feet were inside a wall, in another room! It was weird: his feet were in one room and his body was in another. He tried finding something he could anchor his left foot on so that he could maybe get some leverage ... and then his mouth dropped in horror.

He twitched his left foot. The gum-stained foot on the monitor above him moved. He turned his right foot to the side as much as he could, and the right shoe on the monitor did the same. Holy shit: a camera was pointed directly at his feet, which were in another room altogether. He moved his feet up and down as much as he could and looked at the gallery monitor, and ... there he was. His feet were sticking out of a wall at about chest-level, and they were apparently a part of some ... gallery? He looked closely at the monitors and saw that, in fact, there were several other pairs of feet sticking out of the wall, all belonging to guys that were probably just as helpless as he was. Ryan had a bit of a panic moment: this wasn't right. This was ... insane. HE WAS A PIECE OF ART ON DISPLAY AT A GODDAMN FETISH GALLERY. Ryan spent the next 10 minutes screaming at the top of his lungs and struggling as much as he could, but all that came of his efforts was sweat percolating underneath his plaid button-down that he couldn't wipe away. Dread started creeping into his brain, and he had no idea what to expect next.

After a few minutes passed, Ryan heard faint music. A low, sexy pulse of some electronica music, coming from the hallway where his feet were on display. He looked up at the gallery camera, and suddenly saw a large group of men enter, most wearing formal clothes, all of them wearing masks like they were at a masquerade. A waiter in a white tuxedo (and no shoes, Ryan noticed), walked around with champagne, and the gentlemen milled about the large gallery space, joking and talking amongst themselves. Ryan tried screaming for help, hoping that his words could somehow escape through his pantlegs and out to the room at large, but this proved futile -- he couldn't be heard over the throbbing dance music playing for these well-to-dos. Ryan eyed the monitor closely, and couldn't make a single woman at all -- just all guys. Ryan was trying desperately to wrap his head around what was going on.

Suddenly, a hand had placed itself around his foot, grabbing at the sole of his shoe, the hand forcibly moving his foot back and forth for no discernible reason, perhaps to examine it.

"Hey pervert! Let the fuck go!" Ryan shouted, but nothing came of it. He tried to determine who was holding onto his foot, but those masks were making it close to impossible for Ryan to determine who was manhandling his left clodhopper. Suddenly another hand began tracing the rim of Ryan's right shoe sole, going around and around at a deliberately slow pace, as if savoring, perhaps guessing was underneath. That hand then began tapping the sole with his fingers, playfully, as if trying to tickle Ryan's foot through his shoe. Ryan fidgeted as much as he could, trying to retract his foot through the wall hole, but to no avail. Looking at the monitor, it seemed that the people standing around his feet in the gallery were quite enjoying the boy's reactions. Before more people could gather, some sort of whistle went off and all the masked men met down at one end of the gallery, as the mingling time was over -- they were now going to be traveling in a group. Ryan didn't like the look of this at all.

He saw the men gather around one pair of feet sticking out from the gallery, and they were gathered so tight that Ryan couldn't make out exactly what was happening on the monitors. Minutes were passing and all he could see was the occasional reaction from the group -- usually something that pleased them. They stuck by that pair of feet for about 20 minutes or so, and each minute they were there Ryan's brain raced around with numerous nightmare scenarios, many way more gruesome, graphic, and bloody than they should be. Suddenly, the men moved on to the next pair of feet in the gallery. Just barely, Ryan could see that the pair of feet they were previously around were now bare and exposed -- a pair of sneakers were strewn about on the ground, and the socks were nowhere to be found (although maybe the guy went sockless? They were skater shoes, so that would make some sense ...). The guys seemed to be equally taken with their new set of feet sticking out of the wall, and judging from the monitors, there was one other guy between where Ryan was now and where the group was. He watched the men closely, trying to see if could figure out anything that they were doing. Suddenly one shoe came flying up from the huddled group of masked men, landing behind them -- apparently, they were feeling a bit whimsical now ... or maybe just somewhat drunk. Ryan wasn't sure if this scared him or not.

The group moved from to the next set after about 10 minutes of playing with the last pair, and Ryan's whole back tensed up -- they were one away from him. Ryan still couldn't make out exactly what was happening, but given how much closer they were to him, Ryan could make out occasional glimpses of that poor soul's soles on the monitor.

Depending on where the masked men moved, he could see the feet being touched and handled ... and the toes distorting in a spectacular fashion, as if they were trying to get away from something or ... oh dear god ...

... tickled.

Ryan had never been so scared. He struggled violently once more, but, once again, was greeted with nothing more than his body releasing more hot, sticky sweat. Ryan was the kind of guy who rarely took off his socks, much less his shoes -- a scroll through his pictures on Facebook never once shows his feet bare or exposed in any way (the few times he wore sandals, he made sure no camera was anywhere in sight). As such, his soles were very soft, pale pink, and, very, very tender. Tickling positively drove him mental, and he's attacked those who've tickled him before. Right here, right now, however, he didn't have that kind of defense. In fact, right now, he was completely helpless.

The men seemed to be finished with the latest pair of tender goslings, and soon formed a circle around Ryan's feet, which were twitching with nervous anticipation. Ryan's back somehow tensed up even more, tighter than a thousand wound coils. He eyed the monitor very closely, and at first, the masked men were just ... standing around his feet. They seemed to just be watching his shoe-covered feet nervously twitch and move like frightened animals in a corner. Every time Ryan got self-conscious about it, his nervousness just made it worse, his sneakered feet fidgeting -- perhaps even groveling -- before the mysterious men. Then, with no warning, a hand began caressing the instep of his shoe. Ryan tried to hit it away with his other foot, but it's at that moment that someone else's hand grabbed his other foot, rendering it immobile. The fondling of his left sneakered instep continued on for some time -- whoever was doing this was quite enjoying it. Then, the man's index finger went underneath the tongue of his shoe, his other hand grabbed the heel, and in one quick motion, that shoe came right off. Ryan couldn't see what happened on the monitor, as the men's faces were now out of frame, but it was obvious that someone was sniffing the collected foot sweat inside his shoe. Before Ryan even knew what was happening, the other shoe came off, and now Ryan's sweaty feet were down to those dark gray socks. The moisture from his socks suddenly became apparent once the cool air of the room hit his helpless dogs, and, strangely, that made Ryan feel even more vulnerable.

His toes curled, as if in fear, and there was some minor deal of movement around the men. One hand descended onto his right foot, cradling it, while another set of hands grabbed his left foot and began kneading his soles, attempting to massage it. His right socked sole was now just being fondled, stroked, caressed, while the kneading continued on his left. Ryan couldn't do much of anything, and found the sensation ... weird. These guys were ... trying to please his feet? Against his will? Ryan's neurons were firing but all that came out were dull sparks: he couldn't figure out what the fuck was going on.

Suddenly, the man who was caressing his foot got down to his knees, so he was eye-level with Ryan's socked toes. Ryan couldn't make out much, but all he could tell was that the man was younger, handsome even. The man, still wearing his mask, pressed his nose right into the base of Ryan's big toe and inhaled. Ryan could feel the air rushing in between his big and first toe, and it was odd, to say the least. From what he could gather from the video feed, the young man really seemed to enjoy it, and proceeded to do it again. Another man bent down next to Ryan's other socked foot and after lightly caressing the sensitive sides of his left clodhopper, leaned up a bit and proceeded to suck on Ryan's big toe through the sock. Ryan's foot immediately tried to fidget away, but the guy's hands firmly held the foot in place. The sucking was slow, deliberate, and very, very sensual. Suddenly, his moist left sock was starting to get damp, and he had no idea what to think. Ryan may have even felt a tingle inside himself -- one of *those* tingles -- but immediately ignored it.

As the intensity of the toe sucking increased, fingers reached out to the rim of his left gray sock and began slowly snaking it off the boy's foot. Ryan desperately fought this as much as he could but it was pointless: the sock was off in seconds. His toes instinctively flexed a bit, adjusting to their new freedom, and just like that, his much-sniffed right sock also came off. His bare feet were sticking out the other end of a wall, and whatever the men on the other side were seeing, it was quite obvious that they liked it.

Being barefoot, his left toes especially moist from the soaked-through saliva of his mysterious foot friend, Ryan had never felt so naked in his life. This includes the times he was actually naked in the locker rooms at high school, yet for some reason to have his shoes and socks forcibly removed at the whim of what seemed like a dozen professional foot fetishizers ... it was almost too much for him. While he wished he could've retracted his feet into the wall before, he now simply wished he could pass out and have the whole thing over with.

That, however, was not the case. The two men who were already kneeling in front of his feet were then joined by two other men who knelt down. They seemed to be evenly-divided: two men to a foot. Ryan's toes once again curled in terror, and even Ryan's own face grimaced a bit in anticipation. Then, after each silent second creeped by as if it was an hour in length, the licking began.

Tongues planted themselves at various parts of his feet and proceeded to slither up his soles, across his too-sensitive tops, around his heel, and oh, especially at the toes. Whoever was working the toes of each foot were clearly enjoying themselves, their moist, horny tongues savoring each and every flavor, texture, and detail. Those tongues polished the toenails, lapped at the toepads, and slithered in-between each toe like a hungry snake. The tongues sneaking between each toe began driving Ryan bonkers: they were so wet they seemed to just glide, tickling him intensely. Ryan didn't want to be tickled, and fought it as much as he could, his face distorting and his arms moving at sharp angles, despite being tightly bound. Ryan closed his eyes and clenched his lip as the warm tongues played with his index toe, his too-helpless pinkie toe, and the base of his big toe, but as their speed increased, so did the moist tickles, the little taste bumps on each tongue scraping at the sensitive spaces in-between each digit.

The worshiper on his left foot then did something utterly devious: his tongue darted in and out of the spaces between Ryan's middle toes over and over again, quickly, quickly, tickling more and more each time. Suddenly, Ryan couldn't fight it anymore: the laughter burst out of him, and he resembled a Muppet gone wild. His body seizured to each side, he leaned forward as quickly as he could before slamming back down again, his body doing everything it could to combat the laughter issuing forth from his mouth, but it was all a wasted effort. The other tongues circled his heels and slowly traced his arches, but tongues between his toes were tickling way too much, saliva dripping down the sides of his feet like a melted ice cream cone. Ryan's eyes were firmly shut, as if holding back tears. His head titled back, and his high-pitched cackles came jutting out. Mixed in with them were please of "Stop!" "Don't!" and the ever-classic "It tickles!!" Of course, with a wall between him and his tormentors, Ryan's pleas fell on deaf ears. If those mysterious men even could hear the boy, they'd probably just be turned on by what they heard: honest-to-goodness helpless laughter. Not a firm enjoyable chuckle, or high-pitched whine, no; genuine laughter. Laughter that had to be forcibly removed from its subject, which sounded like it'd do anything for its torment to stop. It was laughter that couldn't enjoy itself; it was laughter that was forced into being laughter.

A half-hour passed.

The slurping stopped, as if all at once. Ryan's feet were simply coated in saliva, his toes exhausted from their wiggling. Ryan's own chest began heaving heavily, his voice scratchy and hoarse, his body spewing out the occasional laughter aftershock completely against his will. With sweat forming on his brow that he positively couldn't wipe away even if he wanted to, all Ryan wanted to do was pass out. He was so weak, he couldn't even fight back when he felt the guys doing something to his toes, as if wrapping something around each one. He knew it was pointless to fight at this time -- it's like his own feet were no longer his.

Then, the cinch came. His feet were now completely flexed back. Ryan looked at the monitor: on the wall in the gallery, there were eight hooks located right above where Ryan's feet were sticking out of the wall. Every toe was tied back to a hook, all seemingly using the same piece of rope, which explains why when they cinched it tight, all his toes moved back at once. The cruel masked men, however, left his pinkie toe on each side completely free to move, giving him the horrible illusion of movement. Ryan, fearful, watched the monitor ahead, doing his best to curl his toes even a half-inch -- and they couldn't even do that. He was completely immobile, save his pinkie toes, which flexed and moved just a little bit, all cute and helpless. He then saw that two of the masked men had grabbed feathers and were nearing closer and closer to his immobile feet. Ryan screamed once more, and then ... he felt it.

The tiny scrape of the tip of a feather against the ball of his left foot. It ... almost didn't tickle. It was so slight, indiscernible. He felt a light wisp on his left foot, but, again, it was fleeting. Slowly but surely, the feather strokes became more apparent, just calmly tracing the balls of his feet on a horizontal line. Wisp. Wisp. Wiiiiiiiiiiisp. It was excruciating. In fact, this was worse than tickling: it was "almost tickling," and it was putting Ryan's exhausted mind in a state of perpetual tension, preparing itself for the full-blown tickles that weren't coming. This went on for five excruciating minutes, and Ryan's feet began to tingle with anticipation. "Just tickle me already!!" he kept thinking, but all he was greeted with was Wisp. Wiiiisp. Wisp. Another three minutes passed, and Ryan was about to lose it.

Then, the feathers stopped. Out of nowhere, a single fingernail glided up the arches of his left foot, and Ryan jolted. It was so unexpected, so -- AHHHH! It happened on his right foot. Then another on his right foot. And then Ryan realized his fears had come true: the tickling had begun.

A bevy of fingers descended on his bound soles, and they were enjoying their soft and fleshy playthings. Some fingers scraped, some lightly poked, some traced circles, some scratched the sides of his feet, some wiggled in front of his toes, and all of them fucking tickled. His bare size 11s were on fire with electricity, processing through a million different ticklish sensations at once. His nerve endings were practically screaming at him, but all he could do was just unleash more torrents of laughter. Tickly tickles. Ticklish tickles. Tickle tickle tickles -- this was all his brain seemed to be capable of thinking. The more he laughed, the worse he got. Every time his lungs drew in to catch his breath, a finger went horizontal across his toepads and a laugh jumped into his lungs. Ryan's brain was buckling under the pressure. The person on his right foot apparently was trying to spell out letters on his soles, his fingernail no doubt leaving a trail of white as it drew across his pink soles, spelling out Q's and fancy S's with too many loops. Ryan pretty much went on cackle auto-pilot. His sanity slowly began to slip, and had he known this was going to continue on for 20 minutes more, his brain would've prepared itself more.

In Ryan's feathery fever dream, years must've passed. His brain had lost all sense of space and time -- he could be a medieval knight for all he knew. The only thoughts that were going through his brain consisted of only one or two syllables: Tickle. Feet. Toes. Tickle. Laugh. Lungs. Water. Ticklisssssssh. Tickley! Tickles. Tooooooooes. Feet. Scratchy. Laughy. In truth, the tickling had actually stopped for a few minutes, but Ryan's brain didn't even detect it until long after.

When his eyes readjusted to the monitors above him, he could see that the men had moved on to maybe three other pairs of feet since he last checked. Ryan couldn't make sense of many things right now, but all he could tell was that the other poor souls (and soles) locked in the gallery right now did not have to suffer as long as his did. While all the men were huddled around their latest foot toy, one of the masked men broke from the pack and seemed to approach Ryan's feet. A hand reached down and briefly tickled Ryan's left heel. Instinctively, it flinched. A feather then came out and proceeded to tickle only that left pinkie toe -- it tried its damndest to escape but that toe was too limited in its movements to do anything. It just danced with the feather, accepted its tickles, and only pretended to escape. For some reason, having his pinkie toes free to move about despite their limited capacity to do so was probably the most frustrating part of the whole thing. The masked man knelt down next to his bound feet, and, from what Ryan could tell through his fuzzy eyesight (hard to regain vision after you've teared up from laughing so much), that man was the same one who so passionately sucked his big toe through his sock earlier. The man leaned in, sniffed that left foot, and then planted a simple kiss on Ryan's left sole, then the right. The masked man reached into his pocket and pulled out what appeared to be a black sharpie marker, and proceeded to press it into Ryan's right sole, and really began to write something. The letters tickled, and Ryan's last reserve of laughter just jumped out of him. This was weak laughter now: high-pitched and craggily. Laughter of the truly defeated. The slightly moist marker swooped in and out, made all sorts of shapes, and simply made Ryan go bonkers just one more time. FUCK Ryan hated whoever was doing this to him right now. When the marker seemed to reach the bottom of his left foot, the ticklish writing stopped. The young masked man got up and walked back to where the rest of the group was torturing some other helpless young man. Ryan, about to pass out, still managed to look up at his bound boyfeet on the monitor and make out what was written:

"I hope you learned your lesson, Ryan. Don't make us come back for you ... unless you want to join us ..." There was a smiley face at the end of that sentence, as well as the image of a crudely-drawn feather across the bottom of Ryan's heel. Ryan tried to make sense of it, but his brain couldn't fight his physical exhaustion much longer. At long last, Ryan -- with his feet in another room and his toes tied back, moist marker ink still drying on his soles -- passed out.

+ + +

Ryan's eyelids fought very hard to remain closed, but Ryan could sense himself gradually waking up. All his body was telling him right now was how much it hurt, especially his feet. Ryan looked around: he was still wearing the same plaid shirt as before and the same pants, but he was very much barefoot. He looked around: he was in his own room again, but not underneath the covers, actually on top of them. Suddenly, Ryan shot up: he instantly remembered everything that happened to him immediately before: his feet in a wall, his socked toes being sucked on, a feather teasing his pinkie toes with absolute relish, him completely losing his mind. Ryan instinctively grabbed the soles of his feet with his hands, as if to protect them. Then he calmed down a bit -- was that all a dream? Did ... did that all really happen? After all, his toes still hurt a lot ...

Ryan looked around his room, just to make sure everything was OK, and then noticed that his computer monitor had a note taped to it. He got off of the bed, his bare feet making contact with his too-familiar carpet at long last, comforting him, and he leaned forward, eying what was taped there. It seemed to be a card of some sort, and all it said on the front was "You are invited ..."

The boy then opened up the card, and couldn't believe what he saw inside ...

THE LETTER
(originally appeared in *Getting Off on the Wrong Foot*)

+ + +

There's loving your fetish, and there's loving your fetish when you're absolutely stoned out of your mind. I'm not an everyday pot user (I gots ta work, kiddos), but the times when I do, I really go for it, getting so high you become stupid, wherein your horniness absolutely takes over and destroys any remnant of rational thought you may have. The orgasms that can be reached are nothing short of transcendent, but I'll be first to admit I've done some stupid things while intoxicated, as we all do: sending out the occasional TMI text message, writing up the too-revealing email that was never meant to be sent, etc. Chuck Klosterman had a great line about this: what aggravated him about writing drunk emails to girls he shouldn't be contacting in the first place wasn't the fact that what he had written was false or untrue; in fact, to the contrary, what he had written hit way too close to home, revealing darker truths he never wanted to. I have a good portion of insanely horny, wildly illogical ramblings stored in email draft folders and various Word docs that will never see the light of day -- the "recipients" that are intended assuredly never, ever, ever need to see them. However, what if one slipped out? What would happen? How utterly, desperately humiliating would it be? When exploring other galaxies with my brain one night, I came up with this idea that -- at the time -- seemed hotter than all get out: to actually be the sandals of your most sought-after foot fetish obsession. To be pressed against his warm feet every day, to feel those toes wiggling around on top of you -- nothing short of foot fetish heaven, am I right? Thus, there seemed no better time to write a quickie such as this, going into all sort of detail about such delirious (and devilishly delicious) idea ...

His cock was throbbing through his jeans, delirious with horny thoughts. After all, Kevin had already had several beers that night -- all while attending a light social occasion with some friends earlier in the evening, although even coming home he didn't feel like he sobered up in the least -- but when he got through his front door, buzzed like a honeybee, he just felt his horny thoughts take over. They dominated every neural pathway and thought. Willingly and with a smile on his face, he submitted to his own naughty fetishes, and they completely dominated him in return.

Kevin sat at his computer, a new beer freshly popped open, checking his bookmarked list of gay foot and tickle blogs, his dick no doubt happy to see many of them were updated. Videos, pics, a cavalcade of candid barefoot and and sandaled photos: it was just nothing but a buffet spread of heavenly delights. Kevin began rubbing his hardening cock through his jeans as he saw video after video of young, sexy college boys slowly peeling off their socks, revealing the tender, tasty foot flesh underneath. This was a very common occurrence for the young man, and even after years of dutifully nurturing this fetish, letting it grow in size and scope, it didn't get any less boring.

Now that Kevin felt completely engulfed by his horny, glorious insobriety, precum no doubt already bleeding through the fabric of his boxers, Kevin defaulted next to a favorite activity of his: writing out e-mails that never get sent. He opened up another draft in his Gmail account, his cock pulsating in approval. He had over 60 e-mails saved in his drafts folder, all with friends names filled out in the "To:" field: dirty, naughty fetish confessions filling the e-mails' body. All these names of would-be recipients was a mish-mash of unobtainable eye-candy: current friends, co-workers, friends from school, etc. They were never sent because, well, Kevin never once wanted to actually ruin any one of these friendships, much less humiliate himself for real. It was a lot of fun, still, to fantasize about what he couldn't have, and by writing out actual e-mails -- naughty, humiliatingly candid missives that were written entirely in the heat of the moment -- he truly was indulging his love of self-inflicted (but tightly controlled) humiliation, of living on the edge, of almost being dangerous. It was a small act of horny submission to his own fetish, but few things truly got him harder.

Thus, a new page was open, and it didn't take long for Kevin to immediately think about his best friend Eric's feet. Those goddamn sexy hipster feet. Incredible for a twenty-something, truly in their prime. His perfectly shaped toes, his tender soles, those lickably curved arches, Eric's constant desire to be either sandal-clad or barefoot any given moment -- it gave the devious Kevin oodles of inspiration. One slightly unusual thought had been encircling his head as of late that concerned Eric's feet: just how jealous he was of that boy's sandals, getting to constantly hug and be pressed against those sweaty size 10s day in and day out. Thus, taking another swig of brew, Kevin got to writing yet another cum-fueled confession, touching his own denim-bound hardon in between paragraphs just to make sure he was still in the moment. His e-mail was as follows:

If I had a genie, Eric, you know what one of my first wishes would be?

I would love nothing more than to be your sandals for a day.

It's a strange concept -- I know how it sounds -- but there is absolutely nothing that I want more. You know I have a foot fetish, but I frequently wonder if you know how bad it is. I pop footboners on a daily basis, and the thing is: I fucking love it. I am conscious of how my fetish works, but I love feeding it, of finding that new batch of tender foot flesh that I want to submit to, praying I can trace the curve of those arches with the tip of my cock time and time again. Surely you know that you've been an unwilling participant in it. After all, you're barefoot around someone with a cripplingly powerful male foot fetish -- at some point it has to click for you. In many ways I'm glad we don't talk about it, but at the same token, part of me wishes you'd take advantage of me one of these days, of propping your exposed feet right in my lap, ordering me to massage them while making unrealistic demands that I would have to submit to, utterly hopeless to say no as you have simply handed me the Holy Grail of Horniness and who am I to say no? I value you as a friend, and as such I'd never do anything to violate that, but oh, if I could. Oh the things I'd do ...

... starting with actually becoming your sandals. I'd love to be the ones you have now: a solid slab of leather that has begrudgingly accepted the imprints of your bared feet, your toes in particular leaving ghost versions of themselves on there. To have those feet imprinted on me, to exist with their shape, their smell, even their taste tattooed on my person -- I truly can't think of anything I'd be prouder of wearing: existing to be under you, existing for the purpose of holding and comforting your sexy soles and toes and doing absolutely nothing else aside from wishing you wearing me when you weren't.

I can imagine how a typical day would go: you'd be sleeping, breathing quietly, and I'd be laying there on your cold hardwood floors, eagerly anticipating the moment when you'd wake up. I'd be eying the foot of your bed with great interest, hoping to catch a peak of your toes sticking out, your arches exposed, vulnerable, tender and delicious. You'd stir, you'd rise, you'd be groggy and run your fingers through your tussled brown hair. I'd wait for that moment when you swing your legs around until both feet are together, inches off the ground. I'd replay what happens next over and over again in slow motion: your toes landing first on the floor, the toes adjusting to the surface, the rest of your sole slowly pouring onto the hardwood, the heels landing like an exclamation point to a very sexy sentence. I love those moments when your toes unconsciously twitch, curling ever so slightly, adjusting to the coldness of the ground. You weren't expecting the floor to be this chill, even in the summer, were you? It's OK. You'd stand up and start to walk by me, myself getting excited that I might be lucky enough to come in contact with your foot flesh at so early an hour: but you never, ever do. I know you too well by now: you'll go to your computer to check your e-mail or go to your kitchen to grab breakfast or even take a shower, washing all that delicious footsweat away.

Yet, since I absorb your sweet, tasty footsweat on a daily basis, I assure that you're doing a great disservice to the world. That salty, tangy footsweat needs to be preserved, collected, sold in large quantities, used as icing on cakes. I practically take a bath in it every day, and it makes me want to explode with pleasure. I tingle the second it comes into contact with me, sending lightning bolts of pleasure through me. I wish I had a refrigerator filled with nothing but water bottles of your chilled footsweat. I'd soak in a bathtub full of it if not just so I could soak it up, imbuing me with the world's first permanent erection. Yet I digress ...

You'd clothe yourself, you'd fritter about as you do most mornings, applying to a schedule albeit haphazardly. There are days, I am loathe to admit, where you toss on some year-old ankle socks and the same black-and-white tennis shoes you have been wearing for ... hell, I lost track of when you got them. Still, in tandem, those pieces of manufactured footwear do a great job of capturing your enchanting footmusk, but I would argue I capture the essence of your bare feet far, far better: your sweat takes some time before it actually begins leaving an impression in me, showing time and dedication. There's a true permanence to how we work together, and I enjoy being a part of that history. You might walk by again, and I'll monitor every aspect of that step: your foot extending out an angle, the heel casually hitting the floor, that sole filling out, your toes angling the foot upward for takeoff again: it's quite the incredible sight. You may not see it, but your pinky toe never actually makes contact with the ground, and for some reason I find that unbelievably hot.

Then, of course, comes my favorite moment of all: you decide to go out for the day, and you pick me as your traveling companion. You wear your t-shirt and jeans, and casually walk yourself over to me, your whole godlike presence standing before me. I tremble at the thought of those feet being inches away from me, of ultimately completing me. Then, one foot lifts up barely off the ground and heads towards the toehold. My day is already made. That sexy big toe leads the way, every other raw toe following suit, slightly splayed, anticipating the fact that they'll be gripping onto me soon. Then, they make contact: the toehold, long soaked in your glorious footsweat, is gripped by your toes once again, and the rest of the the foot follows, aligning with its imprinted shadow in me once again. Made for each other, practically. The other foot follows, and we are one. Harmonious existence has been achieved.

As you lock up the door to your apartment and head outside into the hot summer air, my absolutely favorite part of the day begins: your feet begin warming me whole. I feel the warmth radiate all over: from heel to toes, those toes wiggling a bit with each boner-popping step. I go from the cold temperature of the morning hardwood to the same heat as your warmblooded feet. What an honor. What a privilege Those sweat-blackened footstains on me are only going to get that much darker, and I thrill at the thought of it.

You continue to go through the rest of the day wearing me, sweating all the more, wiggling your toes unconsciously while you think, each toepad tapping against me, teasing me, exciting me. I keep thinking that these toe-tappings are actually some sort of Morse code I have yet to decipher, but I haven't figured it out. I keep thinking, however, that if there are messages, they simply would be acknowledgments along the lines of "Yeah, these toes keep you up at night, don't they?" No one could ever argue with a statement like that.

After a whole day about the city, your warm feet strapped to my person, imprints deepening, embedding me with your smell, you walk home and a sprinkler with bad placement covers me with a light film of water, which makes each step you take a little more frictionless, your toes sliding across my surface, touching areas that to this point have yet to he honored by the touch of your sexy digits. Moments like this I cherish. I goddamn love having new parts of me exposed to the downright greatness that is your feet and toes.

You get home and we head to your apartment. Even with your shortened indoor steps, I still get to make that sexy slapping sound of myself hitting the bottom of your heel time and time again. I wonder if after all these years I've had the privilege of shaping the bottoms of your heels in even the slightest of ways. To be a part of the history of feet so intensely orgasmic as yours is nothing short of a true honor. Sandals don't get the privilege of picking their podiacal partners in crime, but I feel blessed to be smeared with your footstink on a daily basis.

You open the door to your apartment, and in the foyer, do the one thing I absolutely hate: you casually kick me off. And then there I am on the floor, your footwarmth gradually fading from me. It's the saddest part of the day, and unless there's the chance of a late-night food run of some sort, I know our interactions are done for the night.

Yet even as you sleep, I dream of serving your masterful feet again. I dream of your toenails accidentally scraping against my surface, of the fingerprint-like ridges of your toepads rubbing against me, deepening that imprint just a little more, of your footsweat baking into me for all eternity.

Until then I wait, your loyal servant in the wings. I exist solely for your soles. Tomorrow, thankfully, is another day when I can do what I do best, and get to touch your bare, bare feet ...

Kevin's beer was drained down to not even half-a-swig. He ran spell check on the e-mail once again, pleased with the eloquence he was able to accomplish even while drunk. He did feel like those sandals sometimes: existing simply to serve, worship, and honor those deliriously erotic feet. There were fewer fantasies as utterly delicious, devious, and boner-inducing than what he thought about Eric's soft, pink feet. Man, this was turning into one hell of a great night.

Suddenly, he heard a little e-mail beep in one of his other e-mail accounts. He Alt-Tab'd over to his e-mail program, only to see that a piece of spam had worked its way into another account. Not in need of pills that would guarantee to increase his manhood, Kevin flipped back over to his browser to look at his wonderful new piece of horny fantasy ... but saw something odd. A little browser pop-up that said "Your message has been sent." Then, in a flash of intense horror, Kevin suddenly remembered something about Gmail: Alt-Enter is a hotkey for sending an e-mail. He knew he hit Alt-Tab, but if in his intoxicated state he completely forgot ...

Oh fuck.

The next day, Kevin's private fetish life was forever altered, and little did he know that his ultimate humiliation had only just begun ...

ONE FINGER
(originally appeared in *Getting Off on the Wrong Foot*)

+ + +

As mentioned before, fetishes evolve and change over time, sometimes in unexpected ways. When I first started out really developing my foot fetish dreams, they were all about guys who were around my age-group at the time, and as I've gotten older, so has my desirous median age. I was never really a fan of guys much older than that, truth be told, partially for aesthetics, partially 'cos it just didn't jibe with my mentality all that much. However, as time has gone on, that has softened, and it's kind of great hearing from the guys who legitimately have been at this for years, knowing exactly *how to tease and torment footpigs until they're out of their wits and become babbling foot-servants who will do just about anything to help out their obedient 10-toed gods. Thus, I really wanted to have the challenge of writing a story of a cocky young guy run up against a much more powerful and thoughtful older guy, this young dude's own ageism showing through, only before he has his expectations completely turned on his head, his life never being the same afterwards ...*

123

"Oh fuck ... oh *fuck*!"

Angelo looked on, smiling, his hand slowly working the cock of the hipster boy that lay naked beside him. The boy's head tilted back, unable to take in the rush of ecstasy his body was experiencing as Angelo worked the swollen, trembling cock like a pro, the side of his index finger rubbing back and forth over the lip of the boy's cockhead, the motion made all the more frictionless by the copious amounts of sticky-moist precum that were flooding from his member. The brown-haired boy with the ten-o-clock shadow had never been worked so good, and before long, a full-grown lust monster took over, and the boy shouted desperately: "Yes ... YES! FUCCCCK YESSS!" And with that, rockets of sperm fired out of him, getting in his chair, then his face, and then down to his chest and stomach as they decreased in intensity. His panting was almost as loud as his orgasmic cries, sweat appearing everywhere on his skin. His heavy breathing slowly turned into normal breaths, but his very spirit wouldn't be so lucky, that orgasm having shattered just about every notion he ever had about pleasure. He reached around for his glasses on his night stand, and when he put them on, he saw his young Latino friend getting ready to leave.

"Oh -- hey!" he shouted, almost desperate, all while suddenly feeling weirdly embarrassed that he was naked. "Where are you going? What's ... what's going on?"

"I'm leaving," Angelo said, a leather jacket covering his bare chest and he finished buttoning up his tight black pants.

"But I ... I mean ..."

Angelo shot a glance to his latest conquest. "What, you want me to stay?"

"Yeah, I mean, especially after something like that, it just makes sense that ..."

"What? We kiss? I hear about your secret fantasies of boning one of the guys from Arcade Flames?"

"Arcade Fire, actually."

"Whatever. I mean, what do you think tonight was, boy?'

The lightly bearded collegiate lad looked around for the words he was trying to think of, slightly hurt. "I just thought that tonight -- as random as it was -- " (Angelo rolled his eyes to that) "was the start of something. Maybe something special, even."

Angelo took a heavy breath and a stern face. "Listen, I'm going to say this only once, and I don't care how hard it hurts: you're gay, honey. I know that's not what you tell your girlfriend, but judging by how you still have cum in your excuse for a beard, her mouth could never do what my hand just did. You're going to deny that you enjoyed this for weeks, maybe even months, and you're going to think that what we had was special. As you keep looking out for more guys to blow you and fuck you and turn you inside out, you'll realize that while women look for love, gay guys are looking for an honest fuck, without strings and without whatever you're about to say to me after I'm done speaking."

Visibly shaken, the boy struggled to make sense of what was being said to him: "I just thought ... I mean, I just thought that ..."

Angelo held his finger in the air: "I'm gonna stop you right there before I get bored. Drop it, move on, and whatever." Angelo walked out the room and walked down the hallway of whatever dorm he was invited into no more than 90 minutes ago. Right as he was about to leave, he heard the boy's voice calling from way down in the hall. Angelo didn't even want to turn around, but did so, seeing the pathetic newbie chasing after him in boxers with precum stains in the front, showing just how bad a boner he had earlier.

"Hey -- come back!"

"Leaving," Angelo said, turning and exiting once and for all.

"Will I ever see you again?" the hipster boy shouted.

"I'd worry about the cum in your hair first," quipped Angelo as the door shut behind him, leaving the boy all dejected and sad. Shame too -- Angelo really liked this one.

+ + +

An hour later, Angelo was at Swing, the local gay bar in town, sucking down another bottled beer, his eye darting around the room, lazily: nothing intrigued him. He recognized all the types: the recently-liberated jock boy reveling in his newfound status as a hunky sex god, the introverted goth types who didn't just fuck -- they practically worshiped the chance to suck a cock for way longer than necessary, and (of course) the guys over 35 who Angelo couldn't give less of a fuck about. He took another sip of his beer even though he knew he'd have to work out a bit more in the morning so not to reshape his already-sightly abs. Starting to feel buzzed, his eyes drew upward, staring at the lights above and how, despite his hundreds of visits here, he never noticed how perpetually dim they were. Was it mood lighting? Was it supposed to be (gag) romantic? What a weird setting, he thought. He took another sip, catching glimpses of "rubbers" (guys he fucked once and then effectively "thew away") and his regulars who became less and less interesting as time bore on. Angelo, once again, was bored.

He started thinking that perhaps it'd be more fun to go home, put in some poppers, and jack off to whatever was new on Xtube while making remarkably explicit Casual Encounters posts on Craigslist when he noticed someone sitting by himself in of the booths in the corner of the bar. This man was definitely older -- at least 40 judging by what he could make out in the soft-hued corners of this rainbow-colored watering hole -- but he was ... staring right at Angelo. Right at him. Like a target. Angelo's head tilted back a bit in disbelief, but the man's gaze didn't flinch, instead taking a steady sip of his own beer. Angelo would normally tease older guys like that by saying "Pervert!" in passing, knowing it'd piss them off, but something was profoundly different about this guy. The look he was giving him wasn't one of carnal lust or curiosity -- it was just ... knowing. That alcoholic buzz now officially reaching cruising altitude, Angelo thought "Why the fuck not?" He set his beer down and walked on over to the man's booth. As he approached, the man adopted a slight smile, but it was very faint, very controlled. Angelo stood at the edge of the man's table, striking a pose, almost.

"So what -- you like what you see?" teased the tipsy Latino boy.

"It's suitable," the man said, taking another sip of his beer. Angelo eyed his features more closely: thin glasses, his hair already graying a bit, his teal polo shirt assuredly showing a man who was not in "the scene" much at all. Still, the comment stung Angelo a bit. For a man who was lusted after by both gay men and straight women, this was the first time he could ever remember someone not falling for his spell right away.

"Suitable?" Angelo quipped, his voice drenched in sarcasm, "I'm sorry, did they you run out of *Women of Wal-Mart* DVDs recently? That more your speed?"

"Not really, much as how 'bitchy queen' isn't your default setting either. In fact, it's not even a setting for you -- it's a pose."

"A pose?"

"Yeah -- it's a lot more fun being dismissive than it is being dismissed, isn't it?"

Defiant, Angelo said "Um, I've never been dismissed from anything, honey."

"And therein lies your problem," said the man, taking another sip from his beer, casually.

"What?" said Angelo, who would be in a huff if he wasn't so confused.

"Sit down, boy."

Angelo didn't take too well to direct commands, but there was something about the cadence in this man's voice that compelled him to figure out what this man's deal was.

Angelo quietly slid into the opposite side of the booth, wondering what was about to happen.

"So, why is it bad that I've never been dismissed from anything?"

"'cos it's boring," said the man.

"How could a never-ending plethora of chocolates ever be boring?" asked Angelo, pleased with his choice of analogies.

"'cos it's repetitive. Because you can have fuck after fuck after fuck, but what's really so good about that? I'm guessing that most of them are pretty average, right? Every once in awhile you find one that's half-way good, and you reward that boy with what? A date? One of your patented handjobs? Please. When was the last truly good orgasm you had?"

"Well, last week, I was playing around with this exchange student ..."

"No, that's not what I'm talking about," the man interrupted. "I'm not talking about the last really fun one you had, or even the last repeat visit you had. I assume you blew that heteroflexible boy you met earlier?"

"Who?" said Angelo, genuinely not aware of who he was talking about.

"The one in the Arcade Fire T-shirt."

"Oh, him. No, I just gave him a handjob."

"And how did he react?" the man asked.

"Heh, it was like he saw the stars for the very first time."

"And when was the last time someone made you see the stars?"

Angelo paused. On one hand, all he could do was wonder what the fuck this guy was getting at. On the other hand, he was somewhat stumped by that last exchange. Not one to show signs of weakness however, his bitchy queen started up again:

"You know, I don't take advice from guys who should be in the old folks home. Your time has come and gone."

"As has yours."

"EXCUSE ME?" Angelo shot back, vain and defiant.

"Yeah, boy. I've seen you here for a few nights now, and I've seen you try every flavor of man that there is in this bar. You're insatiable, and for that very reason, you're unsatisfied. You think you know so much about the scene but the truth is you're bored as hell, and that's largely because you're boring. Your primary function in life right now is to fuck and be fucked, and somehow after each climax you think, briefly, that you're happy. And then you go home to your bed, still alone, unfulfilled, downloading porn illegally because gay men have suffered for dozens of years so why shouldn't you get a well-made fisting video for free, right? You've been unhappy for years and you convince yourself otherwise and you don't fuck guys over how old: 30? 28?"

"35, actually." Angelo said, a bit flabbergasted.

"That sounds about right. It's a lot more fun to have playthings than it is to have experience or even meet someone who would know what to do with you but that invisible tiara you place upon your own head is ready to slip at any moment. You can sling as many snarky remarks as you want with me but I can clearly see that you're the shaken one, and however clever you think you are, I've heard whatever you're going to say a hundred times over, so you might as save it.'

Angelo's mouth parted, words ready to come out, but nothing did. Half-words almost formed, but the traffic-jam of information that hit his brain was just too much for him to handle. He wasn't sure if he was angry or apologetic or pissed or excited or what. After a minute of sputtering out barely-there syllables, Angelo finally said something coherent:

"So ... what ... do you want with me?"

The man grinned, and took his final swig of his beer. "I want to show you what you're missing.'

"And what, pray tell, am I missing?"

"I'm going to make you beg to cum with nothing but a finger, boy."

"Um, for your information, I've been fingerbanged before, old man," he said.

"Oh I know, boy," the older man said, getting up, "and what I want to do is nothing even remotely like it." He then leaned in and whispered into Angelo's ear: "I'm going to break you like a wild stallion, and you're going to love it."

The man, now standing, pulled out his wallet, and produced a business card from it. He handed it to Angelo and began speaking as he walked towards the front doors of the bar: "Be there, tomorrow. 7PM."

"Not tonight?" Angelo said, almost pleading.

"You're drunk."

Stunned by how blunt this man was, Angelo just froze there for a moment. Right as the man was leaving, in a moment of desperation, Angelo took a few steps towards him and shouted "My name's Angelo, by the way!"

"I don't care," the man said as the door closed behind him, not even looking back for a half-second.

Angelo didn't know what hit him: he sounded ... desperate. "My name's Angelo, by the way!" Who the fuck says that? He knew exactly who said that: first-timers, rubbers, desperate scenesters. What the hell made him say that? What took over? He was so mad at himself right now. He looked down at the card in his hands, and it had an address that appeared to be just outside of downtown. A building filled with studio apartments if he wasn't mistaken. Despite his curiosity, Angelo made a solemn promise to himself: he would not show up at this man's apartment no matter what.

+ + +

Knocking on the door of the man's apartment, Angelo, strangely, felt nervous. His pants were the same from last night but this time around he wore just a form-fitting black T-shirt and put a little more product in his hair. He never felt this nervous about a meet before, but then again, this was the first time he was really at someone else's mercy.

There was no answer, no sound of movement, even, coming from the other side of the of the door on this building's large third floor. Angelo knocked again. He heard the echoes of each rapt sound bounce against the walls of an apartment that sounded very spacious. He stood there, waiting, impatient, and was about to walk away when the door opened and the man greeted him.

"Come on in," the man said, with a smile.

Angelo did, and the site was a dream come true: spacious and minimal, this massive abode had dark hardwood floors, kitchen counters made of white tile, and an island fireplace. It was incredible. The couches were also white, but aside from a few magazines on the coffee tables, there wasn't much in terms of decorations. There were a few bookshelves -- all filled with books that appeared well-worn -- a vinyl player, a large plasma TV against the wall, and a few art-deco paintings, but overall, the aesthetic was pretty direct. There were large wall-sized windows that allowed a small outlook over the city as well, which made Angelo feel like he was in some sort of movie. As he looked around in total awe, he failed to notice that the man had walked up right next to him with two glasses of white wine -- one for him, one for his guest.

"Please," he said, kindly placing the long-stem in Angelo's hand. He extended his own glass out for a toast: "to our health," which Angelo clinked to without even thinking before taking a sip of the luxurious liquid.

"So," Angelo started, "how strong is the roofie you mixed into this?"

The man scoffed, smiling. "Oh please: roofies are used by guys who don't have a real shot at anything." Angelo laughed at that comment, largely because he agreed.

The guys made small talk while staring out the window onto the dusk-lit city below. It was actually kind of pleasant. Once the guys were done with their glasses, however, the man set them on his kitchen counter and then gestured with his fingers to Angelo, saying "Come with me."

Angelo followed and the man lead Angelo to another room in his studio, and in it, there was a simple wooden structure which housed -- a slightly above-ground-level sex swing. There was a small white credenza next to it, but seeing the sling was all Angelo needed to scoff.

"Really?" he said, turning to the man. "That's it? A sling?"

The man smiled again. "When was the last time you trusted someone wholesale, boy?"

"My name's Angelo."

"Again, I don't care, boy," the man said rather bluntly. "When was the last time you really trusted someone without question?"

"I'd say ... never," said Angelo, a bit of fire coming back to his words.

"Then trust me this one time," the man said, the proposition hanging in the air. Given that Angelo's take so far of this older gent was that he knew what he was doing every step of the way, he said something that he only previously said in desperation: "Why not?"

The man instructed Angelo to strip down to his boxers and socks and nothing else. (Angelo made some cocky remark about why the man didn't want to see his "massive" member, but the man cut him down to size simply by saying "Whatever you're about to show me, trust me: I've seen bigger.") Instead of getting in the sling so that he was face up, the man strapped Angelo into the sling so that he was actually face down. Instead of being a relaxed, reclining position, he was at somewhat of a 45-degree angle, belly out, his whole body sagging from his arms, as if his ribcage was a pinata of some sort, just sagging there while his arms and legs held up the weight. There was a bit of a strain (of course) but it wasn't anything Angelo couldn't handle. Angelo tried moving around, but with his arms and legs stretched out at the angles they were, he couldn't do much in the way of escaping anything that came into his personal bubble.

"Snug?" the man asked as he adjusted one last strap.

"Yeah. I've been tied up worse," noted Angelo, thinking casual mentions of his own experiences might impress the man. The man looked at Angelo and then looked away, not even as much acknowledging the comment in question. Out of the corner of his eye, Angelo could spot the man grabbing something from a table that was set up nearby, and as he walked closer to Angelo, the boy could see what it was but only before it was too late: an incredibly sturdy leather blindfold. Without even asking, the man placed it over Angelo's eyes, adjusting the strap behind his head, brushing some of Angelo's jet-black hair out of the way as he did so. The man wasn't playing around or even taking in moments for himself as he fixed the strap tightly around Angelo's scalp, no: he was all about efficiency, which Angelo wouldn't admit frightened him just a little bit.

Angelo's vision was pitch black. The inside of the leather mask had these soft pouchy bumps that fit snugly into his eye-sockets -- he couldn't even open his eyelids if he wanted to, but he wasn't necessarily uncomfortable either. The man was truly limiting the boy's senses. Angelo could hear the sound of a wooden chair being pulled up in front of the boy. Angelo's body was tense, as all it was doing was simply swaying ever so slightly in the dead air of the room. He literally had no idea what was about to happen next.

Some 30 seconds or so passed. Then 30 seconds more. Then a minute. "Um, you going to do anything?" asked Angelo in a tone that simply oozed sarcasm. Nothing. Not even the creaking sound of the man adjusting himself in the wooden chair. Just, silence. As time pressed on, Angelo felt his body subconsciously tense up more and more, growing ever-fearful of what was being planned. The more tense he got, the more desperate the scenarios in his head spiraled, a rare tinge of doubt creeping in to his mind, thinking that perhaps he is actually in the clutches of a conniving serial killer or someone who wants to turn him into a full blown leather boy or was hired to do a number on him after he dumped some guy cold blooded-ly ("That's a word, right?" Angelo thought) ...

And that's when Angelo quickly shuddered "*Oh God*!", his body spasming. On his left nipple, he suddenly felt this chill, cool cream get applied. A huge gob of it too. It must be ... moisturizer ... that had been refrigerated That was the only thing it could be. And now, it was hanging from his nipples and boy was it a shock to the system. Even with his black ankle socks still on, Angelo could feel the chill all the way down to his toes.

Then, with almost the same level of surprise, a gob of the cool cream was placed on his right nipple. It wasn't five seconds before he felt both his nips jutting out at full attention. Already he could feel those dirty, dark tingles start to form at the base of cock, but there was no immediate movement. For now, it was all chill sensation.

"Now," started the man, his voice cutting through the silent air with authority and volume, "What was the deal we made last night, boy?"

"Ohhhhh," Angelo shuddered, his body still adjusting to its new nip-temp, "we ... we no you were going to ... ohhhh ... get me off."

"Nope, that wasn't the deal."

"You're lying then! You said ..."

"I said I was going to get you off with a finger, boy. And that's exactly what I'm going to do."

"Well," started Angelo, sounding like he was on the verge of another gasp of pleasure, "isn't the moisturizer cheating?"

"Not really," said the man, "as the only other liquids I need are going to come from you."

Angelo was almost scared, but that didn't last for long: the man's index finger was suddenly inside his Angelo's helpless bellybutton. The boy yelped. Even though he couldn't see it, Angelo felt as if he somehow knew the man was smiling right now.

At first, the well-manicured finger just stayed there in Angelo's bellybutton, but very slowly, it began to wiggle a bit, twisting around inside Angelo's sensitive tummyhole. A few boyish giggles bled out of Angelo's mouth. "Hehe -- stop it! Stop! That tickles!"

"I know," the man said, coldly.

The finger wormed its way around, the wiggling slowly and steadily growing intensity. It scratched the sensitive inside of the boy's button, but each little scrape of his fingernail unearthed a few more tickles than the last scratch. Over and over again, scratchy scratchy scratchy, tickle tickle tickle. Angelo's arms strained and flexed to try and get his body away from the wiggling finger, but nothing could be done: the finger was in there too deep, and it was tickling like its life depended on it.

Just when Angelo couldn't take it anymore, the finger removed itself from Angelo's belly button. A minute passed, and already, Angelo could feel sweat forming on his body. Then, out of nowhere, he felt the finger fondle his left earlobe a bit. "Hey, cut that out!" Angelo said, once again in a boyish fashion that surprised even himself. Yet the finger wasn't happy with his head movements. It went out to fondle that earlobe again, softly, before tracing behind his ear a bit, then playfully poking a bit on the inside. "Stop it!" shouted Angelo, through laughter, but the constant exploration of the finger wasn't stopping. The finger's favorite thing to do right now seemed to be lightly flicking the lobe back and forth before exploring the ins and outs of the ear itself, poking around like a miniature bloodhound's nose, not caring where it ends up. All of this playfulness was still getting Angelo to laugh. The finger then went around to the other ear and did the same thing, fondling and fondling the ear like it was its own precious, ticklish thing. Angelo couldn't remember the last time someone was this playful, but for whatever reason, those tingles in his loins continued to mount because of it.

The finger then began tracing along the smooth sides of the boy's neck, but one it began running underneath Angelo's chin, he lost it. "Ahaha get out of there!" he screamed as he did everything he could to bring his chin inward, but it was to no avail: the finger could travel wherever it wanted to, but playing with the boy's sensitive chin was actually tickling him.

"I got you by the hair of your chiny chin chin," the man said, glee in his voice as he played with his toy. The childish talk, for whatever reason, was really getting to Angelo. After all, he was often the dominant force in all of his scenarios, so for someone else to be taking the reigns, much less treating him like a helpless child, was only adding on to the psychological torment, as if each degrading phrase somehow increased the boy's ticklishness. Tickle tickle went the finger, and no matter what awkward position Angelo put his face in, the finger somehow was able to scratch somewhere new and exposed at a second's notice and conjure even more tickles out of the boy.

Without warning, the finger left Angelo's chin and then dived right into the little mountain of moisturizer on the boy's left peck and began fondling the pointy nip tip with absolute relish. Angelo screamed, his body lurched to one side, but soon came back into position, the finger circling the sensitive circle of pink flesh as the base of his nipple, then tracing up the protruding center and then down the other side, doing this over and over again, sometimes wiggling around on the very tip for a few seconds just to see what kind of reaction it would get, before flicking the pointy mound a bit before circling it again. It was just constant nerve-ending stimulation. When the finger jumped over to the right nipple, Angelo felt a wave of erotic electricity simply surge through his body, feeling it all the way out at the edge of his fingertips. His body flexed and almost leaned into it against his better wishes, almost asking for the nip to be played with all the more. Angelo couldn't believe it, but he felt as if his nipple was almost trying to grow larger. It loved being played with, tormented, fondled. In the back of his mind, he somewhat wished that the man had promised to get him off with at least two fingers.

The finger stopped its devious torment. "You had enough yet?" asked the man. Angelo, panting a bit, said, "What ... what do you think you're doing?"

Without even answering, a fingernail scratched one of Angelo's ribs no his right side. The boy let out a laugh. It poked and wiggled again, although this time a few ribs lower. Then it started scratching the side of his tummy. Angelo, ticklish as all fuckout, clenched his teeth together, defiant to laughter, but the finger wasn't having any of that. It jumped over to his left rips, wiggled there. Then the right ribs. Then the top of his right ribs. Then it traced a left rib back all the way to Angelo's sagging spine. Then the finger just began wiggling and poking wherever it pleased, finding great joy in the deep-seated laughs that could be found by scratching right in-between Angelo's ribs.

Angelo fucking hated this. His teeth were practically grinding against each other to fight off the laughter, but the fingers were too good, poking him in his vulnerable areas, scratching his sexy, sweaty skin, sometimes even working its way up into his hairy armpit, diving into the fleshy center and unearthing metric ton's worth of evil, evil tickles. Right now, the finger was doing serious tickle damage to his left armpit, twisting the hairs around before prodding and poking the center once more, and finally, at the very edge of sanity, Angelo lost it:

"HA HA HA FUCK DEAR FUCK THAT TICKLES PLEASE HA STOPHA!"

It was music to the man's ears.

Now that Pandora's box of laughter was cracked wide open, the finger grew ferocious: the armpits were now being prodded aggressively, a few new nip-flips were thrown in, and those terribly effective between-rib pokes all shot Angelo into a new stratosphere of sexual torment. He was almost dizzy, spending more time exhaling laughs than he was inhaling air, his brain and body now switched over to tickle-input mode and having little time to process anything else. Angelo was getting lost in this stratosphere of half-consciousness ...

... but a single swipe of his cock was all it took to ground him again.

So distracted by his futile attempts to contain his own maniacal laughter, Angelo failed to notice that he was sporting a massive boner through his underwear, and it was already dripping a bit of precum. The finger's smooth run against his shaft was almost like a slap in the face: it almost made him sober up. Before he could even realize it, a pair scissors was cutting off his underwear rather quickly, and before long, Angelo was naked in midair save for his socks. His large, fat cock flopped out, the air of the room surrounding his sweaty balls, giving him a sigh of relief after being cooped up in that underwear for so long. Angelo could sense the man moving, getting behind him, which honestly scared Angelo a bit.

Without warning (as always), the finger dove right into the middle of Angelo's gooch, that too-sensitive fleshy patch between his ass and his scrotum, wiggling and scratching and teasing away. The shock of the sensation made a high-pitch shock-laugh fire out of the boy's esophagus, all before desperate pleas of "No! Pleeeease stop!" followed, mixing in with reticent moans. The finger sometimes strayed and began slowly tracing the gooch down to the underside of the boy's balls, hanging there, exposed.

"I hope, for your sake," started the man, "that your balls aren't ticklish."

For the next hour, the finger teased and traced every curve and crevice of the young man's nutsack, sometimes touching the very bottoms of the balls ever-so-softly, sometimes wiggling their way up the glands that connected to the base of his shaft, sometimes wiggling in-between the two balls just to see if that cause Angelo to emit some sexy little laughs (they did). Dear fuck this finger was having a love affair with the boy's balls. After about 20 minutes of non-stop stimulation, Antonio discovered that, in fact, it was tickling behind the balls that got him the most, as that area was just so damn sensitive. Angelo had been naked in front of guys dozens of times before, but when the barely-touched back of his balls were teased like that, he felt something he had never felt before: vulnerable. Fully, 100% vulnerable. This man was controlling his eager, throbbing cock like a ticklish puppet, each wiggle and light fingernail scrape causing his member to throb or twitch or lift upward on its own, the tingles accumulating in his beet-red cockhead. By the end of that hour of non-stop ball teasing, not only was precum leaking out of the Latino lad, but it had formed a straight, uninterrupted line of the clear manjuice that went from his cock to the floor, where it was beginning to pool. Angelo, truly had never been more horny in his life.

The ball-teasing stopped and not a moment too soon. Every once in awhile, Angelo's blindfolded head would whip around, trying to shake off the constant threat of horny explosion that was forming in his skull. He sensed the man moving around, moving in front of him, and somewhat underneath him. The finger reached up and took a swipe of moisturizer of the boy's right nipple, and then rubbed that moisturizer right in-between where Angelo's cockhead the front of the shaft met. The finger slowly worked the moisturizer in, not focusing on any other area aside from that pinnacle of sensitivity. Stroke. Angelo took in a breath. Stroke. Angelo gasped a little. Stroke. Angelo felt his balls shudder just a bit, but not enough where anything was about to happen.

Then nothing.

Angelo's cock was practically begging for release, his entire shaft having turned as red as his helmet, the whole thing ready to burst if as much as a light breeze rolled through the room. In the back of his mind, Angelo was simply begging for a nipple fondle. Or a rib poke. Or maybe, oh please, a ball fondling? Please? That's all it'd need ...

"Do you want to cum, boy?"

"Fuuuuuck yes," Angelo said, sighing, desperately, defeated.

"OK," said the man, "but only under one condition."

"Yes, please, anything." Angelo was eager to get this over with.

"Once you cum, I get to play with you for as long as I want, no matter how much you beg me to stop."

"*Fine!*" Angelo screamed. "Just. Make. Me. Cum!"

"Your wish," said the man, ever so sly.

He walked behind Angelo, kneeling in-between his suspended legs, and the finger did what it knew the boy liked best: it lightly scratch-tickled the backs of his balls. "Tickle tickle tickle," the man said, teasingly.

He lost it.

In one surge, Angelo felt his cock jut out, rocketing out a cum shot that was as intense as anything he ever felt. Instantly, tingles overtook every square inch of his body. The man's hand suddenly reached around to the shaft and the fingers wrapped around it. It began jerking the boy off mid shoot. The second shot felt about equidistant to the first, the sheer velocity of it making Angelo feel like he was swinging backwards. The hand, especially the the soft side of the index finger, began rubbing back and forth over that sensitive lip of the cockhead, the one that connected with the front of his shaft where the moisturizer was applied earlier. Except now that the moisturizer was worked in, that lip took on a bit of a rubbery feeling, and being stimulated while he was cumming was a sensitivity nightmare. The man's hand continued to jerk furiously as each shot of piping-hot cum came out, and as the pleasure shots died in intensity, the hand kept jerking. Slowly, the lightning bolt of pleasure that was Angelo's cock was becoming more and more a no-touch zone. His sensitivity was through the roof. The tipping point was crossed, and the boy began squirming.

"Please," Angelo said, "please stop!"

"That wasn't the agreement boy," said the man sternly.

"No, please, ha ha this is just ... he he too sensitive!"

"I know."

"No, really!" shouted Angelo. "I'm too sensitive!"

"I know."

"STOP!" he screamed, his body fidgeting with whatever remaining energy it had left.

"No," said the man, watching as the blindfolded boy's next thoughts were drowned out by his own helpless laughter.

The sensitivity jerking was actually tickling poor Angelo, and now his mind was lost in a world where "tickle" was the only word it knew.

+ + +

Angelo's torment lasted for three more hours. He passed out by the end.

+ + +

Angelo was once again sipping a beer in Swing, his leather jacket on, unzipped, with no shirt underneath, as per always. Angelo was looking around, looking for new meat, but right now, even the rubbers he once disposed of so fecklessly were now intriguing to him. That night with the man (whose name he never caught) was life-changing. For the first time in his life, he was at someone's complete and utter mercy, and the overwhelming desperate intensity rearranged a lot of things in his brain. He realized that even with his hundreds of experiences, there was still much to learn, and new lessons could come from any place. Angelo put the moratorium on his "over 35" rule for now. He'd take anyone who seems to know what they're doing. In fact, right now, he was ...

"Hey there, Angelo!"

Angelo turned around. It was that hipster boy from a few weeks ago. He was wearing a red flannel shirt that made him look like a lumberjack, but ... something was different about him. He had a confidence to him.

"Um, hey there," Angelo said, unsure of how to react.

"How are you man?" Dear gods this boy was excitable.

"Um, I'm good. How ... how are you?"

"Listen," the boy started. "I wanted to apologize for, um ... our last encounter. I'm sure I seemed desperate and pathetic to you, but that's only because, well, I was. It's ..."

"Stop right there," started Angelo, "don't even say another--"

"No no, let me finish!" the boy said, eager. "A lot of those things you said were ... very true. Very cold, hard truths that I had really ..."

"No," Angelo said, softly. "They weren't."

The hipster boy paused and cocked his head, curious. "What?"

"I was wrong to try and demean you like that," started Angelo, sounding more sage-like than he ever had before. "You're new to the scene, you're young, and a lot of the things I said were reactionary. I was playing the role of the stuck-up queen and I was playing it well. It was wrong to say those things to you."

The boy looked at Angelo, confused. "I ... those things were life-changing. I promise to never be like that again."

Angelo put his beer down, got off his barstool, and grabbed the front of the boy's shirt and pulled him close. "I don't want you to act like a stereotype, boy. I want you to act like you." He pulled him in for a deep kiss, and the hipster boy didn't know what to do, but somewhat leaned into it.

Their lips unlocked. They now stood facing each other, Angelo smirking a bit, which in turn caused the other boy to do the same. Angelo smiled as he spoke: "Tonight, I'm going to change your life boy."

And hours later, he did.

FOOT FETISH HELL
(new to this collection)

+ + +

As previously mentioned, I take some of my cues from several brilliant writers, but there is perhaps none more potent than that of Eddie, the devious mastermind behind some of the most relentlessly evil stories to ever grace Jack's Male Tickling Rack, one of the finest foot fetish sites to ever exist in history. His stories were otherworldly, and one of them, "The Fiend", was about a demon designing the most pitch-perfect torture device to torment his latest new damned soul with. It was beyond evil and beyond horny and I loved it to pieces. Writing a "quickie," I loved the idea of somewhat modifying and applying that idea to specifically foot fetish terms, and the result, never before published in a collection prior, is one I quite, quite enjoy ...

Sam awoke, a tussle of his stringy blond hair sagging in front of him. His eyelid were having a hell of a time trying to lift open, but they eventually got there. Sam felt groggy, like he got slammed around pretty badly, his body probably bruised. His mind was hazy, his memory wildly unfocused and largely inaccessible -- what the hell happened?

It was at this moment that Sam realized he couldn't move his arms. He looked up: both of his wrists were strapped into those large leather restraints they use at insane asylums, and the straps for each wrist were attached to the ceiling above him. Sam fidgeted a bit, but no, he was tied up good. Gradually, Sam began to realize things: mainly that he was completely naked and that his feet weren't touching the ground. He craned his neck around as best as he could, and from the strained glimpses that he could muster, Sam's feet were in similar restraints but were tied back to a mid-point on the wall behind him, causing Sam to simply be suspended there, his body arced like a crescent moon of pasty flesh. The strangest thing about this, though, was that Sam didn't exactly feel panicked or in danger. Admittedly, he wasn't in a state of harmonious peace either, but he wasn't deeply terrified -- just very aware of his state of being, almost as if he subconsciously expected to be here.

Sam begin drinking in the rest of the room: it was very small, very dark. He could see the room was barely wider than your average double-doorway and about as long as your average house kitchen. A single bare lightbulb hang down a foot or two in front of his face while the walls, ceiling, and floor was all painted black. There was a door on the far end of the longwall on Sam's left, but it looked like it had been boarded up and then painted over -- all ink black, just like everything else. Directly in front of him was a mounted table on an angle, leaning so it was almost perpendicular to Sam's very vulnerable tummy. There weren't any straps near the head nor foot of the table, but at the base there was a small iron lip -- perhaps to prevent people from sliding off it if they felt inclined to get on it. In any other context, someone could mistake this for a medieval-styled torture rack, but it seemed to be modified for ... some unknown purpose. Sam's arms unconsciously tensed thinking about it, but they soon sagged back into the submissive state they were in. The fight in Sam never even appeared: he was just existing while restrained.

Sam waited.

Some 20 minutes had passed with nothing happening, Sam's mind only marginally worried about what was going to step through that boarded-up door on the other side of the room, instead far more intrigued by how the person was going to enter the room what with the door all boarded up and painted over. Sam also noticed something about the room that was legitimately concerning: the complete and total lack of sound. Not just inside the room, but also outside: no sounds of trucks passing over highways, no other doors being opened from adjacent hallways -- just nothing. Sam suddenly had a bit of a tickle in his throat and turned to cough, pressing his mouth into his left bicep as he did so. When he turned back, someone was sitting on the table directly in front of him.

"The *fuck*?!" he screamed in a moment of terror, his body jerking by the fright and causing his suspended frame to sway ever-so-slightly.

"Hello Sam," the person said back to him.

Sam took a moment to get his barrings: what the fuck just happened? Sam's brain quickly scanned up and down the shape of the person in front of him and -- he realized that he knew who it was. It was Pat. His co-worker Pat. Sam's head involuntarily shook a bit, trying to piece together exactly why he was suspended naked in a room with Pat all of a sudden. He looked up and down at Pat's frame: about six feet tall, slight bit of a burly build, kind face, ink-dark hair with a well-trimmed goatee, glasses for reading -- yeah, this was Pat from work, decked out in a casual green button-up shirt, blue jeans, and his teal felt sneakers pressed up against that metal lip at the foot of the table. Pat's knees were bent, almost touching Sam's chest, Pat's arms leaning on their elbows as Pat was leaning back, Pat's face smiling at Sam, very calm.

"Pat!" Sam shouted. "Holy shit, what are you doing here?"

Pat continued to smile at him, unmoving. "Hello?" Sam shouted, but Pat again didn't move. He blinked, but didn't move any other muscles. "Pat," Sam continued, "what's going on? What are we doing in a place like this? Can you help me get out of these things?"

More silence. Pat then cleared his throat and began to speak: "Sam, I am going to tell you something right now that you're not going to believe. What I ask is that you trust me, OK?"

"Um ... OK?" Sam intoned, unsure of what to make of such a lead-in.

"There are two things you need to know, Sam," Pat started, "one of which is that you are dead."

Sam's head shook involuntarily, this time rejected what it just heard. "No I'm not," he retorted. "I'm alive. I'm right here. Suspended in a weird way for some reason, but very much alive, thank you."

"Think back," Pat said, calmly.

Sam's forehead scrunched in, as if digging for memories. Then, like a sledgehammer to the face, there was an instant shock in Sam's brain. The memories starting flooding back, clear as day: his time in college, in his Frat house, still half-way through his year of being the official Secretary/Treasurer for his brothers, happy, content. The flashes continued: that foot fetish of his. That uncontainable, uncontrollable male foot fetish. Seducing straight and gay guys all across campus to bend to this whim, to let him suck on their toes, tie them up, get them off, buying their used socks and their worn flip-flops for private masturbatory sessions later on -- it was bliss. He had a reputation that he was beyond happy to maintain, even if he was dismissed as "that foot freak" by some outsiders. People in the know didn't think of Sam in such a way, however: he was charming, charismatic, and probably hornier than half the people on campus, his fetish close to insatiable.

Then, Sam's mind focused on that night: two years out of college, living on his own, a high-end sales rep job paying for his studio apartment as well as allowing him to indulge his most base of urges. In fact, that's the last thing Sam remembers: being in his apartment, some sweet young thing named Brian over, dressed like he had a fancy job like Sam did, wingtips kicked off in front of Sam's island fireplace, Sam in the kitchen, making drinks. Sam wasn't opposed to sometimes aiding his evening every once in a while, and proceeded to mix the two Jack & Cokes that he and his guest were about to consume. Sam reached for one of his counter drawers, pulled out an extremely small vial that contained a very fine, white powder. Sam knew it was safe unless mixed with certain medications like the kinds that he had to take. Sam remembers placing the powder in one of the glasses and stirring it so it was undetectable, and -- what happened after that? Did he drink the wrong one? If so, that'd be fatal, which ... oh.

"That's right," Pat said, as if reading Sam's thoughts, "and because of that one poorly-planned act of indiscretion, congratulations: you're here now."

Sam's arms pulled on the restraints one more time. "What do you mean? Where am I?"

"In Hell," Pat said.

A stern silence filled the room as Sam's mind started reeling.

"I'm ... I'm ... I'm in Hell?" he stuttered.

"Yes," said Pat, smiling, "and it's my job to get you to agree to stay."

Sam's face contorted in surprise. "Why -- what ... why would I ever agree to that?"

"Well," Pat started, still barely moving, "remember how I said there were two things that you need to know? Here's the second one: if I can't get you to agree to stay in 24 hours -- well, 23 by this point -- then you are free to go, Sam. You will go back to Heaven or the Hereafter or whatever you believe in. Hell, however, is kind of universal, and the rules are the same for all: everyone who comes in is set aside in a room with a Demon for 24 hours. The Demon gets to research every second of the Punished's life and gets to use that information against them, devising the single most devious torture that they can imagine to get someone to agree to stay.

"For example," Pat noted, "I'm not really Pat. I'm a Demon that's taking Pat's form, and boy am I going to exploit your relationship to Pat to the nth degree."

Sam was starting to feel genuinely frightened by what was happening. "What are you talking about?"

"Well," Pat continued, "for some people that come here, it's easy to get them to submit to eternal damnation. Sometimes you just have to flood the Punished's head with all the memories of all the bad things they've done and 'lo and behold: they agree to stay here in Hell til the end of time. Self-doubt is a wonderful thing, let me tell you. They think that they *deserve* to be kept down here, as punishment. For some people, you simply have to exploit their greatest fear until their soul snaps and breaks. Some Demons just use pain and torture to get them to submit, but I find it too messy. In truth, those guys are more cut out for everything that happens after eternal damnation: just an endless, boring routine of what everyone hates the most, over and over and over again. Here, Demons like me get a new victim on a regular basis, we have 24 hours to find whatever it is that makes them tick, and get them to submit in that time. The variety is a treat for the senses, and let me assure you of one thing Sam: I fucking love my job."

Sam then saw Pat sport the most evil and wicked of grins, his eyes burning with foul intent.

"And now," Pat continued, "I get to make you submit. I can definitely do it within the hour but some of us really relish these moments, often going a full 22, 23 hours before making the Punished submit because it can be just so much fun. Thus, when I started reading up on you Sam, I got really excited. The more I dug up on your, the more devious and twisted I saw you to be. Hell, if you weren't a fucking idiot and drank the right cup, you wouldn't even be here right now. But no, all your scheming ways, all your boundless lust -- it's all here in Hell now, never to be seen by the surface world again."

Sam's eyes had grown wide as Pat spoke, and before long he could even feel the panicked sweat that was forming in his hairy, exposed armpits, slowly dripping out and sliding down his chest. Every word that was coming out of Pat's mouth was terrifying to him.

"Part of me thinks you could score a job here," Pat continued, casually, "what with the way you've manipulated those multitudes of men to take their shoes and socks off for you. You got a way with finding people's weaknesses and exploiting them -- which is exactly what I'm going to do to you right now, Sam."

"What ... what are you going to do to me?" Sam whimpered.

"Well," Pat said as he started unlacing the felt sneakers that were containing his massive size 12 feet, "I had a tough decision to make when deciding how we were going to spend our 24 hours together. My research showed me that you were never a fan of pain, and just a few hours on the rack would surely make you break and submit -- but the more and more I dug up about your gigantic sexual attraction to the bare feet of other men, the more I realized just how perfect a tool I had on my hands here. When you get foot-horny, Sam, you don't just turn into an unquenchable lust monster, you become totally helpless to your fetish. It's like it takes over your entire being and starts to run your every thought."

Pat peeled off one of his sneakers and tossed it on the floor, followed by the other, each landing with a soft, dull thud. A pair of new-but-sweaty white ankle socks were all that was covering Pat's wide feet right now, and Sam would be lying if he didn't feel some of those horny tingles start to form in his balls. As much as he didn't want to admit it, he was fascinated by what he saw.

"Thus," Pat continued, "my goal today is to get you hornier than you've ever been before. To get you close to a climax so explosive it will positively rearrange your brain cells. Why else would I decide to take the form of Pat, a man who possesses feet you've long, long fantasized about, jerking off a nearly uncountable number of loads to the simple fantasy of being able to lick his exposed, sweaty soles, to put each one of these plump, hairy toes in your mouth and being able to feel that foot flavor swirl around in your mouth until it's all you can taste ..."

Sam felt his half-mast cock twitch slightly.

"Well it looks like I'm having an effect, aren't I?" Pat coyly quipped. "You like this, don't you?"

In Sam's mind, there was a very strong feeling implying that yes, in fact, he did like what he was seeing. Yet he took a step back, realized he was still in Hell, and this is *exactly* what the Demon wanted him to feel: helpless to his fetish.

"No!" Sam shouted, "I'm not playing your game! I refuse to indulge in my fetish because that's all you need to keep me here forever."

"I know," Pat said, wiggling his toes visibly through his socks. "After all my research, I found that your co-worker Pat was the one person's feet whom you craved the most at your time of death, more than anything else in the known universe. You have gallons of your own seed stored up just for him, and my whole goal is to get you hornier than you've ever imagined, until you're begging for four consecutive eternities of torment just so you can shoot ropes of sticky sperm all over Pat's naked toes."

Another twitch.

It was at this moment that Sam realized that Pat's feet were actually quite close to his exposed, semi-engorged member, those socked feet just had to be lifted up just a bit in order to touch his shaft. Sam suddenly felt a flash of panic, as if the sudden reality of his situation had just clicked with him and he realized he was in no place to move, protest, or do anything to prevent his torment from starting. It was simply going to be a battle against himself, and one he already was uncertain of how it would turn out.

"So," Pat said, "should I take my socks off?"

Sam's cock twitched against his will once again. "No!" he said, knowing that would be one step further to his undoing. "Please just keep them on."

"Oh, but it isn't that what you envisioned?" Pat started, slyly describing the situation. "Isn't the first part of all of your deliriously horny fantasies is to see that elastic rim of the sock slowly come off, exposing just a bit more flesh with each passing second, teasing you, leading you towards your inevitable climax?" Pat's socked left toes tried hooking the rim of the right sock in a grip so it could start pulling them off. They fidgeted a bit more with each attempt, and as clumsy as it looked, it was a very calculated maneuver: the Demon was fully aware of the fact that this actually turned on poor Sam.

Eventually Pat's big left toe managed to get a hold on the rim of his right sock, and awkwardly, it started pulling it down, over the heel. Sam's eyes, wide open and drinking in every detail, noticed the small things: the leg hairs now visible right underneath the cuff of the jeans, the lightly grayed impression of Pat's foot on the underside of the sock, even the very way the sock fabric bunched together the closer and closer it got to his toes. Sam now had an erection, and his will to fight it was diminishing: he was enjoying the sight far too much. Now the sock was past the instep, right above the toe base, and ... off the balled up sock tumbled, right onto the slanted table before rolling slightly to that metal lip, now right next to Pat's bare, exposed right foot.

Sam couldn't believe how clear a view he got of that bare foot. Pat's toes were long, plump, that perfect shade of pink. Pat's ink-dark natural hair color just made the hair on his feet pop all the more, a little bit on the tops, a healthy sprinkling along his toes. Fuck, it was sexy. Just looking at it made Sam fall in love with it, and he could feel his cock starting to strain: it was trying desperately hard to stretch out even farther than it already was, as if hoping that in and of itself would increase the amount of horny pleasure it was getting out of it. His cock was already tingling from base to tip, and he knew that if it got even remotely closer to Pat's foot, it would increase to the point where he couldn't take it anymore.

So hypnotized Sam was by Pat's up-close, bare, exposed right foot he literally didn't even notice that Pat had pulled off the sock to the other one. When Sam realized that Sam's pair of perfectly manly, dominant, sexy feet were in front of him, not that far away from his cock, his member twitched intently. It lifted up three times on its own, pulsing, nodding in agreement to what it was seeing. The Demon could see Sam's cock already reddening, engorging itself with blood, and right in Sam's slit, the Demon could see moisture forming. He knew he had him now.

The Demon, being a playful creature, was somewhat bemused by the fact that Sam wasn't even conscious to the fact that his mouth was agape, and before long, he'd catch himself drooling. Thus, just to take the boy's torture to the next level, he slowly curled his toes tightly. Sam's magic wand twitched again, reacting to the sight instantaneously, its fate intrinsically tied to every single movement of Pat's feet now. Pat then flexed his strong feet as much as he could, those toes spreading so beautifully, the underside of each toe visible to Sam, and in reaction Sam twitched some more and clenched his bound fists as tight as they could. The Demon grinned in approval. He moved his feet up a bit, placing his heels directly on the metal lip, elevating them slightly, and oh, look at that: his big toes now were touching either side of Sam's shaft, causing the boy to gasp.

"Oh, you like that don't you?"

Sam didn't even catch his voice speaking in a higher octave than he was used to, his body almost refusing to release the breath it just took in, his whole body hotwired with sexual tension.

Then, Sam felt the toes move. He could feel the shape of Pat's toes press in to that mighty cock base, and slowly, the moved up to about the half way point of Sam's radiant member, and then went back to the base. Then up to the half-way point again, then back to the base. Sam emitted a whimper of pleasure, his eyes daring up to the black ceiling, overflowing with pleasure. Sam was receiving an honest-to-goodness footjob from Pat's perfect feet right now. He could tell that if the tempo increased only slightly, he was going to completely explode.

Yet having done his research, the Demon knew that already. The tempo right now was deliberately slow, enough to get Sam blasted horny out of his mind. At this point, the Demon remembered yet another aspect about Sam's life that could be very useful here: just how much he absolutely loved to be humiliated with his fetish.

"Sam," Pat said, still slowly jacking the boy's cock with his firm, meaty toes, "you love feet, don't you?"

With a deep, guttural moan of pleasure, Sam's words slowly, haltingly came out of his mouth: "I ... I fucking love feet."

"How much, Sam?" Pat asked matter-of-factly.

"They are my world. They are the ... the whole of my sexual being. Bare male feet are just instant sex for me. They -- ahhhh -- they get me so ... fucking hard. The second I see them, my cock falls under their control."

"What do you want to do to my bare feet, Sam?"

More moans followed. "I want to sniff the base of your toes and fucking cum all over them. I want to coat your bare soles with my hot cum."

"You want to submit to them, yes?"

"YES!" Sam shouted as his body tensed a bit, snakes of pure orgasmic pleasure winding through his body.

"You like thinking about your friends being barefoot don't you?" Sam asked, still jacking.

"So much," Sam confessed, eyes closed now, focusing on the feeling. "I lick their flip-flops for the flavor. I sniff their used socks 'cos they make me cum so hard."

Pat stopped jacking Sam with his toes, causing the boy to whimper: "What? No. Please. Please don't stop. Please, I need your feet."

The Demon analyzed Sam's cock closely: it was beet-red. He could see veins visible all over the shaft. A steady stream of precum was drizzling out to the floor. Oh, this boy was horny. Hornier than he had ever been in his life. The Demon grinned, loving every goddamn second of this.

"Ya know, Sam," Pat started, wiggling his toes a bit, "one thing you didn't count on in this whole scenario is that we *are* in Hell."

"So?" Sam moaned out, still high on pleasure.

"That means we can bend the rules a bit here," Pat smirked. "You like it when I say the words 'bare feet' don't you?"

Sam didn't even respond, except for with a double cock-twitch.

"You want to submit and obey my powerful bare feet, don't you, Sam?"

"More than anything," Sam whispered out, eyes firmly closed, focusing on his pleasure.

"Then watch this."

Pat's feet were now on the lip as normal, not resting on the edge. His feet were just in a regular relaxed position, but Sam couldn't believe what he was seeing: Pat's black toehairs were slowly starting to ... grow in length. Longer and longer and longer they grew, floating in the air, as if they were tentacles. They drifted up like wisps of smoke, slowly getting closer and closer to Sam's raging erection.

"No," Sam muttered.

"Yes," Pat retorted.

The hairs at first stroked the underside of Sam's shaft, but then they slowly twisted around his member, never hurting it, but keep it firmly in place. There hairs connecting Sam's cock and Pat's toes was rather taught. Pat grinned again.

"And now," the Demon started, "you're going to dance for me."

Sam wasn't sure what was going on, but then looked down and saw it: Pat crunched his toes, and the toehairs pulled his cock with him. Not a severe angle, but just enough make Sam pulsate with pleasure. He couldn't believe it, his cock was now going to move whenever Pat flexed or curled his toes, making his cock wiggle and twitch against his own will. Pat's bare feet were his erection's puppetmaster right now -- and it was hot as fuck.

"Twitch twitch twitch!" Pat said, doing three quick toe curls, tugging on Sam's engorged member, making the tingles bottle-necking at his cockhead just swirl around and go crazy.

"AHHH!" Sam screamed. "Fuck. Fuck. Fuck. I'm gonna cum."

"Not yet you aren't," Pat said. Without even touching them, the two balled up, sweaty Patsocks floated up in the air, slowly. "Why don't you take a sniff, boy?" The cotton balls of footsweat inched closer and closer to Sam's face until they were right up against his nostrils. Pat curled his toes slowly this time, tugging Sam's erection slightly downward, holding it there for a few moments, and then releasing until it snapped back to normal. The toes curled again, slowly, keeping Sam's cock at an angle, tense, ready to cum at the drop of a hat.

"Now sniff," Pat ordered.

Sam inhaled the footscent from the two socks, and his body shuddered. Sam's eyes went wide. He could almost see through time. Pat's footscent was 100% grade-A boner fuel. The tingles in his cock were on fire, his base started pumping, and then ...

... Pat's toehairs squeezed a bit around the rim of Sam's cockhead, preventing the orgasm from going through. The rest of his cock was visibly, forcibly pumping, but nothing was coming out. A few arrant toehairs were teasing and tickling the undersides of his balls, feather-whisping the most sensitive of his areas as he pumped in halted frustration.

"FUCK LET ME CUM LET ME CUM I NEED TO CUM!" Sam shouted at the top of his lungs.

"First," Pat said, "you need to agree--"

"I'LL STAY I'LL STAY LET ME FUCKING CUM!!"

Pat paused for a second, smiling. He tugged the toe hairs quickly twice, teasing the horny boy, and then the toe-hairs released.

GUSH went the first, massive onslaught of milk-white cum. Sam actually screamed: to have that much backed-up semen start shooting out of him at once, it almost hurt (hurting in the good way, admittedly, but he knew he was going to feel this tingle for days afterward). Then, the second wave came, and it was *just* as massive as the first. Then another one. Then another one. Then Sam started to really feel the post-orgasmic sensitivity of his cock kick in.

"Please!" he shouted to Pat, "Make it stop cumming!"

"You wanted to submit to my feet," Pat said, tops of his feet and the front of his jeans now caked with loads of Sam's seed. "This is just the start of it."

Another load came out. Then another. Sam actually started crying, whimpering pathetically. "Please!" he pleaded. "It's not stopping!"

"You love feet don't you?" Pat shot back.

Even with the horny pain he was feeling in his cock, tears streaming down his face, Sam shouted out his confession: "I still love feet. I love feet. Feet. Feet. Bare. Bare feet."

Finally, the waves of horniness were reducing in intensity. One more pump. Then another. Then ... it stopped. Sam's body absolutely sagged in his restraints. Desperate bodysweat was now pooling on the floor. Sam had never, ever, ever experienced anything quite like that, and his cock felt like it was positively beat-up. There was literally no energy left in him. All his brain could focus on was his exhaustion and feet. He couldn't even comprehend that he actually just agreed to spend an eternity in Hell.

"Sam," Pat ordered, "look at my toes."

Sam slowly craned his neck to see: and there were Pat's perfect feet, gobs of his white, sticky cum mixed in with his flesh and black toe hairs.

"Is that hot as hell?" Pat asked, knowing full well the answer.

"Yes," Sam said, meekly. "That's ... actually really, really hot."

"Good," Pat said.

A pause filled the room.

"Pat?" Sam said, still weak as a bean.

"Yes, Sam?" Pat said, still unmoving.

"Am I going to eternal damnation now?"

"Well," Pat said, "not yet. You see, there was one little thing I didn't tell you about: those 24 hours? Those are *my* 24 hours. You can submit during it at any time, but even after you do, I get the rest to do what I want with you."

Sam's eyes opened wide, anew with the energy that's derived from fear.

"Pat," Sam said, even in tone, "how long did that last?"

"One hour," Pat said, bluntly.

"Does that mean ..."

"Look at how well I can wiggle my toes for you, Sam," Pat said.

Pat could hear those joints moving. That flesh contorting just for him. Sam knew full well he couldn't go through that again. Not ever again. Especially not 22 more times in a row. He looked at the ceiling in defiance. He refused to look at Pat's toes. He refused. He couldn't.

"Hey Sam," he heard Pat say, "you're missing out on looking at my big, bare ... feet."

It was hopeless. It was too hardwired into his system. Sam's eyes dragged his gaze downward, right to Pat's cum-covered toes, and as much as he hated it, the process started all over again ...

THE CRIMESCENE
(new to this collection)

+ + +

For whatever reason, in looking for a good new TV show, I wound up stumbling upon the Idris Elba U.K. crime drama known as Luther. *It's not a great show by any stretch of the imagination, but it's good enough. The title character is a clichéd brilliant police detective with anger issues but the ability to see well beyond the obvious to put a stop to crimes. That's fine and good, but creator Neil Cross, who wrote every single script in the entire series, had a knack for really writing psychopaths. Every pasty young would-be actor in England landed plum roles playing the downright psychotic, and, yes, there was even one episode about a foot fetish killer (F/M, but still). I was really intrigued by having a story about a devious serial tickler, and somewhat using that show as a jumping off point, felt like there was a lot that could be explored with one sexy idea like that, as evidenced by this story, never before seen in any of my books. Enjoy, footpigs ...*

Scott was trying so hard, but he couldn't help it: tears were rolling out of his eyes. Again. For the third time that evening.

There he was, in the bed of his own home, gagged, mummified tightly, only his cock, nipples, eyes, and bare feet exposed. He wasn't sure what it was, but he just woke up with this gauze wrapped around him, but something was painted on it to make it harden. Not completely, but enough that he literally couldn't move. A sock was shoved in his mouth before he was encased in his mummified realm of terror, all so that he could see his captor walking around him, cocky as fuck, twirling that stiff white feather in his hand. It was obviously synthetic -- white feathers have never been that stiff, that ... tingly -- but it was doing a number on him. On his feet, on his shaft, on his soft, sensitive nipples. It was all too much fun.

The reason Scott was crying was because this was his third go-around. He had already been tickled, teased, edged for a really long time, and made to cum twice already. Scott would like to tell you when his ordeal started or what caused him to pass out in the first place, but that knowledge had disappeared a long time ago. Well before his first cumshot, even. He had cum before, but never to *just* the touch of a feather. Especially one that stroked his 6" shaft *while* he was cumming, much less continue stroking for a full 30 minutes afterwards. Feeling those tingly featherwisps glide across the soles of his bare feet was torture. They'd start at the heel, inch their way up to his sensitive arch, trace the curve of the arch, grace across the balls of his feet, and then just go to town on the undersides of his sensitive toes. Scott was ticklish as all fuckout and couldn't stand it. He had screamed into his sockgag more than a few times, and his captor seemed to enjoy it more and more.

Scott didn't know why he was here, what he had done, or why he was being tickled and edged over and over again. All he knew was that he wanted it to stop. He wanted it to stop so badly. Hence the new set of tears that were welling in his eyes: his captor was dragging that feather across his nipples again. Light, tender strokes over those pink little nubs of flesh, over and over as they got firmer and firmer, and, against his own desires, his manhood started to inflate, twitching slightly. Scott moaned. There was no way in hell he could survive another round.

"Aww, you enjoying that, Scotty?" his captor teased, Scott's sensitive nipples being mercilessly teased. "You ticklish there? Does someone have ticklenips? Is someone tickling your ticklenips right now?"

Scott screamed into his gag, but that scream quickly devolved into a sob. He was broken. He was done. He would give literally anything for this to stop right now. Literally. Anything. Yet with the gag soaked in his saliva and the hardened gauze around his mouth, it appears that his captor couldn't care less about what he had to say.

Twitch.

Already, Scott's cock was half-engorged. Scott was moaning in disagreement: how could his own penis betray him like this? No matter: the tip of his captor's feather pressed into his the tip of his shaft ... and forcefully, carefully moved down it. Those sensations returned to Scott's hardon: that sensitive tingle, so tingly it actually made him laugh. It was making him giggle against his will.

"I love how ticklish your cock is," his captor teased. "I love how I know what it wants better than you do."

Scott muffled something in response, but it was no matter: he was at full mast now. His captor turned the feather to its side, and stroked the feather longways up Scott's shaft, which was already caked with dried cum from his last two climaxes.

"Oh Scott," his captor said through Scott's moans, "what are going to do with you? You run one of the largest hedgefunds in Philadelphia and yet you spend so much time screwing other people out of their money. You abuse your power, Scott, and I don't like that. Boys like you need to be punished, which is why I enjoy overpowering you, using your own penis, no less. Your sensitive penis wants tickles. It wants to be teased. You've cum twice already, Scott, and I'm going to get you to cum again, and again, and again. I'm going to tickle your feet after this next orgasm Scott. I know how badly you want to pass out and simply hope this ordeal is over, but I'm not going to let you do that, Scott. I'm going to make you cum so fucking hard. I'm going to tickle the sanity right out of you. I'm going to reduce you down to nothing Scott. That's what I do. Maybe, just maybe I'd stop after three orgasms, but Scott, I gotta be honest ... I'm having *so* much fun right now ..."

A bead of precum was starting to form on the tip of Scott's exhausted member. The tears were welling up again. All he wanted was for it to stop. His captor knew better, though, and the primal scream that Scott let out an hour later, all into his sockgag, of course, was music to his captor's ears. The captor almost felt sorry for Scott -- but only almost.

+ + +

"We got another one," Thompson said, leaning into his boss' office.

"Another what?" asked Clyde.

"Another one of the, um ... ticklers, I guess?"

"Christ."

With that, Clyde, a burly, somewhat muscular black man who had worked hard through most of his 20s and early 30s to get to the position of detective, grabbed his trench coat and was off, Thompson the driver as always.

It only took them about 20 minutes to get to the scene of the crime, a residential house that was cordoned off with police tape as their car pulled up, an ambulance already at the scene. The two investigators got out of their car, the wormy Thompson still a bit desperate to impress his superior, perpetually angling for that promotion that was never gonna come. They walked under the police tape and were greeted by an officer.

"Gentleman," the officer intoned.

"What's going on?" asked Clyde.

"Another one. Found after his wife got home early from a weekend work function. The first responders were able to cut him out of the ... um ... mummy casing?"

"Let's just call it cocoon," stated Clyde.

"Yeah, out of the cocoon, and he's being wheeled out momentarily. It appears just like the others: no signs of a break-in, no signs of any additional DNA being left at the scene, but that's just from our initial sweeps. If the perpetrator mixed his semen with the victim's at all or left saliva anywhere, we could find a match pretty quickly, but--"

"How's the vic?" interrupted Thompson.

"Well," the officer said, "babbling like an idiot. I don't know what the prep put him through, but the guy's brain is gone." The officer glanced to the driveway briefly. "Oh, they're wheeling him out right now."

The three men cleared way between the medics and the ambulance, and Clyde saw the Vic being wheeled out on a stretcher. His gaze was lazy, his head bobbing left and right, looking at nothing in particular. The paramedics were proceeding to prep the stretcher to be lifted into the ambulance when Clyde approached the man.

"Sir," he started, "are you OK?"

"Tickle ..." drifted softly out of the man's lips, his brain clearly dazed. "So ... much ... tickle ..."

"This person who did this to you," Clyde started, whipping out his notebook from his inner-jacket pocket, "what did he look like?"

Scott chortled a bit. "Ha, oh man. Just ... tickle. So much ... tickle. Tickle. How could you let him tickle me so much? How could you? Just ... tickle."

"But the man who did this to you," Clyde pressed on, a bit more aggressive in tone, "what did he *look* like?"

Scott then started laughing, with no external stimulation, just laughing, his psychological scars running deep, his mind entrenched in madness. Clyde frowned, recognizing he wasn't going to get anything out of this poor man, and proceeded to walk back to his car with Thompson by his side, both of them hearing the desperate cackling of the victim behind them, his life forever changed.

+ + +

"So what are we looking at here?" Clyde said, stroking his ink-black goatee with his feet on a desk in the main bullpen of the station, almost a dozen other cops scattered around, all staring at the bulletin board with all three previous tickle vics' faces up, strings connecting them to their locations on a map and various personal ephemera from each Vic scattered about.

"Well," started Thompson, "these area all men. Are we dealing with a homosexual?"

"'Gays' is fine, Thompson," Clyde insinuated. "And maybe. We can't say for sure at this point, but yes, so far, all men."

Gretchen, one of the department's newest hires, chimed in: "Yet look at the ages we're dealing with here: 42, 39, today's Vic was 28 -- there's no immediate correlation of ages, much less locations."

"You're right," Clyde said, standing up and walking over to the board, staring at each picture closely. "There's no correlation to imply this prep is in any specific location -- but these are all targeted. These men were very specifically targeted on nights when they aren't home. He stalks his prey. The question is: why does he choose the men he chooses?"

"He got a fetish?" Thompson chimed in.

"No duh," said Clyde.

"Wait, what do these men do?" asked Johnny, one of the smarter detectives at the office.

"That's a good question," said Clyde. "Thompson?"

"Well," Thompson said, scrambling over his files, "it appears the first Vic was the CEO of a big health food chain of stores, the second was a prominent high-level banker, our most recent one ... helped run a hedge fund based in Philly."

"Ah-ha," noted Clyde. "So these are political targets."

"But," Gretchen said, "none of these guys had any political affiliations as note."

"No no no," said Clyde, staring at the board, not breaking for a second to look at his colleagues. "This man is trying to make a point. He's taking these men in positions of power and breaking their minds, apparently through being ... really good at tickling I guess. Whatever the breaking point is of the human spirit ... he figured it out a long time ago. That's why he's aiming for people in powerful organizations. He's power-hungry. He wants to make a scene."

"So what do we do?" asked Thompson.

"Simple," Clyde said with a grin, "we step up to the platform first."

+ + +

The reporters all huddled around as the TV cameras positioned themselves, focusing on Clyde at the table that was used for media events such as this. He took a swig from his glass of water and faced forward. He was ready.

The director of the broadcast signaled we were on air. The reporters all fell silent. Clyde, with his concerned gaze, looked directly into the camera.

"Ladies and gentleman of Philadelphia," he started, "right now, we are dealing with a sexual menace. A man of terror who has been stalking prominent members of the financial and business world, torturing them sexually to make his own sick point. We here at the police would normally try and figure out what the goal is of such attacks, but we what we're dealing with here: not a man of great political intellect, but, instead, a sick and lonely pervert who is trying to use politics as a cover for his own sick fetish."

There was murmuring amongst the reporters, a bit aghast at how frank Clyde was being while his message was being broadcast across the entire city.

"This sad man, who will no doubt strike again, needs help, and then needs to be brought to justice. If you know anyone or suspect anything about this perpetrator involved in this case, please, call your local police department and provide them with that information. Any information that leads to an arrest will carry with it a $50,000 reward. We look forward to bringing this deviant to justice. There will be no time for questions at this time. Thank you."

The reporters broke out into a sea of crying voices anyways, but Clyde knew better: the trap was set, the public was aware, and although a lot of manpower was required to go through each and every tip received, it may very well lead to the arrest his department was looking for.

Around 8PM, Clyde's car pulled into the driveway of his house. He had a busy day, having handled no fewer than 20 calls himself since the press conference was broadcast. He was tired, exhausted, but felt a good sense of accomplishment. He went in to his place, so much emptier and cavernous since his wife decided it would be a good idea to separate while they "sort through" their marriage. Naturally, he tossed his keys on his kitchen island, grabbed a bottle of gin, and poured himself a full glass with two ice cubes. He leaned against his kitchen counter in damp light, mulling over today's developments, wondering about this mysterious perpetrator and what his real motivations were. He'd dealt with sex crimes before -- that was nothing new to him -- but for something so specific, it was hard to determine what made this man tick. The second he figured that out, he'd have his man in cuffs within the hour.

Clyde went upstairs to his bedroom, that mattress having used to be shared by his wife every night before the problems set in, before the accusations that his job was taking more prominence in their marriage than their marriage was. He had heard the argument before with various girlfriends, but that didn't mean he liked it.

He sat on his bed, looking at his wife's side. The indents of her body were long since smoothed over with his own tussling about late at night, but he stroked the top of the blanket that she would sleep under, harboring warm memories of what used to be. He wondered what she was up to right this minute.

"Hey." That voice was not Clyde's at all.

He turned around to where the voice was coming from.

THUNK!

Clyde was out cold in a second.

+ + +

Clyde awoke, slowly, groggy and dazed. "What ... what just happened?" his mind thought. His first inclination was to bring his hand to his forehead to rub it ... but he couldn't. Clyde looked down -- but he was ... encased. He was wrapped up. He was ... oh fuck. He was a victim. He was the next victim.

It was just as the previous cases: he was wrapped up tightly in some gauze that had some sort of hardening sealant painted over it. He could *somewhat* move, but by and large, he was just a worm, wrapped up to be played with. His mouth was gagged with a sock (he couldn't tell if it was one of his own), his eyes, muscular nipples, cock, and bare feet were all exposed. He tried wiggling his feet and toes -- he was able to, but man were his legs bound tight. That's about the only thing he could move. He tried bringing his knees up to his forehead, but was unable to do even that. This sick fuck knew what he was doing.

"Oh, hello there."

Clyde's immobile eyes darted around the room. It was late at night, there were no lights on, just the glow of the streetlamp through his bedroom window, which was on the 2nd floor of his place. His eyes were adjusting to the new light situation, but suddenly a figure stepped in front of the window, now backlit, a silhouette Clyde muffled something into his gag.

"So -- you think I'm a sick pervert, do you?" The captor was standing with his hands behind his back, looming over his conquest. For the first time in a very long time, Clyde was worried for his own safety.

"Oh Clyde," the captor continued, now pacing back and forth, eying his new victim, "what shall we do with you? I'm fully aware of what you were trying to do: go out and discredit my intentions to the media. You're very smart, Clyde. Rob me of my power to influence change and you're left with the empty shell of a man with nothing but devious intent. Oh Clyde, it may have worked on a lesser mind, but, unfortunately, not mine."

The captor sat down on the left side of the bed, Clyde's bound body firmly in the center. Clyde still wasn't able to make out his captor's appearance all that much. His captor then brought his arm from behind his back, revealing ... a large, white feather.

"Clyde, do you know much this feather cost? I had it custom made. A 900-fiber count, the lower 80% stiff but the 20% remaining of the tip soft as all get out. It was made to my exact specifications, and given that it's synthetic, it will never wilt or age or show holes or any of that nonsense. It cost me a pretty penny, Clyde, and I intend to get the full value out of it. For example ..."

The captor leaned over and scraped the super-soft feather blade against Clyde's nipple, and Clyde's eyes instantly widened. That light scrap felt like a million little microfibers, all of them so soft, so teasing, scrape against his nipplebuds, his tips, his everything. The scrape then happened again. And again. The speed wasn't increasing, but the captor was making sure that Clyde felt ever single aspect of that featheredge, tingling him to an absolutely insane degree.

"Oh, you like that, don't you?" teased the captor, obviously pleased with Clyde's bugged-out reaction. "Guess I'll keep doing it then." Clyde's other nipple was teased next, those light scrapes scuttling along, and Clyde violently shook his head back and forth, trying to reject the sensations that were being forced into him -- but there was nothing he could do about it. That feather just worked its magic over and over. Tingle and tickle, one nipple and then the next, teasing and teasing and teasing him. Unable to speak or move, Clyde tried everything he could to shake the sensation: closing his eyes as tight as he could as if to will it away, shaking his head again -- but nothing worked.

Then he felt it. The tingle. The one ... down there.

Slowly, surely, blood was starting to engorge his cock. Nothing much was happening right now, but it was more than just flaccid. As embarrassed as Clyde was by this, all that was on the front of his mind was STOP TEASING MY NIPPLES. Yet his captor was unrelenting, and Clyde knew all too well as to why: he was enjoying this. Enjoying this way, way too much. He wasn't tickling Clyde specifically to punish him: this man just happened to like to see grown men go insane.

Clyde's cock swelled a bit, his cock and balls being the only part of his torso that wasn't elaborately bound in the cocoon his captor had wrapped him in. "Oooh," his captor said, "looks like that thin blue line is getting a little wider, ain't it?" Clyde could see his captor smirking a bit -- he fucking hated that smirk.

Mercifully, the teasing of his nipples had stopped. The captor stood up now, and Clyde could get a better look at his face, his eyes finally having adjusted to the dark room a bit more: this guy was young. Mid-20s at the oldest. His hair was dark: a bit spikey/swoopy, almost like an emo kid, but he was also wearing a casual suit. Clyde's mind was trying to wrap around why this guy was wearing such as specific costume, thinking it was just a fetish thing, but then he realized: his eyes were open. All of the victims could clearly see their captor. Maybe he was daring the odds: driving each innocent completely insane and hoping they'd forget his face, or maybe he was trying to make a statement, letting his face be known to his victims only (at first), slowly expanding his power and influence as time went on, his legend preceding his visage. Maybe this guy was smarter than he looked, but Clyde grew somewhat fearful as his captor walked to the end of his bed ... right where Clyde's exposed feet were. He stood facing the mummified detective, once again the streetlamp casting his captor in silhouette.

"I got this theory," the captor said, twirling the finger between his fingers, menacingly. "I think that office slaves like yourself are ticklish. You're not athletic aside from the times you're on the job, but you're not a beat cop, are you, Clyde? No, you're a detective. You spend your time at work all day, wrapping your brain around the sociopaths you deal with on a daily basis. As such, you know what happens with your feet? They are trapped in shoes and socks All. Day. Long. All that sweat kept there, softening the soles, making them ... ticklish, perhaps?"

Clyde tried not to show his terror -- his captor was speaking a truth.

"Let's test my theory, shall we?"

The captor then slid the featherblade in-between Clyde's left big and index toe. Clyde screamed into his gag, arching his body as much as he could in his cocoon.

"Aww, that's that I thought, Clyde!" sneered his captor. Clyde noticed his brow breaking out into a panic sweat as he saw his captor kneel down, becoming eye-level with his soles.

What followed was hell: the captor spent a half hour sawing that feather in and out of each toegap, Clyde doing his best to clench or twist his toes away from his torment, but FUCK THAT FEATHER. It was so soft, so expertly made, it was drawing tickles out of him. For some reason, when it dragged slowly across his ring and pinkie toe -- that's when it tickled the worst, sending Clyde into howls. For some reason, that little bit of tickle lightning on his pinkie toe drove him insane, and it felt like he was being violated. For someone to play with your feet is one thing, but to be so intimate in touching and feeling and teasing that one vestigial toe, it felt like an invasion of space, someone playing with a part as intimate as that. After a half-hour, Clyde himself was losing focus of his goal.

"Awww, you really hate having your toes tickled, don't you?" his captor teased. Clyde didn't even bother to respond -- it was totally true. "How about your soles?"

The feather started scraping the bottom of Clyde's right heel, and it was merciless. His captor was employing a slow drag, making sure every single part of that featheredge could be felt, and it just lightly worked its way up his sole, digging in to the curve of Clyde's masculine, prominent arches, and all Clyde could do was bite down on his sock a little more. The feather dragged, the tickles scraped along his foot, and despite his best efforts, the closer the feather got to his toes, the more Clyde felt the corners of his mouth being dragged upwards, into a ridiculous smile. Fuck it tickled. Clyde didn't want to show any weakness. It got to the ball of his foot, to the base of his does, and his brain was screaming at him to laugh. Clyde, smiling against all odds, clenched his mouth even tighter, praying for mercy ...

... and then it stopped. A few moments passed. Then that fucking feather started scraping up his heel again. The smile came back even sooner than before, but christ that feather tickled even more than last time. Clyde couldn't believe it. He didn't want to laugh, but the second that feather hit the middle of his arch -- he caved.

A flood of insane laughter flooded his gag, and there was nothing that could be done. All his captor could hear was just an onslaught of indiscernible muffled sounds, Clyde's head shaking left to right in a violent fashion, the laughs exploding out of him like a loose firehouse at full blast. "There we go," teased his captor. "Everyone gives in in the end -- there is no shame in it, Clyde."

Clyde couldn't help it: the giggles! He couldn't stop giggling and laughing and doing nothing but have his body just accept tickles and process them into laughter. The captor's feather now dragged along his other foot, and it felt even worse, every second slowing down due to tickles, each drag feeling like an eternity in hell, scraping along, teasing his flesh, breaking down Clyde's resistance more and more and more. Clyde's brain couldn't think straight: it was too focused on laughing uncontrollably, alternating between various pitches, each one more desperate than the last. The scraping, the scraping, the scraping. It was too much. Then, just to be cruel, his captor dragged the feather in-between his toes once more. A whole new wave of desperate energy overwhelmed Clyde: he couldn't take much more of this.

Finally, after what felt like an eternity, the tickling of Clyde's bare feet had stopped. The captor stood up and walked over to the side of the bed again, sitting down. Clyde was panting into his sockgag, sweat forming on his brow. The young captor lightly brushed some of those beads away, faux-tenderly.

"Aww, look at you Clyde," the captor said, "it's OK. I know you're a big tough guy that has to assert his dominance around the office, but the feather is the ultimate leveler. Everyone falls under its might the same way, bending to ITS whims and desires. Is the pen mightier than the sword, Clyde? If it's a quill, then absolutely yes."

Clyde tried speaking to his captor, but all that came out was muffling sounds.

"I fucking love it when you try to talk to me, knowing full well it's useless. Besides, our evening is just beginning. You live by yourself, don't you? It's going to be a long, long time before I let you go. I think the longest I've had a victim is, oh, 18 hours. He wound up passing out at that point, despite the poppers I gave him. From what I read of the medical report, he slept for three full days after that. They had to feed him through a tube 'cos they simply couldn't get him up on his own volition."

Casually, mid-conversation, the captor slid the feather right underneath Clyde's balls, and lightly "flicked" his undersides with the feather. Clyde's eyes bugged out again, as his balls were quite, quite sensitive. Each flick was ... indescribable, but his entire body was invested in the sensation.

"You see," his captor said, continuing the flicking as he spoke, "the other men I've gotten a hold of were pretty weak. Oh sure, they had positions of power, but it was a no contest kind of situation -- I knew their reactions before they even had them. For a big, burly intimidating police officer such as yourself, well ... I dunno. I really like seeing men like you being brought down a peg."

At this point, Clyde's cock was growing erect. He couldn't help it: the ball teasing was stimulating him, and he had no control over it. Clyde couldn't remember if he had *ever* been hard in the presence of another man, but, well, his captor didn't seem to care much as to what he thought.

"You have power, Clyde," his captor continued, watching Clyde's cut cock grow, turning into a mighty oak of horniness. "I like reminding men of power that they will never be powerful enough, as their 'noble causes' and 'philanthropy' are just fronts for the fact they screw people out of their livelihoods every day. My own grandma got kicked out of affordable housing after our government decided to make it not as affordable anymore. My own grandma. I researched and found out which companies were responsible for such injustices, and I made sure the people in charge paid their dues."

Clyde was at a full erection now, completely against his will.

"And you, Clyde, you're getting in my way."

With that, his captor took the feather and started dragging it up the front of Clyde's shaft, and Clyde gasped. As the featherblade dragged along, Clyde could feel his cock getting firmer and firmer. The sensation was overwhelming, his cock radiating with tingles after just a single half-stroke. Clyde started to whimper; he wanted to cum, but not like this ...

"Oh Clyde," the captor continued, relishing Clyde's obvious desperation despite his cock's occasional twitch, "you had no idea your experience would be like this. And let's see: your wife is no longer here -- never be a public servant in the Google age, my friend -- so you probably haven't cum in days." Clyde's dick was already throbbing. "So, if I did this ..."

The feather began lightly "licking" the front rim of Clyde's bulbous pink cockhead, ignoring the rest of the shaft, just flicking and flicking and flicking, making Clyde moan, plead, beg, and then scream in slow motion as ...

"Unnnngggghhh," Clyde moaned, little spurts of white cum firing out of him, after what felt like the shortest tease session in history. The cum was so thick, milk-white, and coming out in gobs. The captor continued stroking the shaft as it kept pumping out its juice, encouraging each pump by enhancing the sensation all the more. Stroke, pump, stroke, pump. What a terribly efficient machine for delivering manseed. Clyde had never felt more helpless in his entire life.

Without a moment's hesitation, the feather went back to teasing Clyde's nipples, which were now incredible sensitive post-climax. Clyde, his strength fading from his body, screamed in sensitive agony.

"Oh, you didn't think I was done, did you?" his captor teased. "You got ticklish little nips there, Clyde. And a ticklish cock. And very, very, very sensitive bare feet. Oh, man, I don't think I've ever seen anyone cum that quickly. It was pent up for awhile, wasn't it Clyde? I usually drag the first climax out for much longer so the victim feels like the ordeal is over at long last, but this has its advantages too: if you cum that quickly, then you're that much more sensitive now, and we might be able to fit that many more orgasms in before your brain breaks in twain. Oh, this is gonna be fun, Clyde!"

It was hard to listen to his captor while his nipples were being mercilessly teased, but Clyde tried to annouciate as clearly as he could with his mouth stuffed full of sock. "AH HAF OO OH OO TH BAHRM" Clyde said through his gag, as clearly as humanly possible.

"What's that," his captor said, stopping the nipple-torture momentarily.

"AH! HAF! OO! OH! OO! TH! BAHRM!" Clyde almost screamed, his voice hoarse.

The captor looked at Clyde carefully, noting the urgency in his eyes. "Ya know, I rarely do this, but you're you, so let's show just a little bit of mercy ..."

With that, the captor whipped out a switchblade he had, and very, very carefully started cutting the area just below Clyde's eyes, opening up the face, already drenched in too much sweat. Once the hardened face portion was removed, the captor grabbed the bit of sock sticking out of Clyde's teeth and removed it.

"Now," the captor said, twirling that feather still, "what did you want to say?"

"Ieh ... ieh nah ..." Clyde started, very, very faintly, sapped of strength and his voice hoarse.

The captor leaned in very close to his victim's face. "What was that, slave?"

With all of his remaining strength, Clyde slammed his head forward as much as he could in his restraints, right into his captor's face, knocking him out cold. Despite being on the bed, Clyde could hear how hard the captor's head hit the floor.

Clyde started panting, his nervousness diffusing, his strength still mostly absent, having been spent on one daring move.

Now, however, came the conundrum: his captor was knocked out cold, but the rest of his body was still encased in a cocoon. No one knew that his captor was here. Could Clyde find a way out ... or would his captor wake up first? That's when the panic set in ...

... and it wasn't going to go away for a long, long time ...

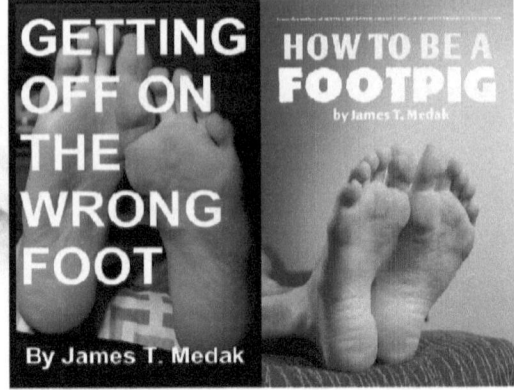

OTHER WORKS BY JAMES T. MEDAK

+ + +

How To Be a Tickle Slave (2010)

My, What Ticklish Feet You Have (2012)

Getting Off on the Wrong Foot (2013)

How to Be a Footpig (2014)

www.ingramcontent.com/pod-product-compliance
Lightning Source LLC
Chambersburg PA
CBHW030228180626
46810CB00008B/3030